THEY RAN TOWARD THE FIRST LINE OF NEAT BAVARIAN-STYLE HOUSES...

...and into a hail of machine gun fire.

Chiun leapt high above the blast to the left, Remo jumped to the right. Hitting the eaves of the roofs with one foot, they pushed off and forward. Twisting in midair, they landed on their feet behind the startled IV troops.

A few guns fired feeble bursts of lead into the clear blue sky as Chiun ripped through the men. Diet-and-exercise-hardened fingernails clawed vicious strips through chest muscle and bone.

Remo had torn into the crowd from the other side, spinning like a top on one foot, barely seeming to change position. As he whirled, an arm or foot would fly out of the twisting blur. In their wake, streaks of blood would erupt from throats and chests.

In a matter of seconds, the attackers were dead.

Created by
WARREN MURPHY
and RICHARD SAPIR

THE Destroyer™

FAILING MARKS

A GOLD EAGLE BOOK FROM
WORLDWIDE®

TORONTO • NEW YORK • LONDON
AMSTERDAM • PARIS • SYDNEY • HAMBURG
STOCKHOLM • ATHENS • TOKYO • MILAN
MADRID • WARSAW • BUDAPEST • AUCKLAND

First edition February 1999

ISBN 0-373-63229-0

Special thanks and acknowledgment to
James Mullaney for his contribution to this work.

FAILING MARKS

Printed in U.S.A.

AN IMPORTANT MESSAGE FROM CHIUN

Remo eats beef Stroganoff!? Chiun watches soap operas!? What has happened to our beloved Destroyer series?

These are but a few of the many questions inspired by some of the recent entries in the books, which have for years chronicled the adventures of the Master of Sinanju and a few other lesser characters. In one novel in particular (was it number one billion and eighty-three?) I am depicted as a White-hating old man obsessed with daytime dramas. This is simply not so. I am neither old nor a fan of these programs. Oh, at one time I enjoyed them. But it has been many years since cruel fortune stripped this single pleasure from my bleak life.

Is there an explanation for this lapse, you now ask?

The answer is yes. There is an explanation.

The explanation? Sloth.

This story obviously was from an earlier time in my dubious association with Remo Williams, my slug-brained pupil and purported "star" of this series. Somehow the fools at Gold Eagle (whose gold is scarce and whose eagles, I believe, are actually pigeons) mixed in an old manuscript with the new. What should have been billed as a "classic" Destroyer novel was thrown in with the rest.

Do not bother to ask me how such a thing could happen. Just look at the copyright page of the book you now hold.

Canadians. Need I say more?

Apparently there were modern elements added to the old story to update it. Again, do not bother to ask. If these nitwits were to publish a biography of Nero he would doubtless be wearing Air Jordan sneakers and racing around Rome in a dune buggy.

Oh, what will happen next!? Master of Sinanju, help us!

Although you are undeserving and have never done anything nice for me, I shall honor your request.

To those of you who care about such things, the problem has been addressed. I have enlisted the aid of a particularly dim American to relate my epic adventures. Apparently he has been hovering like a servile dog at the periphery of this dreadful series for many years, and so understands what has gone on before. This new scribbler is quite dense. As Americans weaned on "The Gong Show," you should be very happy with him. And do not despair; if he fails in his duties, I will flay him and move on to the next. There are many more where he came from. Unfortunately. You Americans have yet to understand the term "family planning." (A suggestion from one who has been forced to live among you for many years: Look it up.)

As for Remo's diet in the book that inspired the most mail, it was awful, was it not? Omelettes, stews, fried eggs, bread, coffee... Back then he would have eaten a yak on a stick as long as it was first dipped in Twinkies.

There. I have addressed your inane questions and silly concerns. You may go back to using your typewriters to pester the editorial departments of your local newspapers. One parting suggestion. Change the ribbon.

> I am, with moderate tolerance for you,
> Chiun, Reigning Master of Sinanju

For Mark Mullaney, who likes them in spite of the abuse.
And for Madeline Osgood, a queen among aunts.
And for the Glorious House of Sinanju, which now recognizes
the e-mail address: Housinan@aol.com

Twenty-first century. No later.

PROLOGUE

At the precise moment his killer was sharpening the sword that would sever his head from his body, Durthang of Saxony was carefully applying the finishing touches to what he considered his finest creation.

Gnarled craftsman's hands lovingly buffed the surface of the wood carving. Weary eyes peered intently at the deliberately uneven surface, searching for any flaws.

There were none. He had carved the wood to perfection.

Nonetheless, Durthang took from a nearby stone table a long, curved, flat implement forged for him by Gull the Blacksmith. The hook at the end was gradual, the iron end pitted with thousands of tiny indentations. Each dent had been gently tapped into the surface by Durthang's own hand.

He picked up the wood block that was, unbeknownst to him, the reason for his impending murder. He placed the block carefully between his knees, clamping them tightly together. Taking the curved tool in one hand, he drew it down to one of the interlocking furrows in the center of the block.

Durthang drew the iron implement back and forth gently across the wooden block. The delicate pitting of the tool's surface acted as sandpaper.

After a short time, Durthang blew gently on the wood. A puff of dust escaped down the deep furrow and out into the cool air of his forest workshop.

He repositioned the block between his knees and repeated the procedure, this time on a second line. Together, both lines formed a cross in the center of the block. The four separated areas outside the indentations were part of a larger map.

Durthang knew the precise spot that the entire map indicated. Of course he would; he had carved the map to the exact specifications of his noble employer. And he was no stranger to this area that would one day be part of modern Germany, having lived in the region for more than sixty years.

Until that morning, however, the white-haired carver didn't know the significance of the location. This knowledge was the reason for his impending death.

In each of the four corners, above the elaborate fleur-de-lis pattern in which were hidden the hissing heads of three sinister serpents, Durthang had been instructed to carve a single runic mark. It was the symbol for gold.

He couldn't entirely believe that this simple block carving he had been hired to create truly represented what he suspected it did. He was too insignificant a person to be involved even peripherally in something so great.

But still. The thought was there.

Durthang blew the last of the dust free of the block. Placing his sanding tool down with his other implements, he lifted the piece of wood from between his knees and held it upright to examine the lines of the map.

He knew where the place was. It was close by.

And the symbols at the four corners. Gold.

It could *not* be.

Durthang jumped as he heard footfalls behind him on the stone floor of his cramped work area. So engrossed in his handiwork was he that he had not heard the old wooden door creak open. He quickly lowered the carving, turning to the intruder.

A lazy burst of early-evening air sent a twirl of sawdust spinning before the glowing hearth fire.

His fat ruddy face relaxed when he saw who had entered. Durthang rose, bowing deep reverence.

"Forgive me, noble sir. Your servant did not know the lateness of the hour."

The visitor stood before Durthang, resplendent in his silver chain-mail tunic. A skintight chain headdress rose up around his neck, enclosing his entire head with the exception of his face. A shining silver iron battle helmet sat atop his head, nestling down over his ears.

Perched at the peak of his armor helmet was a metal-hewed falcon, its wings spread back and frozen in perpetual flight. The bird stood as high as the ceiling, its beak open in a still-life menacing cry.

The regal intruder stood a few feet inside the open doorway, his hooded black eyes staring intently at the simple peasant carver.

Although Durthang had met his lord on several occasions now, the man's presence was still awe-inspiring to the carver. And why not? For this was a god among men. His exploits were legendary. Siegfried, son of Siegmund, husband of Brunhild. Slayer of Fafner, the dragon. King of the Nibelungs.

Possessor of the Nibelungen Hoard.

Siegfried regarded the dusty interior of the tiny peasant hut with regal disdain. He looked from hearth, to kitchen table, to cot, to work area with equal contempt. At last his eyes alighted on the nervous Durthang.

"It is complete?" Siegfried intoned.

Durthang nodded anxiously. "'Tis surely so, sire."

Siegfried didn't say another word. He stretched out an open palm to the carver. The hand was encased in an expertly crafted chain-mail glove. The gauntlets stretched halfway up his forearms and were attached around the back with elaborate metal fasteners.

Durthang obediently placed the block of wood in the hand of the Nibelungen king.

The wooden piece was heavy and flat. Though Siegfried's hand was large, the wood was larger.

With his fingers splayed, his hand was only as big as one of the four equal-sized sections. He nodded his approval as he scanned the details of the map.

"You have done well," Siegfried said with satisfaction.

Durthang the Carver sighed in great relief. When he had accepted this special appointment, his worst fear was that his work would dissatisfy his lordship, and that Siegfried would condemn him as an inferior craftsman. His business among the nearby villagers—meager as it was—would surely suffer from such a condemnation.

"I thank you, my lord," Durthang said, again with a polite bow.

While his eyes were downcast, the carver heard a sliding sound. It was that of metal against metal.

When he glanced up, he found that Siegfried had placed the hcavy wood carving on a chair. The sound Durthang had heard was that of Siegfried's famous sword. The king had drawn it from the chain belt that was slung below his hip.

Legend had it that the king had forged the weapon himself from the fragments of his father's own sword. It was the blade he had used to slay the mighty Fafner. This terrifying implement of death was aimed now at the simple peasant wood carver.

Durthang looked in fright at the sharpened tip of the huge gleaming sword. It was half a hand from his face. So powerful was Siegfried that the weapon did not quiver, though it weighed more than forty pounds. Orange firelight danced along the length of the broadsword.

Eyes locked on the tip of the sword, the carver threw himself to his knees. "My liege, I beg you!" he pleaded. "Spare my life!"

Siegfried shook his head. "You have done well, carver. Would that I might do as you request."

"Please, Lord. I will forget that which I have seen."

"How can you forget?" Siegfried stated, a note of sadness in his voice. He raised his sword in two hands as if to slaughter the peasant.

"Please!" Durthang cried. "Blind me, that I cannot see to find the spot. Cleave out my tongue, that I cannot speak of what I know. Remove one hand, that I will be unable to duplicate in memory that which I have crafted for you. But please, O Lord, I beg of you. Let me live."

Siegfried seemed for a time to consider the impassioned words of the simple carver. After a moment, his deliberations ended. He nodded ever so slightly. As he did so, the falcon on his helmet tapped softly against the great crossbeam at the center of Durthang's small hut.

The carver fell to the floor in relief and homage. He prostrated himself at the feet of the great, beneficent king.

"Let me sing praises of your lordship till my dying day!" he cried with joyful passion.

Tears streamed down his face, dropping to the dirt

and sawdust on the floor of his simple hut. Remnants of years of hard work. As he wept, Durthang saw the armor-encased feet of Siegfried shift slightly. One arched upward while the other braced itself firmly against the flat stone floor.

Durthang's brain did not have time to process what this might mean before his brain became incapable of processing any information at all.

The peasant carver felt the weight of the mighty blade against the back of his neck for only an instant. In half a heartbeat, the sword passed through his spine, his throat and sliced out through his Adam's apple on the other side.

As Durthang's aged body collapsed to the floor, his severed head dropped and rolled, tumbling end over end to the simple stone hearth. His long white hair scattered among the gray ash and glowing orange embers.

Near Durthang's bleeding, headless corpse, Siegfried replaced his sword in his belt. He gathered up the engraved block of wood, placing it atop the carver's table.

Searching quickly, he found a hammer and chisel among the tools. Collecting the hammer in one hand, he steadied the chisel atop the carving with the other.

With a single great crack, he shattered the wooden map into two sections. He gathered up the two remaining sections in turn, snapping them each in half.

By this time the embers from the hearth had ignited the hair of Durthang. The fire burned up around his scalp, catching onto the thatch of the walls. Yellow flames raced up to the ceiling.

As the tiny hut was engulfed in flame, the king of the Nibelungs collected the four sections of the map beneath one powerful arm. Flames burning an inch above the splayed falcon wings atop his gleaming battle helmet, he hurried from the ratty, burning cottage.

And into the final day of his life.

THE SERVANT BOY FOUND the body of the king. It lay facedown in the river, arms spread wide. Only the head was submerged. The rest of the body was on dry land.

There was an area of what appeared to be rust on the back of Siegfried's chain mail. It flaked off when touched. Dried blood.

Closer scrutiny showed a small breach in the armor. Just wide enough for a single knife thrust. Someone had crept up behind the king while he drank from the river and murdered him.

"Was it the work of bandits, O Master?" the servant boy asked, his razor-slit eyes grown wide with wonder.

The man he addressed was the Master of Sinanju. Only once in a generation was a man deemed worthy to hold that title. From the village of Sinanju in the far-off land of Chosun had Master Bal-Mung come. He was a tall man with thick black hair and the flat face of the East. Squatting, he was examining the body of the king.

"No, it was not a true bandit who did this thing," the Master of Sinanju intoned. "Would that it was," he added. And after thus speaking, said no more.

The Master of Sinanju shook his head gravely as he looked down at the body of the slain king.

Siegfried might have survived the attack had he not been dressed so foolishly. His ridiculous metal gloves weighed several pounds each. His idiotic iron helmet, with its insanely ornate iron bird, weighed much more.

After the assault from behind, the king had fallen into the water. The battle gear had weighed him down, effectively finishing the killer's job. Due to his absurd choice of wardrobe, great King Siegfried had drowned.

The Master of Sinanju was about to turn away from the scene when something odd caught his eye.

There was an object a few feet away from shore, resting amid the slick stones at the bottom of the river. It was obviously man-made. The normal human eye wouldn't have seen it beneath the rapid currents. Indeed, the Master of Sinanju had nearly missed it.

Using a stick broken from a nearby tree, Bal-Mung pulled the object from the cold waters of the stream.

It was a flat block of wood. Two of the edges were rough, and two were smooth. A section of a larger puzzle, if the pair of jagged borders was any indication. The Master of Sinanju grew excited when he saw what it represented.

Clamoring into the waist-deep water, he searched the silty river bed for nearly an hour. All in vain. The one piece he had found was the only piece that was there.

Dripping wet, he climbed back up out of the cold water. He passed the body of Siegfried and crossed over to where he and his servant had left their horses.

Bal-Mung had forbade the servant boy from entering the water to aid in the search, insisting that the boy would only stir up more silt. Even so, the young man had waded ankle deep to collect the helmet of the slain Siegfried. The falcon-in-flight headpiece was already tied in with the Master's bedroll when he reached his pony.

Master Bal-Mung took the river section of the wood carving and tucked it inside a leather pouch near the helmet.

His young servant craned his neck to see what the Master of Sinanju had hidden away. He saw only a flash of carved roads and rivers. Places traditionally represented on maps.

"What is it, O Master?" the servant asked.

The Master of Sinanju was swinging up atop his steed. In his saddle, he looked over at the gently bobbing corpse of the legendary Siegfried. Bal-Mung's tan face could have been carved from the oldest petrified wood from the darkest heart of the surrounding forest.

"It is my undoing," Bal-Mung said gravely.

He tugged the reins. Together, the Master of Sinanju and his servant rode away from the body to vanish back into the thick forests of ancient Germany.

His stalker came from the West, though his skills were born of the East.

Adolf Kluge had met his pursuer once. At first glance, Kluge might have thought him an average man. He was a thin Caucasian with dark hair, approximately six feet tall, perhaps 150 or 160 pounds. Other than a pair of abnormally thick wrists, he didn't seem exceptional in any way.

But he *was* exceptional. Of that, Kluge had no doubt.

The latest proof of this had been faxed to him not ten minutes ago. Among the documents were several black-and-white photographs that showed the bodies of men who had been killed in horrific ways. Kluge singled out a photo of a man whose head had been crushed by some massive force. He looked like a tube of toothpaste squeezed in the middle. In his mind, Kluge couldn't help but see himself as the victim in the photo. The thought froze his spine.

"The description by those left alive lends the appearance that this is all the work of a single assassin,'' said Herman, an aide. ''I would venture that this is not possible. Do you concur, Herr Kluge?''

Eyes hooded as he looked up from the gruesome photo, Adolf Kluge gave his assistant a baleful glare. ''Of course it is one man. Where else but in this village could one find an army that wears the same face?''

The aide frowned. ''But it seems too incredible to believe,'' he insisted.

''That it does,'' Kluge admitted. His voice had an edge of annoyance.

Kluge dropped the photo. In the other hand, he still clutched the envelope containing the latest intelligence. With a world-weary sigh, he looked around the room. Involuntarily his gray-blue eyes alighted on the life-size painting of Adolf Hitler—Kluge's namesake—that graced the main wall of the large stone conference room. The führer's flinty eyes had been painted so that they glared unapologetically at anyone who might enter this mountain fortress. As if the chancellor stared with disdain from a realm beyond death.

Kluge tore his gaze away from the painted eyes of Hitler. He found his aide staring at him, a puzzled look on his broad face.

Kluge was aware on some level that Herman had been talking to him while he was in his trance. He shook his head as if to clear out the cobwebs.

''Forgive me, I was distracted.'' Kluge waved his hand that held the latest information. ''Continue.''

"I was saying, Herr Kluge, that our friends on several police forces in Germany are searching for fingerprint records. I thought we might involve Interpol in the matter."

"Do not bother."

The aide seemed confused. "Herr Kluge?"

Kluge dropped the dossier to the gleaming table. "Tell them not to bother," he repeated flatly.

"But he has killed many of our men."

"Not *our* men," Kluge snapped. "They were not from the village. They are therefore not my responsibility."

"Nonetheless," Herman persisted, "they were sympathetic to our cause."

Kluge laughed bitterly. *"Our cause,"* he mocked. "Thanks to our old friend Nils Schatz, we no longer have a cause. We have a pursuer. And he is getting closer." Kluge shook his head. "No. I fear now all we can do is await the inevitable. Please go." He sounded defeated.

Without another word, the aide gathered up his paperwork from the large oaken conference table. Dress shoes clicking a loud complaint on the highly buffed stone floor, the young man left the room. The big door echoed shut.

Alone, Kluge felt his shoulders sag as if drained of life.

The old portals in the ancient stone outer wall of the conference room had been filled with expensive paned windows. Around the edges were panes of beautiful stained glass depicting various struggles from different periods of German history.

Kluge's tired, roaming eyes ignored these. He had no great desire this day to dwell on the great Teutonic past. That was precisely what had brought them all to this dismal state.

Instead, his gaze moved to the clear glass at the middle of the nearest window. He stared out the slightly frosted panes at the nearby peaks of the Andes.

The air was thinner here in the mountains of Argentina, but his body seemed to have gotten used to it over the years.

It was a shame he had to leave. This had been his home for much of his life. The home of IV, the community of renegade Nazis that Adolf Kluge led.

An ultrasecret organization founded by the ragged losers of the Second World War, IV was to represent a rebirth of the fascist dream—the Fourth Reich, a Teutonic dynasty spanning generations.

That had been the ideal at its founding, and in his early, idealistic days as IV's third leader, it had always been the ultimate plan of Adolf Kluge. However, Kluge was nothing if not pragmatic. As he grew older, he realized that it would be impossible in the modern world to achieve the original goal of the secret Nazi organization.

With the abandonment of his youthful dreams and the approach of middle age, his concerns became more realistic. IV had a great deal of wealth at its disposal, riches looted from some of the finest families in Europe. During his tenure, Kluge began an aggressive covert campaign to involve IV in the financial markets of the world.

At nearly every turn, he met with rousing success.

Kluge, it turned out, was a financial wizard. When it came to investments, he had the Midas touch. In the years of his stewardship, IV's business portfolio burgeoned. The money he made was used to meet the expenses of the village in which the founders of the organization—now retired or deceased—had come to live.

The building in which Kluge sat was an ancient structure, possibly Aztec, that had been constructed on a mountain peak that neighbored the IV village. A stone bridge connected the office stronghold with the main village. It was in this great old building that Kluge had made the first tentative steps toward the ruination of IV.

Of course, it had been accidental. When the downward spiral had started several months ago, Adolf Kluge had no idea where it would lead.

Back then, one of the many corporations in which IV had a financial interest was a technological giant, a German company called PlattDeutsche. The company's subsidiary in the United States, PlattDeutsche America, had developed a system that was able to create a link to the human brain with a computer via an electric signal. While refining the system, the company had run across a pair of agents in the employ of the U.S. government. One of these men was the legendary Reigning Master of Sinanju.

According to the old men of the village, the Master of Sinanju was truly responsible for the death of Hitler. It was said that when the führer learned that the wily Korean was on his way to Berlin to dispatch him, the German leader had taken his own life.

The Master of Sinanju was said to possess remarkable physical powers. Kluge had foolishly approved a plan to use the computer program of PlattDeutsche to download the abilities of the Master of Sinanju and his protégé.

The scheme had backfired completely. Sinanju had triumphed, and IV's operatives in America had been killed. It was only sheer luck that Kluge had been able to sever all connections with PlattDeutsche before the neo-Nazi group could be uncovered.

In the days that followed, Kluge was certain that the men from Sinanju would eventually show up on his doorstep. But as time went on, he realized that he and IV had stumbled into a bit of good luck; either Sinanju wasn't interested in him or didn't realize the extent of the Nazi organization's holdings.

Whatever the reason, he was left alone. In spite of the loss of a major company, IV had survived.

Adolf Kluge had breathed a sigh of relief. But this relief proved to be short-lived.

All hope of anonymity for IV had been lost three months before. That was when the world as Kluge knew it ended and the entire delicately stacked structure of the decades-old organization had collapsed around his ears like a house of cards in a hurricane.

One of the old founders of the village had left Argentina with the impatient hope of creating the vaunted Fourth Reich in his own lifetime. In a campaign that had played out before the entire world, the bitter old Nazi had created a modern reprise of World War II, complete with bombs dropping on London and the surprising takeover of Paris. Nils Schatz had financed all of this with stolen IV funds.

The Master of Sinanju had again arrived on the scene, and again he and his heir vanquished IV. This time, however, they knew. In the months following the events in London and Paris, a definite pattern of violence had begun erupting in neo-Nazi groups throughout Germany. Always the description of the attackers was the same—an old Asian and a slender white man with thick wrists.

The Master of Sinanju and his protégé. Lately, in the reports he was getting, the old Korean was seen less and less. Adolf Kluge was not certain why this was. It could be that the Reigning Master—who looked quite old and frail—had finally succumbed to age.

He could be sick. He could even be dead.

What really mattered to Adolf Kluge was that the young Master of Sinanju was still alive. And he was coming for Kluge.

Kluge glanced away from the distant mountain peaks, drawing his gaze across the sparkling crystalline pattern of ice on the transparent window panes.

As he continued to reflect on his dire future, he found that his eyes had refocused on one of the stained-glass panes in the surrounding edge of the window.

He recognized the image out of Germanic legend.

Ironically, like the pictures of the murder victims on the table before him, a body lay sprawled on the ground. Bits of red, blue, yellow and green glass—polished to a great luster—depicted an outdoor scene.

There was a river running near the body. The brilliant sunlight that eased across the Andes illuminated the strip of painted water, causing it to sparkle hypnotically. The effect as one stared at it was almost that of real running water. A vibrant testament to an artistic genius.

There was a small streak of red running down the stream.

Funny. Kluge had never noticed that before.

He saw now the slit of a knife wound in the back of the body. A smile of blood. According to myth, Siegfried, the great Nibelungen king, had been stabbed from behind by the mercenary Hagan.

More legends.

It was the legend of Sinanju that had brought Kluge to this sorry state. Would that *that* legend had not been true.

Kluge slapped his hands atop the table in impotent

rage. He got to his feet, shoving the paperwork roughly to the floor.

He marched over to examine the stained-glass rendering more carefully.

It was foolish, really. Staring at a window that had been imported from a centuries-old European castle. But Adolf Kluge had little else to do while he awaited death.

The stained-glass Siegfried had been designed by the artist to be a big, burly man. The creator of the scene had been able to capture a sense of strength in the ancient hero even in death.

How old was the window? Kluge wondered.

Several hundred years at least.

The detail was exquisite. He had never really taken the time to study it in all the years the castle had been his home.

Something at the hand of the dead king caught his eye.

Kluge leaned back, surprised. He peered in more closely.

It was there. Plainly evident beneath the gauntlet. To Kluge, it was rather like noticing for the first time one's own passport photograph in the background of the Mona Lisa.

He frowned.

It probably meant nothing. But his experience lately had proved that there was fact in some legends.

Kluge strolled to the door, deep in thought.

He paused once, looking back at the ancient death scene. The windows all along the wall shone like a thousand painted diamonds. For some reason, only one caught his attention.

Since he had been stabbed in the back, Kluge wondered briefly if Siegfried ever knew who his murderer was. Adolf Kluge at least knew who his killer would be. He had met the man who was coming after him.

He even knew his name.

2

His name was Remo and the tenement rooftops of former East Berlin stretched out before him like the sun-bleached surface of some giant concrete checkerboard.

He stood on the flat tar roof of a tall high-rise and surveyed the city with a disapproving eye.

Remo had been to the eastern bloc countries many times before the fall of the Iron Curtain and had always found them to be dismally depressing. This was his first trip to this part of Germany since the Berlin Wall had toppled, and he was surprised to see that things hadn't changed much.

There was a little more color here now. On the streets below, as well as in the apartment windows. A few blocks away, Remo saw a billboard featuring the red-and-white logo of a famous American soft drink.

But the place was still as somber as a funeral parlor. Of course, the Russians were to blame. Decades of Communist oppression had a tendency to take the fun out of anything.

Remo wasn't certain what building he was looking for. The sameness of the tenements was startling and more than a little disconcerting. To him, it looked as if some Titan with an enormous square bucket and a limitless supply of beach sand had spent a lazy afternoon scooping up and plopping down building after identical building.

Remo didn't realize how true this analogy was until he leaned against the upper rim of the roof he was standing on. The cheap mortar crumbled to sand beneath his hands.

Jumping back toward the roof's center, he slapped the dust from his palms and shook his head in disbelief.

"Good thing this isn't an earthquake zone," he muttered to himself as he surveyed the half-crumbled wall.

The structure he was trying to find was somewhere east of Grotewohlstrasse beyond the location of the old Wall.

Remo's best course of action would have been to stay on the ground and head east until he ran into a helpful pedestrian. But there were two very important reasons why he couldn't ask directions. The first was simple enough: Remo didn't speak German. The second reason was a bit trickier. The number of bodies Remo had been leaving in his wake lately had begun to attract undue attention. He had been given explicit instructions to eliminate only those who were absolutely necessary.

Of course, all of this would be simpler if Chiun

hadn't stopped coming along with him. *He* understood German. If Remo's teacher had come *with* Remo rather than sitting like a Korean lump in their Berlin hotel room, the two of them would probably be back home by now.

Thanks to Chiun, Remo's only hope was to find the place himself. And so here he was, standing alone amid the seemingly limitless sea of cheap, Communist-era buildings.

With a put-upon sigh, Remo climbed gingerly atop the crumbling four-foot wall that rimmed the roof.

He was an average-looking man with deep-set eyes and dark hair. He wore a dark green T-shirt and a pair of tan chinos that fluttered in the early-winter breeze. Although the thermometer hovered around the forty-degree mark, Remo seemed unaffected by the cold.

Just beyond the toes of his loafers was a five-story drop into a filthy alley. Thirty feet across the empty air was an identical roof.

Remo hopped over to it.

It was an impossible jump even for an Olympic athlete. Remo made the leap with ease.

One instant he was standing; the next he was airborne. He landed atop the neighboring roof a second later.

Even though he had dispersed his weight in flight so that upon landing he would be no heavier than a handful of feathers, the mortar promptly crumbled beneath his weight. He hopped down to the main roof just as the avalanche of bricks and mortar slipped out from underneath him, landing with a terrible crash in the alley far below.

An angry shout rose up from one of the apartments beneath him. He ignored it.

Remo continued forward.

He picked up speed, running to the edge and leaping for the next building. As he ran, he glanced all around, looking for something in particular. Something the last man he had killed told him would be there.

Building, alley, leap.

Run.

Building, alley, leap.

He covered blocks in a matter of minutes.

While he leaped from rooftop to rooftop, Remo found himself thinking of the city's recent history.

It was pretty disheartening.

First the fascists, then the Communists. Which was worse? It was a testament to the utter evil of both philosophies that he had a hard time deciding.

Remo finally chose the fascists as being the worst of the two. After all, they were a better reflection of the dark souls of the indigenous population. The Communists had ruthlessly seized control after the Second World War. The Nazis had been *voted* in.

Remo was above a street parallel to the main concourse of Unter den Linden, leaping to the next building, when something far ahead caught his eye.

Movement. Briefly, he spied someone with a gun.

Remo landed softly and skittered crab-like over to a massive vent cap. Twirling slowly in the soft wind, the cover resembled a tin chef's hat.

He peered out from behind it.

Remo didn't know where precisely his leap-frogging had taken him. The man he saw was several buildings away. For all he knew, it could be a guarded government or bank building. It wouldn't help the low profile he was supposed to be keeping for him to assault a few innocent bank guards. Upstairs would blow a gasket.

Remo waited until he spied what he was after.

The man turned slowly away from him, scanning the rooftops to the north.

There it was. In plain daylight.

A red armband was wrapped tightly around the armed man's biceps. Within a white circle on the crimson band, the crooked black lines of a swastika were clearly visible.

No doubt about it. This was the place.

He came out from behind the vent cover and strolled casually across the roof. At the edge, he hopped over to the next building. He continued his harmless amble toward the distant rooftop.

Remo didn't want to alarm the sentry. If the man saw him too soon and Remo was running like a maniac in his direction, the neo-Nazi might have time to warn others. This way, as long as Remo wasn't spotted actually jumping from one building to the next, he would look like nothing more than an underdressed apartment dweller who had gone up to fix his antenna.

As it was, the sentry failed to see Remo until after the final leap from the adjacent roof.

Remo dropped down directly in front of the startled neo-Nazi. He smiled.

"Hi. I'm here to kill Gus. Is he in?"

Shock.

The young neo-Nazi immediately swung the barrel of his machine gun in Remo's direction. He tried to pull the trigger but was stunned to discover the gun was no longer in his hands. Looking desperately for the weapon, he found to his astonishment that it had somehow ended up in the hands of the strange intruder.

"No, no, no," Remo admonished, as if speaking to a toddler who had just scribbled crayon cave paintings all over the living-room walls. "Mustn't make boom noise."

As the neo-Nazi watched in horror, Remo took the gun barrel in two hands and twisted sharply. There was a quick groan of metal as the barrel bent in half.

A six-foot-high section of wall nearby was dotted with ancient rusted hooks that had been once used to secure lengths of clothesline. Remo hung the U-shaped gun barrel around one of the hooks.

Immediately a large section of the wall collapsed

under the relatively light weight of the gun. Some of the debris fell to the alley. Most fell to the roof.

When they hit the roof's surface, the slabs of concrete continued downward. They crashed through the rooftop, landing in a heap in the apartment directly below.

"Well, crap," Remo griped, peering down into the hole.

There was shouting from the apartment. Through the dancing dust, a wide, pale face peered up through the opening. When he saw Remo, the man grew panicked. The face hastily withdrew.

Since landing on the roof, Remo had been between the guard and the stairwell door, which was rusting on its hinges in an alcove beyond the toppled wall. With Remo's attention redirected momentarily, the guard made a break for the door.

Remo grabbed the man by the back of his brown shirt collar before he could take two steps. He held the man several inches off the roof. "Hold up a second, Frankenfurter," Remo said.

"No, no!" the young man screamed in heavily accented English. "Let me go! Let me go!!"

"In a minute," Remo promised. "First things first. Where's Gus Holloway?"

"I do not know a Gus Holloway."

"That is a lie," Remo said simply. "Every lie gets a whack. In case you were wondering, this is a whack."

Whirling, Remo slammed the neo-Nazi's forehead

into the remains of the half-toppled side wall. A square section of mortar shattered from the force of the blow, toppling to the alley far below.

When Remo brought the neo-Nazi back from the wall, his frightened face was caked with dust. He coughed, and a puff of concrete powder gusted into the chilly air. A streak of blood trickled down his dirty forehead.

"My next question is surprisingly similar to my first. Where is Gus Holloway?"

"I do not know!" the man cried. He blinked blood and dust from his eyes.

"Wrong answer," Remo said. "Whack time." He slammed the man's head against the wall once again. Again more concrete tumbled away. "I'd feel safer living in a shoe box," Remo frowned, looking down at the rubble in the alley.

"Please!" the young man begged woozily. "I do not know this Holloway."

Remo shook his head. "You *must,*" he stated, firmly. "My last lead pointed me here. And your 'Hi, I'm an asshole Aryan' merit badge—" he nodded to the swastika armband "—indicates to me that you're maybe not being entirely forthright. Hey, I know what might jar your memory!" Remo said brightly. "A whack!"

He slammed the man's head against the wall. This time most of what was left crumbled away, tumbling in long angry sheets to the asphalt five stories below.

Once it was gone, only one four-foot finger of mortar remained upright.

"Gus...Gus," the man wheezed, choking on dust. "Gustav? Do you mean Gustav?" He looked desperately up at Remo, one eye shut painfully. A shard of concrete had gotten stuck beneath the lid during his last whack. By now his forehead was bleeding profusely.

Remo frowned, confused. "Yeah, I think that might be his alias or something. Is there a Gustav here?"

"Yes!" the man cried. "That vas him." Still half-blinded, he pointed at the hole in the roof.

"The fat guy that looked up here?"

"*Yes!*" the neo-Nazi howled in frustration.

Remo shook his head angrily. "Why didn't you say so?" Cupping his hand on the back of the neo-Nazi's head, he drew the man toward the last upright section of side wall.

"Vait! No vack! No vack!"

"That's 'whack,'" Remo instructed even as he slammed the man's head into the remaining portion of wall. It collapsed against the pressure.

Unlike the first three times, the man's injuries did not end with a simple whack. As he passed through the wall, Remo released his grip on the young man's hair. The neo-Nazi continued his forward momentum, sailing out over the alley amid a pile of concrete fragments and a cloud of mortar dust. Bleeding and filthy, he dropped from sight. He landed with a squishy thud in the alley a few seconds later.

Remo did not stay on the roof long enough to see him splatter. As the young neo-Nazi was free-falling to his death, Remo had gone over to the hole in the roof. He hopped down into the apartment below, landing atop the pile of collapsed ceiling.

The apartment was empty. Scowling at himself for allowing his target to escape so easily, he moved stealthily through the small flat and out into the dank hallway.

FOR THE PAST SEVERAL months, Gustav Reichschtadt had been hearing about the pair of terrifying men supposedly slaughtering neo-Nazis throughout Germany. He had disregarded the stories.

Certainly Gustav didn't deny that people were being killed. However, he was convinced that it was the work of the German government out to punish pro-Nazi groups for the embarrassment they had caused a few months before.

Modern Germany prided itself on its intolerance of the underground fascist organizations that seemed to spring up cyclically—like spring daisies in a Bavarian meadow. It was therefore humiliating to the national government when hundreds upon hundreds of its citizens began clamoring to the French border after the covert neo-Nazi takeover of Paris that had occurred the previous summer. Much to the German government's embarrassment, these young fascists made it clear to the world that they wished to join the leaders of that great campaign as soldiers under a unified Nazi flag.

The crisis in Paris had been defused by means that were still uncertain—at least as far as the press was concerned. The men who had eagerly swarmed to join the neo-Nazi forces had returned to their homes, never having set foot on French soil. And Germany was left to squirm in embarrassment as the world looked on in veiled distaste at the country that had failed to anticipate or control its most vile element.

It was at the beginning of this silent condemnation that the first bodies began to show up.

Gustav was certain that German authorities were doing the killing. The government in Berlin was attempting to prove its worthiness to a scornful world by murdering its most favored sons.

This was what he had been telling the members of the Göring Brotherhood for the past several months. He had told them this in English, for—though he dressed as a Nazi, lived in Germany and vociferously condemned the current weak German government—Gustav spoke not one word of German.

Gustav Reichschtadt had been born Gus Holloway, son of "Cap" and Dottie Holloway of the Pittsburgh Holloways. He had lived at home, jobless, bitter and without any life prospects, until his thirty-fifth birthday, at which point his more than tolerant father had thrown him out on his hairy ear.

With so much time on his pudgy hands, Gus had whiled away his youthful days at home as an active member of several American fascist groups. He had even achieved some notoriety for once throwing a chair at the host of the *Horrendo* show on national TV. When his parents finally disowned him, his friends in the skinhead movement took him in.

In a movement that was notoriously undercharged in the sparking-synapse department, Gus Holloway—with his high-school GED and unerring ability to accurately spell *Mein Kampf*—became a shining star.

Eventually Gus renounced his American citizenship and followed the movement to its birthplace. The home of the führer himself. Germany.

He was promptly thrown in jail for distributing illegal Nazi literature. Gus learned the hard way that the current German government wasn't like the one to which he had pledged his undying fascist allegiance.

While in prison, Gus met up with many individuals like himself. After his release, he joined his newfound friends in the underground skinhead movement. He was reborn as the leader of the neo-Nazi Göring Brotherhood. Changing his name was part of that rebirth.

He was working in his capacity as leader of this secret group when the whole world came crashing in. When the dust cleared, Gustav realized that it wasn't the world after all—just most of the ceiling of his apartment.

Fortunately for Gustav, he had been standing on the other side of the room at the time.

The neo-Nazi leader had been running off his latest propaganda leaflets from an old-fashioned printing press that his mother had given to him for his eighth birthday. His fat fingers were smeared with blue ink as he crept over to the pile of collapsed building material.

When he looked up through the hole in the ceiling, he found himself staring into the coldest eyes he had ever seen.

It was him! One of the two men who had been spotted slaughtering members of neo-Nazi groups all around Germany. The German government's politically correct hit squad had finally come to claim the great Gustav Reichschtadt!

The fascist leader had immediately lumbered from the room.

The tenement in which the brotherhood conducted its holy work was overrun by neo-Nazis. Gustav waddled frantically down the urine-soaked flight of stairs to the fourth floor. He pounded a desperate fat fist against the door across from the bottom of the landing. The ink on his hands left marks like toeless baby footprints across the thick metal door.

"Help me!" Gustav screamed in English. He was hyperventilating. "They're here! Good God, they're coming to kill me! Hurry!" He pounded harder.

Finally the door opened a crack. A suspicious eye peered out at him from within the apartment. Somewhere unseen, an aged scratchy recording of Wagner's "Ride of the Valkyries" was building to a warped crescendo.

"What is it?" a voice asked in thickly accented German.

"The killers!" Gustav hissed. "The government hit squad that's out to destroy all our work. They're here."

The eye peered first left, then right. It finally looked back at Gustav.

"I do not see anyone."

Gustav flapped a large mitt toward the ceiling. "They're on the roof. Let me in!"

He forced his meaty palms against the door. Although the old man within the apartment was far from strong, he didn't need to be; there was precious little strength behind the push. Gustav only succeeded in spreading more ink across the face of the door. He pulled away, panting at his exertions.

"I need help," Gustav begged. He was on the verge of tears.

There wasn't a hint of sympathy in the eye. Obviously its owner had had a run-in or two with Gustav Reichschtadt before. But that was not to say that there was no sign of emotion in the orb. It suddenly blinked once, as if in great surprise. All at once, the door slammed shut.

Gustav wheeled around, ready to run panting for

the next door. He didn't get an inch down the hallway before he saw what had made his fellow neo-Nazi slam the door.

The government killer with the dark, dead eyes was coming down the stairs from the fifth floor. He steered a path to Gustav.

Gustav broke into a dead run down the corridor. To his horror, his pursuer trotted easily up beside him.

"Are you Gus?" Remo asked as they both ran.

"Nein, nein!" Gus insisted, wheezing heavily. It was the only German word he had mastered in his nine years in that country. "Me no Gus. Me German."

They had come to the end of the corridor. Gus's face was coated with a sheen of sweat. His few remaining strands of hair were plastered to his pasty scalp. He looked desperately for a place to run, but there was nowhere to go.

Remo stopped before him.

"The guy on the roof said you were Gus Holloway."

"Me Gustav," Gus panted.

"Yeah, and me Jane," Remo said. "Tell you what. I think you are Gus. What do you think about that?"

The chubby neo-Nazi's eyes darted first left, then right. Blank walls stared back at him. There was not even a window behind him. He spun back to Remo, his ample belly jiggling like a sackful of kittens. Desperate, he opted for a different approach.

"I am an American citizen," Gustav Reichschtadt insisted. "I demand to see the United States ambassador." He tried to stick his chest out proudly, but even at its farthest point it remained a full foot behind his enormous stomach.

"That and bus fare will get you to Oktoberfest," Remo said flatly.

"I'm serious," Gus said arrogantly. "I want my lawyer. I know my rights as an American."

"Okay, let me explain your rights," Remo offered.

Reaching over, he grabbed a slick, glutinous mass of puffy flesh at the side of Holloway's neck. To Remo, it felt as if he had just grabbed a handful of shortening.

Remo squeezed.

A piercing feminine scream stabbed up through the mountain of semidigested pastries that filled Gus Holloway's ample pot. His eyes grew wide in pain and shock.

Remo eased off on the pressure. "Your rights at the moment are simple. You have the right to feel pain. You have the right not to feel pain. Do you understand these rights as I have explained them to you?"

Remo squeezed again for emphasis. Gus shrieked, nodding his understanding. Three chins waggled helplessly.

"Good," Remo declared. "I need some information on a neo-Nazi organization called Four. What do you know about it?"

Gus licked his thick lips as he tried frantically to think of a clever lie. None came. He decided to bluff his way through.

"Never heard of them," he insisted.

The pain again. Far worse this time—it felt as if every nerve ending in his neck were being buffed with acid-dipped sandpaper. He howled in agony.

"I don't know!" Gus screamed. "They're a shadow group. In deep cover. I've only ever heard rumors." He was panting, swallowing thick, mucous-filled saliva.

"Tell me what you've heard," Remo pressed.

"They were responsible for the Paris takeover."

"I know that." Remo's expression was dark.

"And the London bombings."

"Ditto."

Gus's head was clearing now. Remo had eased the neck pressure. The pain wasn't as severe.

"That's everything I know," Gus said feebly.

The pain came in a white-hot burst. It shot up his spine, exploding in his brain. Gus sucked in his breath as his body contorted. He slapped his ink-smeared palms against the wall behind him, leaving streaks of sweat-soaked blue.

"There's a man," Gus hissed, "in Juterbog. He knows." He was breathing heavily now against the pain. "He's Four. He can get you to them."

"What's his name?" Remo asked.

"I don't know," Gus replied. The pain came again, as he knew it would. "I *really* don't!" Gus cried. Tears streamed down his swollen red cheeks. "It's Kempten Olmu-something. It's a really long old German name. I can't pronounce it. I've never been very good with German."

All at once, the pain stopped. Gus sucked in a tentative breath. It was truly gone. He had never before realized how good a feeling it was not to be experiencing agony.

His torturer was still standing before him. His brow was furrowed, casting an annoyed shadow over his dark eyes.

"Do you have a phone?" Remo asked.

Gus nodded fervently, anxious to remain on Remo's good side. "Yes, yes. Absolutely. It's upstairs." He waddled past Remo deliberately—Gus was now a man with a mission.

"Good," Remo said, following him. "Because we have to call someone who's good with German."

3

Harold W. Smith was submitting to the latest in the interminably long line of physical examinations he had been subjected to over the past three months.

He sat in his spotless white T-shirt on an examining table in one of the doctor's offices of Folcroft Sanitarium, a Rye, New York, mental-health facility of which he was director. Smith breathed calmly as the physician inflated the blood-pressure cuff around his left biceps.

The doctor watched the indicator needle on the gauge in his hand as he gently released the air from the bag. He nodded his approval.

"Your blood pressure is good," he said.

"I assumed it would be, Dr. Drew," Smith responded crisply. There was an icy edge in his voice.

The doctor looked up over his glasses as he slipped the cuff from Smith's arm.

"Forgive me, Dr. Smith, but you were the one who insisted on these examinations."

"Yes," Smith replied. "However, they appear to be no longer necessary."

"You were in rough shape a few months ago," Dr. Drew cautioned, as if Smith had forgotten.

Smith hadn't. There was no way he would ever forget his recent trip to London.

"It was a very stressful time," Smith admitted.

"Yes," Dr. Drew agreed, dragging his stethoscope from his ears. "I imagine it would be. It's a shame that on the first vacation you took since I came to work here at Folcroft, you wound up in the middle of a war zone. Do you and your wife plan to take another?"

Smith pursed his bloodless lips. He didn't appreciate the informal tone Drew had taken with him over the past few months. After all, the Folcroft doctor was Smith's employee.

"I fail to see how my private life is your concern," Smith said, getting down from the table.

Drew stiffened. "I didn't mean to pry, Dr. Smith," he said tightly.

Smith didn't even seem aware that he had insulted the physician. The older man had already found his shirt on a brass hook near the door. He had pulled it over his creaking shoulders and was in the process of buttoning it.

"If that is all, I will return to work," Smith said absently as he fastened the top two buttons. He drew his green-striped Dartmouth tie from the same hook and began knotting it around his thin neck.

"Of course," Dr. Drew replied without inflection. "Same time next week?"

"That will not be necessary," Smith declared officiously.

Drew raised an eyebrow. "If you wish to postpone, it's obviously at your discretion. Remember, my day off is—"

"Thursday," Smith supplied. "And that does not matter. Our appointments are no longer necessary." He finished with his tie, checking the perfectly formed four-in-hand knot with his aged fingertips. Satisfied, Smith took his gray vest and suit jacket from another hook.

"Are you sure?" Dr. Drew asked.

"Of course," Smith sniffed. "I will let you know if there are any changes in my physical condition. Please excuse me."

Without so much as a thank-you, Smith left the office.

Dr. Drew stared at the door for a few minutes.

"You're welcome," he said with a sarcastic laugh.

He didn't know why he was surprised by his treatment at the hands of the sanitarium director. The real surprise was that Smith came to him for help in the first place. But the old man had been in pretty rough shape back then. Now that he was better, Smith was back to being his old nasty self again.

Dr. Drew realized that it was his own fault for expecting anything more than being treated as a servant. At this stage, there shouldn't be anything that

Dr. Harold W. Smith could do to surprise him any longer.

With a sigh, Dr. Lance Drew began labeling Smith's latest blood sample.

HAROLD SMITH WALKED briskly to the administrative wing of Folcroft. He took the stairs up to his second-floor office.

Mrs. Mikulka, his secretary of many years, smiled maternally as he entered the outer room of his small, two-office suite.

"Dr. Smith," she said with a concerned nod.

Smith didn't appreciate the familiarity her smile represented. Some in the staff had been treating him differently since he had returned from his week-long European vacation three months before. Dr. Drew and Mrs. Mikulka were the two worst offenders.

Smith found it easier to remonstrate Drew than Mrs. Mikulka. After all, doctors were a dime a dozen, but good secretaries were impossible to find in this day and age.

"I will be in my office for the duration of the morning," he noted crisply as he passed her tidy desk.

There was no need to ask her if there had been any calls while he was downstairs. Eileen Mikulka was efficient enough to let him know immediately if there was anything that required his attention.

When he pushed the door closed on the world a

moment later, Smith felt a tide of relief wash over his thin frame.

This was Smith's sanctum sanctorum, his haven from the foolishness and trivialities of the outside world. In this sparsely furnished room, Harold Smith had created for himself a perfect, orderly environment.

He crossed over to his desk, taking his seat behind the smooth onyx slab. The desk was the only hint of intrusion by the modern world into the decidedly low-tech room.

Smith's arthritic fingers located a rounded button beneath the lip of the desk. When he depressed it, the dull glow of a computer screen winked on beneath the polished surface of the large desk. The monitor was angled in such a way to make it invisible to anyone on the other side of the desk.

Smith raised his fingers above the edge of the desk's surface. Immediately the orderly rows of a computer keyboard appeared as if summoned by magic. In actuality, the capacitor keyboard needed only to sense the presence of his hands above it in order to activate.

Smith began typing rapid commands into the computer. His fingers drummed softly against the flat surface of the desk. Each key shone obediently in amber in the wake of Smith's expert touch.

To the uninitiated, everything within this office was gauged to appear precisely as it should for the rather bland director of an anonymous private health facility. However, the work that consumed Dr. Harold W. Smith was decidedly atypical for the humorless head of a medical facility. Smith was using his computer to search out neo-Nazi activity.

There was a vast store of data through which to sort. Too much for Smith's liking.

He began scrolling down a list of German names. Some were marked with asterisks. Many more were not.

The delineated names were members of neo-Nazi groups who were now deceased. The dates of their deaths were clearly marked beside their names. All of the dates had been entered since September. Smith knew this for a fact. After all, he had entered the dates himself.

His lemony features grew more pinched as he scanned the list of dead. There were a great many of them. More than he would have liked. And not one of them had been any help whatsoever.

It was slow, slow going.

So far, they had limited the hunt to Germany. Smith dreaded the prospect of expanding the search parameters further. There was so much to sift through in this one country alone that he couldn't begin to figure out how he would approach searching through the files of fascist sympathizers around the world.

As he worked, a dull ache began to grow at the back of his head. Smith did his best to ignore the pain, as he had for the past few months. His work was too important to be sidetracked by a minor headache.

Of course, Smith was not concerned with his work as director of Folcroft. Mrs. Mikulka was able to handle nearly all of the day-to-day operations of the facility herself.

The work that Smith found so important was that which was conducted without the knowledge of any of his underlings. This included his search through neo-Nazi files. Indeed, Folcroft could be consumed in flame and burn to the ground and Smith's true work would continue.

For in truth, Folcroft Sanitarium was only a front. Beyond the high brick walls and the attendant dignified stone lions that guarded the somber iron gates, within the ivy-covered walls of Folcroft itself, beat the heart of an organization so secret its existence was known to only a tiny handful of people.

The organization was CURE, a group sanctioned by the highest level of America's elected government and whose operational parameters granted it virtually unlimited discretion in dealing with the nation's enemies. Smith was CURE's director.

It was a thankless posting for a rigid bureaucrat whose devotion to patriotism was as rock solid as the granite hills of his native Vermont. It was this patriotic bent that had nearly gotten him killed.

Although the press would never know the truth, CURE had been responsible for the defeat of the neo-Nazi force that had taken control of Paris in August. On vacation with his wife at the time, Smith had gotten personally involved in the mission. As a result, he had suffered various scrapes and bruises, as well as a rather severe concussion.

He hated to admit it, but the emotionless Smith had been stirred to passion by a level of revulsion he hadn't felt since his youth, when he had helped topple Germany's Nazi regime. This past summer when he had been thrown in among a crowd of jack-booted neo-Nazis, it was as if the years had been stripped away. Smith had reacted as he would have in his youth.

But he was no longer a young man.

The reckless fury he had directed at the army of young skinheads in August was now channeled to an activity more suited to a man of his advanced years. With the aid of CURE's basement mainframes he was attempting to locate the shadow organization behind the Paris coup.

Smith typed furiously for nearly an hour. When he was finished, he had found nothing. He knew that the group he was looking for was called IV, but there was nothing his computer could turn up that might help him zero in on the organization.

He was only succeeding in covering old ground.

So that was that. The answers he sought were obviously not in Germany. Smith steeled himself for what he knew he must do. He had been dreading the thought of it, but there were no other options left.

He would have to expand his search.

Wearily Smith began typing the preliminary commands into his computer. He was distracted from his work by the jangle of a telephone. One hand remained poised above the keyboard as he retrieved the blue contact phone from its cradle. He tucked the receiver between shoulder and ear.

"Report," Smith said pointedly, returning to his work.

"I think I've got something, Smitty," Remo's voice announced over the international line.

"What is it?"

There was a strange gurgling noise over the line. It stopped abruptly. The instant it did so, a voice that was unfamiliar to Smith wheezed out a foreign-sounding name.

"Kempten Olmutz-something-with-a-hyphen."

The man struggled for breath.

Smith had been accessing police records in the Netherlands, Denmark and Poland. He quickly switched over to his German neo-Nazi file. He began scanning the list of names.

Remo's voice came back on the line. As soon as it did, the bizarre gurgling noise resumed.

"Did you get that, Smitty?" he asked.

"Yes," Smith said tightly. He was having no luck with the known neo-Nazis on file. There were several Kemptens, but none with a last name remotely like the one the voice had given him. "Are you still in Berlin?" Smith asked Remo.

"Uh-huh."

Smith accessed the Berlin phone directory. He scrolled rapidly down to the *O*s. Still nothing.

"This man is in Berlin, presumably," Smith commented.

"I don't think so," Remo said. His voice grew more faint as he addressed someone nearby. "Where'd you say he was?" he asked.

The low gurgle had continued until now. It stopped. "Juterbog," the strange voice rasped. The gurgle resumed.

"Jitterbug," Remo said to Smith.

Frowning, Smith accessed the proper phone book. He found the name immediately.

"Kempten Olmutz-Hohenzollerkirchen," he said.

"Wow. He must have to print that on both sides of his business card," Remo mused.

"Confirm this before you proceed," Smith pressed.

"Okeydoke," Remo said. The gurgling grew very loud now. It was the sound of someone being strangled. "Say that name again, Smitty?" Remo called from somewhere beyond the gurgle.

Smith repeated the name. There was a choked "yes" on the other end of the line.

"He's our man," Remo said, coming back on the phone.

"I will see what I can uncover about him," Smith said. "You and Chiun proceed to Juterbog."

Remo sighed. As he did so, the strangling grew louder. Frantic.

"We'll go there, but I bet I end up doing most of the work."

"Why? Is something wrong with Master Chiun?"

"I don't know," Remo griped. "He hasn't been much of a help lately." The gurgling sound reached a fevered pitch and then stopped suddenly. There was a heavy thump, audible even over the satellite-to-fiber-optic-cable telephone feed. "Are you still keeping a kill record?" Remo asked.

Smith winced at the term. "Yes," he admitted.

"Add Gus Holloway," Remo said, then hung up the phone.

Smith found that his headache had gotten worse during his phone conversation with Remo. He removed an aspirin bottle from one of his desk drawers and took out two pills. He swallowed them without water.

Smith's throat—dry as dust—had a difficult time accepting the two aspirins. He finally felt them drop from a point beneath his protruding Adam's apple. They plopped into his acid-churned stomach.

Medicated, Smith returned to his computer. Calling up his list of neo-Nazis, he located the name of Gus Holloway. Beside his name, Smith wearily recorded the day's date.

4

The old man had been a fixture in the musty corner of the ratty Juterbog beer hall for as far back as anyone there could remember. He sat in the same chair, in the same back booth wearing the same reeking clothes every single night of the week. His yellowed eyes rarely strayed from the door.

A smoldering cigarette hung in perpetuity from between his brown-smeared chapped lips. The blackened stumps of teeth that remained attached to his mucky gums were held in place seemingly by damp ash alone.

He smoked in deep drags, blowing great hazy clouds at the smoke-yellowed ceiling. There his relentless exhalations would join the massive fog created by the assembled drinkers in the Schweinebraten Bier Hall.

Kempten Olmutz-Hohenzollerkirchen stared at the door as the young men around him reported the latest news.

There were three of them, all dressed in skintight black leather with a multitude of zippers. Their heads were shaved smooth, and their noses and ears were adorned with a variety of safety pins, chains and earrings.

"That fat American was found dead this morning," an earnest skinhead named Hirn whispered. The pin and chain in his flat nose wiggled enthusiastically as he spoke.

"How?" asked another.

"Strangled with his own armband."

Hirn tapped his biceps. Beneath his long-sleeved black shirt was a Nazi band similar to the one that had been found wrapped around the bloated neck of Gustav Reichschtadt. Hirn and his companions were forced to hide their armbands when they ventured out in public.

Aged Kempten pulled his cigarette from his mouth. Bits of skin on his lip tore away, stuck to the unfiltered end. Kempten didn't seem to notice the bleeding.

"Where was this latest attack?" he inquired, voice thick with phlegm.

"Berlin."

Kempten nodded. "Did anyone see his killer?" The ball of brown goo that he coughed up and spit to the floor of the beer hall was as large as a small mouse.

Hirn nodded and glanced over his shoulder at the rest of the room. "It was *him*," Hirn said in a hushed voice. Shivering, he took a pull from the large beer stein which sat on the table before him.

No one seated in that cramped booth needed to

ask who "him" was. They all knew the stories of the unstoppable killer who was carving a bloody path through the neo-Nazi underground.

Kempten made a mental note. He had been reporting each of these incidents as he heard them. He would have to make another phone call tonight.

"Have there been any others since then?" Kempten asked.

"Today?" Hirn said. "No, none today. The American was the only one. I heard the killer was seen chasing him at nine o'clock this morning."

"That dumpling would not be very hard to catch," one of the other young men joked.

The group around the table joined in an uncomfortable chuckle. All except Kempten.

The old man made a sudden supreme effort to clear decades of mucous buildup from his smoke-ravaged throat. An awful, ragged wet rumble poured up from deep within his withered chest. Whatever this maneuver managed to dislodge was swallowed back down an instant later in a slippery-sounding gulp. Kempten nodded across the crowded room to the door.

"My eyes are not so good," he said to the disgusted group of young men. "Who is that who just came in?"

Hirn looked back across the hall to the distant entrance. Through the haze of smoke he saw a thin young man framed in the doorway. The new arrival was scanning the room with a pair of eyes buried so deep within their sockets they lent him the appearance of an angry skull.

Hirn turned back quickly, his heart beating madly. He glanced at his two younger companions. They had seen the stranger, as well. All three skinheads were looking anxiously at one another.

"It's him," Hirn whispered anxiously.

Old Kempten was still straining to see the door.

"Who is it?" Kempten repeated. "Is it Rolph?"

He squinted at the figure that was even now scanning the many faces around the crowded room. Try as he might, Kempten couldn't see who the strange outsider was.

AS SOON AS HE STEPPED through the door of the Schweinebraten Bier Hall, Remo's body automatically doubled the number of times he ordinarily blinked per minute. The air in the cramped bar was thick and grimy and his eyes were forced to work harder than usual just to cleanse themselves of the accumulation of smoke and attendant airborne particulates.

He had assumed that he would be bothered most by the stench of fermented grains, but he had forgotten the European love affair with carcinogens. If they weren't mining them, building shanties on them or being irradiated by them, they were damned well determined to smoke them.

Fortunately Chiun had declined to join him on this expedition to Juterbog, preferring the solace of their

Berlin hotel. The Master of Sinanju would have been impossible to deal with in a place like this. As it was, Remo's body was having a hard enough time filtering out the airborne toxins.

He would have to get in and out fast.

Keeping his breathing shallow, Remo began making his determined way across the room.

"HE IS COMING this way!" Hirn whispered urgently.

"Who?" Kempten demanded. The others still hadn't told him the reason for their sudden concern.

"Holloway's murderer," Hirn explained. It was all the warning he planned to give Kempten. As neo-Nazi sympathizers, they were *all* in danger. Hirn included.

Hirn jumped to his feet, joined by his two skinhead companions. Without another word to Kempten, they hurried off through the crowd. They circled over near the bar, cutting a wide swath around the intruder.

The killer was nowhere near them. He was walking through the cluster of tables in the center of the main floor. Although the room was thick with stretched-out legs and bent elbows, the man moved through the tangle without so much as a single sidestep. It was as if he had no more substance than the smoke-filled air around him.

"He doesn't see us," one of the young men said, braver now that the shadowy door loomed closer.

The chain in his nose tinkled softly as he nodded dully.

"Shut up," Hirn hissed.

As he spoke, he watched in horror as the killer's dead eyes turned their focus on him. It was as if he had somehow been able to single out the skinheads' hushed voices in the clamor of beer-fueled shouting.

Hirn's stomach twisted into frozen knots.

"Hurry up," he whispered urgently to the others.

They had seen the change in the stranger, as well. The trio hurried to the exit.

They were two yards away from the door when a terrifyingly familiar face appeared as if summoned by magic from out of the smoke before them.

"What put the goose in your step?" Remo asked, eyes leaden.

"Excuse us, sir," Hirn begged, swallowing nervously. Over Remo's shoulder, the door remained enticingly out of reach.

"Hmm. Polite for Germans," Remo mused, nodding. "I guess you three must be all putsched out. I'm looking for someone. Kempten Oatmeal-Hasenpfeffer, or something like that. His landlord said I'd find him here."

Three index fingers decorated with black nail polish stabbed in unison to the rear booth.

"Back there," Hirn insisted anxiously. "Very old. Yellow eyes. Bad teeth. You cannot miss him."

"Thanks," Remo said. "I don't intend to. By the

way, bad teeth hardly narrows the field in this country.'' He began gliding past them.

There was a collective sigh of relief from the three skinheads.

''That is all?'' one of them whispered, relieved. Hirn could have killed him.

Remo stopped abruptly.

''Actually, this is your lucky day,'' Remo said, turning back to the trio. ''I was told to cut back on my killing.''

There was a look of nervous relief on the faces of two of the skinheads. Hirn remained stone-faced.

''But that doesn't mean I'm not allowed to vent a little righteous indignation.''

Remo's hand shot forward three times. Each skinhead was aware of a blur of movement beneath his eyes and of a sudden, wrenching sensation at the center of his face.

The pain followed at once.

All three skinheads grabbed at noses that were suddenly gushing blood. Loose, frayed flaps of skin hung wet beneath their fingers.

As they watched in agony, Remo dropped three identical nose chains to the nearby bar.

''Hang Hitler,'' Remo announced with a sharp click of his heels and a crisp Nazi salute. Smiling, he headed back across the hall. Toward old Kempten.

THOUGH HIS EYES WERE no longer perfect, they didn't need to be. Kempten Olmutz-Hohenzollerkirchen clearly saw his three companions point him out to the vile Nazi killer.

The old man had hoped to hunker down behind his cigarettes and beer until the intruder left the bar. He saw now that this was no longer possible.

Climbing uncertainly to his feet, he began hobbling quickly to the rear of the beer hall. He was vaguely aware of a door back there. At least there had been one about fifty years ago. He hoped it was still there.

As he walked, Kempten leaned against the side wall for support. He was an emaciated figure in out-of-date clothing. A few patrons glared angrily at him as he stepped steadily over feet and handbags in search of a door that might or might not be there.

He was surprised when he stumbled upon the ancient fire exit a moment later. His discolored eyes squinted suspiciously as he reached for the long metal bar.

Kempten rattled the handle. The door stubbornly refused to budge. He leaned his bony shoulder against the painted door and pushed with all his might. Still nothing.

He couldn't allow his exertions to get the better of him. Every moment brought the assassin closer to him.

Kempten leaned back and shoved once more against the door. It sprang abruptly open. The old man found himself flying out into a garbage-filled alley. He landed in a heap atop a pile of fetid, rain-soaked plastic bags.

Hurrying, Kempten used the grimy alley wall to pull himself to his feet. As he moved, his dry tongue stabbed around the filterless end of his imported cigarette.

Coughing madly, he turned away from the garbage heap...and came face-to-face with the very man he was avoiding. The horrid spasm that racked his lungs froze in his throat.

Eyes flat, Remo allowed the rusted beer hall door to swing quietly shut behind him. The raucous shouts from within grew muffled, replaced with the sounds of distant traffic. Car horns honked angry complaints somewhere away from the alley.

Remo spoke but one word.

"Four."

Still leaning against the alley wall, Kempten made an unpleasant face. Taking a deep drag on his cigarette, he blew a cloud of defiant smoke in Remo's face.

He was smiling contemptuously, showing off his row of jack-o'-lantern teeth, when it occurred to him that Remo was no longer standing before him. The smoke cloud had missed its target. Kempten frowned.

He was still frowning when Remo reappeared beside him.

"Didn't you catch the Surgeon General's warning on these?" he whispered with quiet menace.

Remo reached out and yanked the cigarette from Kempten's mouth. Somehow, half of Kempten's lower lip came with it. As the old Nazi screamed in pain, Remo stomped both lip and butt beneath the toe of his Italian loafer.

"Four," Remo said again.

"Go to hell," Kempten snarled. He spit a bloody glob of phlegm at Remo. Remo sidestepped the expectorated ball.

"Age before beauty," Remo said. Grabbing up a handful of the old Nazi's greasy, yellowed hair, he twisted.

To Kempten, it felt as if his scalp had caught fire. He was acutely aware of each individual hair follicle as it burned a laser-precise hole through to his brain. Pain like nothing he had ever known made him scream in sheer agony.

"Pain on," said Remo, giving the hair a final twist. "Pain off," he added. He loosened the pressure.

The old man was surprised at himself. He had always thought he would be able to hold out under torture.

The words came in a flood.

"There is a village," Kempten breathed wetly. "It is a haven for those who are reviled by the world."

"Why aren't you there?" Remo asked.

Kempten missed the sarcasm completely. He

puffed his chest out proudly. "This is my home," he said. "I will not be driven from it."

"Spoken like a true fascist homesteader," Remo said. "Where is this village?"

Kempten shrugged. "I do not know."

"Not good enough," Remo said, grabbing at another clump of filthy hair. He lifted the old man off the ground.

"South America!" Kempten shrieked. "Beyond that, I cannot say!"

Remo knew the old Nazi was telling the truth. His pain level was far too high for him to be able to sustain a lie. Remo released Kempten's hair. Tangled bits dropped in filthy clumps to the grimy alley floor.

"I do not know where the village is," the old man continued, panting heavily. "That is a privilege reserved only for those who choose to make it their home."

"How do you contact them?" Remo demanded.

"A telephone number. I can give it to you," he added helpfully. He began searching through his grubby pockets. After a moment, he produced a small scrap of paper. Like everything else about Kempten Olmutz-Hohenzollerkirchen, the paper was a sickly brownish yellow. He handed it to Remo.

Remo scanned the numbers. They meant nothing to him. He tucked the paper in the pocket of his chinos.

While searching for the paper, Kempten had removed a battered pack of cigarettes from his jacket pocket. Hands shaking, he tapped one from the rest, pasting it to the clotting blood on his lower lip. With a dirty silver lighter, he ignited the tip. The cigarette burned a bright orange.

Kempten waggled the cigarette at Remo. He shrugged his wasted shoulders feebly.

"It is customary, is it not?" he said, indicating the cigarette with a nod.

Remo nodded. "Knock yourself out," he replied, folding his arms across his chest.

Kempten took a long, thoughtful drag. He exhaled mightily into the foul air of the alley. Beyond the closed metal door, the endless party within the beer hall continued its muffled hum. Kempten knew that he would never see his favorite corner booth again.

When his cigarette was nearly finished, the old Nazi took it from his mouth and stared at the glowing tip.

"The village is well guarded," he said absently. "Even for someone of your abilities, it will be dangerous."

"Yeah, yeah, yeah," Remo grumbled, uncrossing his arms impatiently. "Will you hurry up with that thing?"

Kempten replaced the cigarette. He took one final, great pull. The tip of the cigarette burned brightly, and his lungs filled with the soft, comforting smoke.

Kempten blew the last puff of smoke into the air.

"You will die there," he said smugly. He dropped the spent butt to a filthy puddle at his feet.

Remo smiled grimly. "Maybe. But better there than here," he said as he reached out with a thick-wristed hand for Kempten's throat.

WHEN HE LEFT the alley a few moments later, all that could be seen of the late Kempten Olmutz-Hohenzollerkirchen was a pair of stained black shoes sticking out of an oversized plastic garbage bag.

The old Nazi's body with its collapsed ribs and lungs would not be found for two weeks. By then the anonymous IV village would lie in ruins and an ancient myth would threaten to bring the economy of Germany to the very edge of bankruptcy.

Remo Williams would take credit for the former, but he would swear until his dying day that the latter was not his fault.

5

When Herman brought him the news of the disappearance of old Kempten, Adolf Kluge was in the process of packing up his office. There were cardboard boxes piled on the floor around his big desk. Kluge abandoned the box he had been filling and dropped woodenly into his chair, considering the import of the young man's words.

"When?" the head of IV asked.

"Around three o'clock, Berlin time," his aide replied. "It was him again."

Kluge glanced up. "The Asian was not with him?" he asked.

"The older one was not seen," Herman admitted.

Kluge shook his head unhappily. "That does not mean that he was not there," he sighed.

"So you have said."

"How do we know all this?"

"Our operatives are in place. Per your instructions, they went immediately to his most likely targets. Kempten was on the list."

Kluge's mouth opened in shock. "If they were there, why did they not kill Kempten themselves?"

"They arrived at the beer hall after the younger Master of Sinanju. They could only watch as he led the old one outside."

"And they did not think to follow, obviously," Kluge said sarcastically. He threw up his hands in amazement.

"Those were not your instructions," Herman explained.

"Of course not," Kluge snapped. "If they had killed old Kempten, they might have ended this right then and there. But no. I did not fill out a form in triplicate instructing them to do so." He wheeled around, staring at the ancient mantelpiece stretching along the outer wall. Like many of the other fine antiques in the massive stone temple, the mantel had been imported from Germany. "Freakish dunderheads," Kluge muttered under his breath.

"What are your instructions, Herr Kluge?" Herman asked after an uncomfortably long moment had passed by in silence.

Kluge barely heard the words. He found himself staring at an object on the mantel.

Getting slowly to his feet, Kluge walked over to the fireplace. He took down the item that had drawn his attention, feeling its weight in his hands.

He stared at the heavy article as he spoke.

"He has gotten to Kempten. He is therefore much closer to us," Kluge mused aloud. His eyes never strayed from the object in his hands. "It is only a matter of time before he reaches the village." He turned to his aide. "Tell the fools in Germany to regroup. If he has gotten the information we entrusted to old Kempten, then we know where he will have to go next.''

The aide frowned. ''You wish for them to return to South America?''

Kluge cast a withering eye on his aide. ''No,'' he said with exaggerated patience. ''My hope is that we may stop them before they leave Germany. Send them to the airport. The men from Sinanju will surely go there first before skipping off to South America, wouldn't you agree?''

Herman took Kluge's sarcasm without reaction.

''I will let them know,'' he acknowledged.

''Please do,'' Kluge said. ''For, God help us, our lives are in the hands of those bungling aberrations.''

Nodding his understanding, the aide stepped briskly from the cluttered room.

Only after Herman had gone did Kluge realize that he was still holding the object he had taken down from the mantel. It was a two-inch-thick block of petrified wood with a face approximately one square foot around. Ancient characters had been chiseled in the solid surface of the wood.

Although time had worn some of its carved features smooth, most were still plainly visible.

Kluge stared at the wood for a long time.

When he finally spoke, his words were barely audible.

''There is a kernel of truth in all legends,'' he said.

Frowning, Adolf Kluge tossed the wood carving into the nearest packing crate.

6

The Hotel Ein Dunkles was a tidy little building on Meinekestrasse just off the Kurfurstendamm, which until very recent German history had been the main street in isolated West Berlin.

Remo was whistling a cheery version of "The Star-Spangled Banner" as he pushed into the tidy lobby and strolled across the plush carpeting toward the lone elevator.

From behind his polished desk, the hotel's gray-haired proprietor—apparently still nursing festering wounds from the Second World War—shot him a foul look from over his gleaming bifocals. It had the practical effect of making Remo whistle all the louder.

As the elevator doors were closing, Remo directed a final shrill burst toward the glowering desk clerk.

He had calculated the pitch perfectly.

Remo's final glimpse of the man before the elevator doors slid silently shut was that of the middle-aged German pulling off his pair of shattered glasses. If they hadn't been broken, the desk clerk would have been able to see that his watch crystal was cracked, as well.

Happy, Remo rode the elevator up to the third floor. As the doors rolled quietly open, he paused to listen into his apartment, which was directly across from the lift.

He heard nothing.

Relieved, Remo crossed over to the door. He had just placed his hand on the polished brass knob when there came a sudden burst of wild electronic laughter from inside. This was followed by a merry cackle that was all too familiar.

Sighing, Remo pushed the door open.

The television was on—as he had expected it would be. The bulk of the laughter he had heard came from the small speaker on the side of the set. The balance came from the hotel room itself.

Seated before the TV was a man so old he made Kempten Olmutz-Hohenzollerkirchen look like a toddler. Unlike the dead Nazi, however, this old man had a vibrancy of spirit that belied his many years.

The wizened Asian's tan skin was the texture of dried rice paper. His bald head was framed with puffs of gossamer hair—a single tuft above each shell-like ear. Bright hazel eyes displayed a glint of fiery youth that old Kempten hadn't known since the days when brownshirts marched along the Rhine. Even now the aged Korean was laughing uproariously at the action on the TV screen.

"I'm back," Remo called unhappily.

Chiun, Reigning Master of the five-thousand-year-old House of Sinanju—the premier house of assassins on the face of the planet for as many millennia—turned to Remo. Tears streamed down his parchment cheeks.

"You have missed the funniest program yet," Chiun breathed. He sniffled as he turned back to the TV.

Remo frowned as he looked at the television. On it, a rather thin, gawky Englishman was stumbling around with a gigantic turkey over his head. Chiun shrieked in joy as the odd-looking man attempted to disguise the bird by throwing a blanket up over it.

"I've seen this one before," Remo complained.

"I have seen many sunsets, yet each is always more beautiful than the last."

"In that case, try looking out the window," Remo suggested blandly. At that very moment, the sun was sinking low over the Berlin skyline.

"Shh!" Chiun insisted with an angry flap of one kimono-clad arm. He stared in childlike joy as the strange-looking man on the TV attempted to remove the turkey from his head. The Master of Sinanju clapped his hands with glee.

"I'm going to call Smith," Remo sighed wearily.

Chiun made an effort not to listen.

Remo turned his back on the familiar scene and walked over to his bedroom. He shut the door as Chiun's bald head bobbed in eager anticipation of the impending turkey removal.

Sitting on the edge of the bed, Remo picked up the phone. He began depressing the 1 button repeatedly. It was rather simplistic, but it was the only phone code Remo ever seemed able to remember.

Smith picked up on the first ring.

"I need you to trace a number for me, Smitty," Remo said by way of introduction.

"Proceed," came the tart reply.

Remo gave Smith the phone number from the scrap of paper he had gotten from the old Nazi at the beer hall.

"The country code is for Uruguay," Smith noted.

"What can I say?" Remo said. "Nazis have a love affair with South America."

He could hear Smith's fingers as they drummed against the touch-sensitive keyboard buried beneath the edge of the CURE director's desk.

"The number you have given me is to a hotel in Montevideo," Smith said after a brief pause.

"Geography isn't my strong suit, Smitty," Remo cautioned.

"That is the Uruguayan capital," Smith explained.

"And also where the rest of South America goes to rent movies on Saturday night. What happened when they were naming the place—'Blockbuster' already taken?"

"Actually the name stems from a story that is most likely apocryphal," Smith explained. "*'Monte vide eu'* is what Magellan's Spanish lookout allegedly shouted when he first spied the shore. It means 'I see a mountain.'" Smith returned to the subject at hand. "May I ask what purpose this number serves?"

"That Kermit Ovitz guy bit the dust," Remo explained. "But he gave that up first. It's supposed to be a secret number to contact Four."

"I do not believe so," Smith said. "It appears to be no more than an ordinary number. It is something called the Hotel Cabeza de Ternera."

"That doesn't make sense." Remo shook his head. "I know he wasn't lying."

"One moment," Smith said.

Remo could hear Smith drumming his fingers against his keyboard. A moment later, he was back on the phone.

"The proprietor is not Spanish," Smith stated. He tried to keep an excited edge from his voice. "His name is Dieter Groth." The typing resumed, more urgently now.

"Let me guess," Remo said. "He's a German immigrant."

"Groth emigrated to South America thirty years ago. One moment, please, Remo." He paused. "I've accessed the records of the Committee to Bring Nazi War Criminals to Justice. They do have a file on Groth, but are not actively pursuing him at the present time."

"It's their lucky day. They're going to get a freebie," Remo said. "Book me a flight to Uruguay."

While Remo remained on the line, Smith quickly made the necessary arrangements.

"By the way, Smitty," Remo said after the flight was sorted out, "the old guy said something about a village down there that's supposed to be a refuge for Nazis."

"I will borrow satellite time to search the Uruguayan countryside," Smith said. "In the meantime, you and Chiun follow up the Groth lead."

"Can do," Remo said.

He hung up the phone. As he did so, there was renewed laughter from the living room of the suite. The Master of Sinanju shrieked in joy as a new program began. It starred the same British comic and was one the old Korean had seen at least a dozen times.

Remo wondered how he could pry Chiun away from the TV.

"I wonder if the gift shop sells extension cords that'd reach all the way to South America?" Remo asked with a sigh.

Already fatigued by the battle not yet fought, he got up from the bed.

IT TURNED OUT rousting Chiun was not as difficult as Remo imagined it would be.

The Master of Sinanju's umpteenth viewing of the same British sitcom episode ended an hour before their flight was scheduled to leave from Tegel Airport. Remo rounded up the seven steamer trunks

Chiun had brought from the United States and herded them into two small European taxis. Remo and Chiun followed in a third cab.

As they drove through Berlin's crowded post-twilight streets, the Master of Sinanju detailed all that had occurred on the television while Remo was talking to Smith.

"When the ugly British woman removed the fowl from his head, he found to his delight that the item he sought was in his very mouth."

"Uh-huh," Remo said. He stared out the cab window.

"Did I mention that it was his wristwatch?"

"Yes, you did," Remo sighed.

"I ordinarily do not approve of the use of ornamental timepieces," Chiun cautioned. "They are for those too slothful to develop the inner clock in the minds of all men. However, for comic purposes it was quite amusing."

He looked over at his pupil. Remo remained silent. His sharp features were illuminated at regular intervals by Berlin's streetlights.

"You do not appear to be amused," Chiun challenged.

Remo shook his head. "I'm sorry. It's just that I saw that show before."

Chiun raised an eyebrow. "So?"

"So, I couldn't give a fat flying frig."

Chiun's wrinkled face drew into a deep frown. "You do not have a sense of humor," he accused.

"I do, too," Remo argued. "The first fifty times I saw those shows, I thought they were funny. But we've been in Europe now for over three months, and that's all every country seems to play, day in and day out. I can't take anything twenty-four hours a day, seven days a week."

The harsh frown lines were reshaped into a look of intense pity. "You are a humorless man, Remo Williams," Chiun pronounced sadly. "I knew it the day we met. Not that you made any effort to hide the fact."

"I do, too, have a sense of humor," Remo said defensively.

Chiun raised an instructive finger. His nail was long and fiercely sharp. "If one must say it, it is untrue," he declared. "For only the humorless man is ever accused of being so."

Remo could not think of a clever retort. Unfortunately this didn't prevent him from trying.

"Blow it out your ears," Remo said sullenly. Crossing his arms, he hunched down in the seat and stared at the back of their driver's head.

Chiun clutched at his heart. "Oh, I am stung by your piercing wit," he moaned histrionically. "Forgive me, O King of Comedy, for ever doubting your jovial soul." The Master of Sinanju smiled happily, pleased at having made his point.

Remo felt the blood rise in his cheeks.

"Is it any wonder I'm annoyed right now?" he groused. "You ditched me weeks ago for that hotel idiot box. I've been clomping alone around this backward excuse for a country whacking every knockwurst-fueled spike-hat I find, while you've been having a hey-ho time watching Brit-coms and ordering room service. So forgive me, Chiun, if I've lost my goddamned sense of humor.''

"I did not accompany you because I lost interest," Chiun said simply. "We are assassins, not exterminators. Smith had you scouring the countryside for all manner of vermin. In Germany, that could be a lifetime's occupation. And as for your second point—" the impish smile returned "—one cannot lose what one never had.''

The elderly Korean settled placidly back into the taxi's seat.

Beside him, Remo racked his brain for something witty to say. Most everything he came up with, however, involved surly references to biological functions. Any of these would doubtless inspire further derisive comments from Chiun.

With great reluctance, Remo remained mute for the remainder of their trip to the airport.

WHILE REMO HAD MADE a deliberate choice to remain mute for the duration of his ride to Berlin's airport, the man who intended to kill him had been born that way.

The assassin had been sent from the IV village, accompanied by three colleagues.

Lounging around the main terminal building of

Berlin's Tegel Airport, the four of them were an odd sight. The casual observer would have assumed they were related somehow. And in a very real way, they were.

In order to keep the curious at bay, an attempt had been made to differentiate between them.

One had long hair and was dressed casually in blue jeans and denim jacket. Beneath the coat was a red flannel shirt.

Another man wore dark sunglasses and a tweed blazer. His hair had been pulled back into a ponytail and tucked down behind his jacket collar.

The hair of the third had been cut short. He wore a conservative business suit and a pair of wire-rimmed glasses.

The well seemed to have run dry with the fourth. He, too, wore a business suit, though of a different color than the third man. He had been allowed to keep his hair long, but not at the same length as the first two. It was trimmed and moussed and parted neatly in the middle like a young Hollywood star.

Even after all the effort at disguise, close inspection revealed a rather startling fact. These men did not simply look alike; they were each identical to the next.

Four interchangeable muscular young men with perfectly chiseled Aryan features.

The man in blue jeans was their leader. He watched the glass double doors to the airport terminal with hooded eyes.

They had come here immediately upon receiving their orders from Kluge's underling, Herman. The four men had sat virtually unmoving for almost three hours. Incapable of speech, they had passed the time in utter silence.

Oddly they didn't seem agitated in the least. It was as if nervousness or boredom were concepts completely alien to them. They had been given a mission and were waiting with absolute patience to carry out their assignment.

They were closing in on the end of the third hour when their long wait finally came to an end.

The man in blue jeans spotted the short line of cabs as the three vehicles drew up to the curb outside the door.

The first two cabbies sprang out of their cars. One raced to find a pushcart while the other began unloading his cargo of lacquered steamer trunks to the sidewalk. It was as if they had been rehearsed, so precise was their performance.

Remo and Chiun climbed out of the third cab along with their cabbie. Chiun immediately began issuing orders to the remaining drivers.

The blond man with blue jeans tapped once on his seat, and his three colleagues took note of the activity on the sidewalk.

Like well-rehearsed zombies, the trio got up and walked deeper into the terminal. Their leader remained sitting, waiting for the hectic scene on the sidewalk to spill inside.

The missing cabbie returned with a cart. He and the others loaded up the steamer trunks while Chiun flounced between them in his saffron kimono. The Master of Sinanju made copious use of both hands and feet to ensure that his luggage was properly attended to.

In the end, one unlucky driver was chosen to wheel the cart inside. The other two were allowed to leave. Their tiny cabs made smoking rubber stripes on the asphalt in their eagerness to leave before Chiun changed his mind.

Remo and Chiun followed the least lucky cabbie inside the drafty building.

As they walked past the row of plastic seats near the door, the young blond man got to his feet. He trailed the two targets at a discreet distance.

"Use care, lummoxy Teuton," Chiun clucked angrily when the cab driver hit a bump on the rubber mat that was spread before the baggage check counter. The cabbie cringed, expecting a swat from the old Asian's lightning-fast hands.

"You going to be okay with this?" Remo asked.

"We are fine," Chiun said, eyeing the taxi driver with suspicion.

"Okay, I'll get the tickets," Remo offered. They separated, each going to an end of the counter.

Remo collected the boarding passes Smith had ordered for them. The overly friendly woman behind the desk was more than willing to help Remo and his aged companion. Beaming, she relayed Chiun's pertinent ticket information via computer to the woman operating the baggage-check terminal at the far end of the counter.

"Iss dere someting else?" she asked with a lascivious grin. It was clear from the look on her face that she would have invaded Poland for him.

The look she gave him sparked a thought.

"Actually there is," Remo said.

The woman squealed in delight. "I get off at nine. Actually I can get off right now. I'll be sick. Or I could qvit. I'll qvit. I qvit!" she shouted to no one in particular. A few faces turned her way.

"No," Remo said, easing the woman back behind her computer. She had been climbing over the counter to get to him. "I was just wondering about the menu on the flight."

"Oh." The woman seemed crestfallen. When she glanced around, she saw that the few people who had looked at her were already looking away. Forcing a businesslike air, she studied her computer. "Ve haff bratwurst and sauerbraten sandwiches. Braunschweiger or wienerwurst. Unt beer."

"Any way of getting some shark meat?"

Remo was surprised when the woman nodded. "Ve haff *koenigsberger klops*," she offered helpfully.

"Is that shark?"

"German meatballs," the woman said.

He saw now that she was only half listening to

him. She was staring at his crotch even as she tried to work.

"You're drooling on your keyboard," Remo observed.

"Vant to sit on it unt dry it?" She grinned lewdly at him as she tapped the counter.

"Tell you what—you start, and I'll catch up with you."

The woman did not need to be told a second time. In an instant, she was off the floor. Her Bavarian backside mashed her damp keyboard. As she slid from side to side like a human mop, Remo gathered up his and Chiun's tickets.

As he walked back over to the Master of Sinanju, he noticed that the woman had scrawled her telephone number on the bottom of his ticket. He rubbed his thumb against the handwriting, exciting the particles of ink at the atomic level. By the time he reached Chiun, the pen marks had faded to invisibility.

Chiun had just finished supervising the passing of his luggage through the square hole in the side of the counter. He was dismissing the grateful cab driver as Remo sauntered up beside him.

"I suppose I don't have to tell you we're being watched," Remo announced.

"Since our arrival," Chiun said blandly. He studied his last trunk as it slid along the conveyor.

Their work in Germany was over. Remo had gotten the information they needed to proceed.

"What do you want to do?" he asked Chiun.

"I wish to leave this land of pastry-eaters in peace."

"Me, too," Remo said. "Let's ignore him."

Together, they began walking toward the stairs that would take them to their boarding gate.

They had gotten no more than four feet from the counter when the first bullet was fired at them.

It was aimed at Remo's back. He shifted his weight slightly to his left foot in order to avoid the incoming round. After the bullet had passed harmlessly by, he continued his lazy glide across the main concourse.

The lead projectile thudded between two doors set into the wall beneath the main staircase.

"He's using a silencer," Remo commented.

"It is still not silent enough."

"Not for us, maybe," Remo said. "But at least no one else can hear it."

Another two bullets came whizzing in their direction. This time both Remo and Chiun had to dodge the fat lead rounds.

"He's using a clip." Remo frowned.

"Should I care?" Chiun asked.

"Dammit, Chiun, a clip holds more rounds. He's bound to shoot someone by accident before we can get out of here. Crap," he griped. "What is it with this dingdong country?"

Abruptly Remo dropped back from Chiun, twisting sharply on his left heel. In a flash, he was suddenly walking in the opposite direction.

The shooter obviously had not anticipated a change of course on Remo's part. He didn't have time to slow his own brisk pace before he slammed directly into Remo.

"Oh, sorry," Remo apologized, helping the stumbling man to his feet. As he did so, he tugged the man's gun free. The would-be killer had secreted the weapon beneath a newspaper that was draped over his hand.

They were near the wall struck by the first fired bullets. A waist-high trash receptacle was sitting next to the men's-room door. Remo slipped the gun through the metal lid, dropping it into the pile of trash within the barrel.

"Gee, pal, you don't look so hot," Remo said.

He took the man by the arm as if to support him. With his free hand, Remo tapped a hard finger against the killer's chest. Immediately the man's heart stopped beating. He would have slumped to the floor had Remo not still been holding him upright.

"A little cold water on the face should fix you up," Remo suggested to the corpse. "Chiun, gimme a minute. This poor guy needs a hand."

"Do not dawdle," Chiun urged.

Remo pushed his way through the swinging men's-room door, carting the body with him. The

Master of Sinanju took up a sentry position outside the door.

Inside the bathroom, Remo propped the body up against the line of sinks. He quickly searched the man's pockets for identification. There was none.

"Great," Remo muttered unhappily. He stepped back from the corpse, looking more closely at the face. Maybe Smith would have a photo on file that would help identify whoever this had been. Not that it mattered very much at this point.

As he examined the features, something about the man's face sparked a distant memory.

Leaving the body leaning against the sink, he stuck his head out the bathroom door.

"Hey, Chiun, come in here a minute."

Frowning, the Master of Sinanju followed Remo into the bathroom. Inside, Remo pointed at the body.

"Does he look familiar to you?" he asked Chiun.

Casting a puzzled glance at his pupil, the Master of Sinanju tipped his head, examining the young man's face. His hazel eyes opened wide almost at once.

"He wears the face of the voiceless lout from the place that robbed us of free will." The old Korean sounded surprised.

"That's right," Remo said, remembering all at once. "He worked for what's-his-name." He snapped his fingers. "Holz. He was Holz's assistant."

It was six months ago during what they would

later learn had been their first brush with IV. That man had been a mute. As Remo inspected the features of the corpse in the Berlin airport he realized that he was the spitting image of the man they had encountered half a year before.

"This is eerie," Remo said. "That guy is dead."

"So is this one," said Chiun. He nodded to the door.

"Yeah," Remo said, nodding his understanding.

He took the body and stuffed it in one of the bathroom stalls. Slamming his palm against the door, he crushed the metal lock. It would be necessary for airport maintenance to use a welding torch in order to free the body.

"Let's make like the German band and blow," Remo suggested.

They hurried back out the rest-room door.

They hadn't even gone around to the bottom of the escalator before they were again assaulted. This killer attempted to use a dagger.

The man jammed the knife toward Remo's ribs. Rather than dodge the blade, Remo tightened his muscles at the point of impact, flattening out the skin above as he did so. The knife blade slammed against Remo's back, but—much to his attacker's consternation—his back was incredibly unyielding. The knife failed to even puncture Remo's tight skin.

The abrupt manner in which the knife was stopped caused its wielder to lose his grip. His hand inadvertently skipped up beyond the hilt, gripping down again automatically. Unfortunately the portion of the knife he managed to grab on to was the sharpened, double-edge blade.

Remo was surprised that the man didn't cry out in pain. His mild surprise turned to utter bewilderment when he turned around to face his attacker.

It was the same man as before. This time the young blond killer wore a sedate blue business suit. His hair was shorter, and a pair of glasses sat atop his nose.

"What the hell?" Remo said, glancing at Chiun. The Master of Sinanju seemed confused, as well. That was good. At least Remo knew he wasn't going nuts.

The man was bleeding profusely from twin gashes in his hand. Like the first time, Remo gathered the killer up and carted him off to the men's room. This time he didn't get as far as the bathroom before the third killer attacked.

This assassin used a high-powered rifle. Unseen by passersby, he was on the upper tier of the terminal building wedged between a pair of tall plastic signs that advertised two competing international credit-card companies.

The silenced bullets from the rifle ripped into the wall beside Remo and Chiun, who fluttered and danced to avoid the spray.

"I will attend to this facsimile," Chiun announced sharply. Like an orange typhoon, the Master of Sinanju flew toward the escalator to the second floor.

This was getting tricky. Although the people passing through the airport didn't know exactly what was going on, Remo and his bleeding companion had caught their attention. A few raised curious eyebrows. Fortunately the assassin didn't ask any of them for help.

"Let me give you a hand," Remo said, loud enough for anyone nearby to hear. He was careful to keep this one alive as he led him into the men's room.

Remo was positive he had killed the assassin on the first attempt, but had to be certain. Leaving the man to attend to his bloody hand at the sink, Remo peeked under the stall door just in case. The dead killer was still there. His sightless blue eyes stared into Remo's.

"That's a relief," Remo muttered, getting to his feet. "Okay, spill it," he said as he turned to the second thug.

The man was in the process of binding his injured hand with a handkerchief. Remo caught his reflection in the long mirror that stretched above the row of sinks. His resemblance to the first attacker was disconcerting.

As he examined the face, Remo caught a hint of something sinister in the man's eyes. All at once, the man wheeled around, his unbandaged hand flashing forward.

The knife that Remo had failed to take away flew toward him now, eating up the space between them in a flash. At the last minute, Remo leaned back, snagging the knife from the air. He tossed it over his shoulder, and it landed with a splash in one of the unseen commodes.

"That's enough of that," he said, marching over to his assailant. Reaching around, Remo snagged a knot of muscle at the base of the man's skull. "Who sent you?" he demanded. A hand like a vise squeezed tight on all the neck's pressure points at once.

The killer's eyes sprang open wide. But though the pain should have been unbearable, he didn't even attempt to speak.

Remo was surprised. This technique had never failed to induce a response in the past. He increased the pressure.

This time, Remo got a reaction. The man opened and closed his mouth in a desperate attempt to communicate. No words came out. He gulped helplessly and silently at the air, giving a flawless impression of a fish gasping for breath in the bottom of a boat.

And the light finally dawned on Remo.

"You're a mute, aren't you?" he asked.

There was still no response. The man looked at him with helpless, pleading eyes.

"Great," Remo said. "You're a mute who doesn't understand English."

He tightened his grip on the man's neck. Vertebrae popped away from one another like beads on an abacus. The thug immediately went limp.

Remo carted the dead man over to the stall where he had ditched the first attacker. He threw the second killer up over the top and tucked random protruding arms and legs back in under the door.

Remo quickly left the men's room. He met the Master of Sinanju at the stairs. Chiun was just coming down from above.

"Was your guy mute, too?" Remo asked.

"He did not say," Chiun replied blandly.

"Har-de-har-har," Remo said. "Where did you put him?"

"He will not soon be discovered," the Master of Sinanju insisted. "Unless these cuckoo-clock makers have invented some special means to unseal maintenance closet doors. In case of that eventuality, I would recommend we make haste."

"Yeah," Remo agreed. He and Chiun stepped onto the escalator. "If nothing else, this proves we're on the right track," he said as they rode upstairs.

"Perhaps," Chiun replied.

"Perhaps, nothing," Remo said. "The guy we met six months ago couldn't talk, either. That makes four identical guys who are all mutes. I think I smell a pattern here."

"Here no longer matters," Chiun sniffed. "We are leaving."

The elderly Korean was right. And Remo was surprised at how good it felt to finally be leaving German soil.

They found the proper gate and made their way onto the plane. When they were settled into their seats, Chiun was delighted to find that the in-flight movie was a feature-length version of the sitcom he had enjoyed watching virtually the entire time they had been staying in Europe. Remo hunkered down, steadying himself for a long, long flight.

As the plane taxied for takeoff, neither of them noticed the young blond man seated in the rear of the cabin.

7

Smith wasn't certain if it was the aspirins that had done the trick, but his pounding headache had eased somewhat since morning. He massaged his gray temples delicately with his fingertips as he studied the satellite images that stretched across his computer screen.

Through circuitous means, Smith had gotten time on a military satellite that was in geosynchronous orbit over the massive northern section of South America. The surveillance device was put in place to monitor drug activity in that part of the continent.

The satellite had been redirected ostensibly at the request of the CIA, which was working in conjunction with the Drug Enforcement Administration on mapping the latest U.S. inroads being made by the powerful La Cosina drug cartel. When the order to reposition the satellite came through via computer, no one questioned why the Colombian drug lords would ship their product south when their ultimate destination was north. The technicians simply shifted the satellite as directed.

Smith wore an unhappy expression as he studied

the grainy images. He couldn't seem to find anything in the rolling hills and wide prairies of Uruguay that even remotely hinted at a hidden Nazi village.

At first blush, the existence of such a place was an idea that seemed to border on fantasy. But Smith had seen much recently that lent credence to the claim of the old German from whom Remo had gotten the information. With the facts they had thus far confirmed, Smith conceded that it was very likely there *was* a secret community tucked away in some dusty, long forgotten corner of the world.

But if the IV village was on these satellite photos, Smith didn't see it.

The work was tedious. First he needed broader images to find signs of roads and buildings that didn't match up with any known map. When he did find an area that didn't conform, the satellite had to zero in on the place in question. He would then be able to get a closer look at the unfamiliar spot. At that point, Smith would attempt to judge whether or not the nonlabeled area was the product of a faulty mapmaker or had been deliberately omitted from official documents.

But so far there were no mysterious deviations. Every strip of highway, street and access road was accounted for. He had studied the images for hours. His only break came a few minutes before when one of his special computer programs raised an electronic flag. Some odd deaths had been reported at the airport in Berlin. They matched the Sinanju pattern of Remo and Chiun.

The only truly odd thing was that the dead men were said to be triplets. While Smith found this interesting, he could not fathom its relevance. He vowed to question Remo about the matter when CURE's enforcement arm checked in from South America. In the meantime, he had work to do.

Twenty more minutes passed before Smith's headache began to reassert itself once more. The main pressure area was a spot at the crown of his skull. It felt as if the painful throbbing were connected by a taut and twirled elastic band that ran straight through his brain and out along his optic nerve. He felt nauseous.

Smith pulled his bleary eyes away from the computer screen. He leaned back in his creaking chair. Pushing his glasses up, he gently rubbed his eyelids with his fingers.

The headaches were worsening and coming with more frequency. They had begun in the wake of his return from France after the vacation debacle that was supposed to be a celebration of his fiftieth wedding anniversary.

Smith knew that the headaches must somehow be related to the blow he had received on the back of the head by an unnamed IV operative. At the time, the man had been posing as a member of British Intelligence. Circumstances had been such that no one save the Master of Sinanju had bothered to question the man's authenticity.

Smith was lucky he hadn't been killed. If the headaches continued much longer, he knew he would have to consult a specialist. Dr. Drew was a competent physician, but if there was some greater trauma, the Folcroft doctor would be out of his element.

Smith opened his tired eyes. The queasiness still clung to his stomach and ribs. For an unsettling moment, he thought he might vomit.

Smith steeled himself. He didn't have time for nonsense.

He leaned forward once more in his chair, readjusting the rimless glasses on his patrician nose. The black-and-white images on the computer seemed clearer to him now.

Good. Perhaps it was all simply a matter of determination.

Peering down at the screen, Smith began to once more carefully scrutinize the contours of the current satellite image.

A COUNTRY AWAY from the area of South America that was the focus of Harold Smith's pointless search, Adolf Kluge was touring the silent, tidy streets of IV village.

The pretty little gingerbread houses in their gaily painted colors were silent tombs. They were lined up along the cobbled roads—their doors locked, their shuttered windows closed on dead, black interiors.

A numbing stillness stretched up like icy hands from the mountainous rock beneath Kluge's feet. It wound its arms around everything—houses, streets, even the distant mountaintops. The very air around him seemed wrapped in eerie calm.

Everywhere was silence.

It was the beginning of summer in this hemisphere. Flowers had been planted in the rich black soil of brightly colored window boxes. As he walked along, Kluge wondered if the plants would grow wild and eventually go to seed, or if they would be burned to ash.

He had never seen the village empty. These hills in the lower Andes had not been without activity since the first handful of carpenters hired by IV had put hammer to nail to construct the first block of quaint, old-world homes. That had been in the 1950s.

Now all was still. Every building was empty. And it had happened on the watch of Adolf Kluge.

His sadness was tinged with threads of anxiety as he walked past the last of the small houses.

The mountain fortress that was the nerve center for IV even before the rest of the village had been built loomed on its separate mountain peak before him. It was like something from another world. The long stone bridge that connected the fortress peak with the mountaintop on which the village had been constructed stretched downward until it became part of the road Kluge walked on.

Between the village and the bridge, just before the chasm that separated the two peaks, was a lush, bucolic field. Ordinarily parcels of this land were portioned out to the older members of the village with an interest in gardening. Today, the field was home to Kluge's neo-Nazi army.

Several hundred men were gathered in the meadow. Each of them carried an assortment of weapons. Kluge's aide walked over to him as the IV leader stepped from the road and began walking through the tall grass of the field.

"We are ready," Herman announced.

Kluge smiled wanly. "Are we?" He focused his thoughts. "Any news out of Berlin?"

The aide hesitated. "They…failed."

Kluge closed his eyes. "All dead?"

"Three of them. The fourth has not yet faxed in."

"Faxed," Kluge said sarcastically. "We do not even have agents capable of using a simple telephone."

He looked over at the men lined up in the field. At first glance, an intruder might think that he was seeing some elaborate illusion. A funhouse-mirror army.

Impossible as it might seem to the uninitiated, many of the men lined up in that small Andean field were identical to each other. Azure blue eyes, collar-length blond hair pulled back into ponytails, perfectly hewed, almost feminine bone structure. They looked to have been stamped out, one right after the other, by some bizarre Aryan factory.

It was a disturbing image.

Mixed in with these men were a few other IV soldiers. Like Kluge, they were dedicated young men who had been born into the movement. Some had even been raised here in the village. They were standing here, waiting to defend their home.

Kluge had never felt compelled to dress the soldiers of IV in the maudlin frippery of days gone by. In fact, he had made a deliberate effort to avoid sticking his troops in Nazi uniforms. If someone had somehow managed to sneak a camera up into the village, the last thing he wanted was for his people to be goose-stepping around in SS uniforms.

Dressed in plain brown shirts and slacks, the men in that field looked as if they could have been part of any nondescript South American police force from Venezuela to Chile. That is, with the obvious exception of the small silver lapel pins on each of their shirts.

The pins were bisected by a narrow line. On one side was inscribed the Roman numeral IV. On the other was a simple engraved swastika.

Kluge looked away from the pin on the nearest man. With a bitter grumble, he turned his attention to his aide.

"It is possible that the agent who has not been reported dead somehow managed to succeed in his mission," Herman ventured. "Perhaps he is en route here."

"Yes," Kluge replied dully. "And perhaps *they* are en route here. Did you think of that?"

Herman cleared his throat. "That thought did occur to me," he admitted.

Kluge's blue gray eyes were flat as he turned from his aide. "It is very quiet here," he commented, looking back over the silent village. "Almost peaceful."

"Herr Kluge?" Herman questioned, his voice striking a troubled note. It was as if he wanted to draw attention to the seemingly apathetic attitude of IV's leader without being insulting. His tone worked.

"I have not taken leave of my senses, Herman," Kluge replied tightly. When he looked back from the sleeping village, his brow was furrowed. "Yet," he added. "Have you made certain the other defenses are fully operational?"

Herman nodded sharply. "We will give them more of a fight than they expect, Adolf. And we will prevail."

"Perhaps," Kluge said. He didn't sound convinced.

"Unquestionably," Herman said with a determined nod.

Kluge said nothing. Let the fool bury his head in the sand if he wished.

The head of IV looked out over the sea of identical faces. "Explain to them what is to be done," he directed. It seemed an effort for him to point a world-weary finger at his army. "I do not have the patience."

Clasping his hands behind his back, Adolf Kluge walked back across the field to the road.

Shoulders hunched, the leader of IV strolled up the path toward the bridge.

The huge stone fortress loomed above him, a massive headstone for the grave that had been the IV village.

8

With two connecting flights and various delays in between, Remo and Chiun didn't arrive in Montevideo until after 3:00 a.m. Instead of looking for Dieter Groth in the middle of the night, they decided it would be best to settle into their hotel for a few hours' sleep.

The hotel they chose was the Cabeza de Ternera, the place Smith claimed was operated by the potential Nazi.

Remo never slept in beds any longer, preferring a simple mat on a hard floor. However, since he had neglected to bring a tatami sleeping mat along with him, he instead tossed a half-folded sheet down onto the dull green wall-to-wall carpeting.

He had just settled down on his makeshift bed and was drifting off to sleep when a familiar sharp noise shook him from his slumber.

"Oh, no. Not here, too," he groaned, rolling over.

In the living room of their spacious hotel suite, the Master of Sinanju was cackling loudly. The television hummed softly, with occasional bursts of laughter from a studio audience. Remo could almost see the pantomime antics of the British TV comic.

Moaning, Remo pulled the pillow down from his bed, drawing it down tightly over his ears.

Remo could ordinarily blot out sounds as easily as a normal man might close his eyes. However, he had discovered several months before that the combination of the shrieking canned laughter of the TV soundtrack and the Master of Sinanju's own delighted cackle could penetrate his best auditory defenses.

After a sleepless half hour, Remo finally gave up.

When he walked back out into the living room, another episode of the same sitcom was just beginning. On the television, the odd-looking English actor was driving desperately down the street in his pajamas. Remo didn't want to know why.

"I'm going to look for Groth now," he complained.

A bony hand waved impatient dismissal. "Fascinate the chambermaid with announcements of your comings and goings," Chiun snapped. "I am busy." His face grew more intent as he studied the screen.

Remo rolled his eyes as he stepped into the hallway.

He strolled down the hall past the elevator. Pushing open the fire door, he walked down the four flights of stairs to the hotel lobby.

It was only four-thirty in the morning, so the same night desk clerk who had checked Remo and Chiun in was still on duty. He was a thin boy of Spanish descent. Remo's best guess wouldn't have put him much older than seventeen.

"Me again," Remo announced, walking up to the desk.

The boy grinned earnestly. *"Buenos dias!"* he said.

Remo wanted to resent the clerk for being so cheerful, but the boy's guileless, eager face made it impossible to do.

"I'd like to see Dieter Groth," Remo said.

The desk clerk's cheerful expression evaporated.

"Does *señor* know the time?" he asked.

"Too early for British sitcoms," Remo grumbled.

"Señor?"

"Nothing," Remo said. "Groth. Is he here?"

"Señor Groth does not come in until eight o'clock," the boy said apologetically.

Remo tapped an index finger against the desk. He glanced over at the stairwell door, considering. Did he really want to go back up and listen to Chiun's incessant hooting for the next three and a half hours? After a long, thoughtful moment, he shook his head.

"I'll wait," Remo insisted. He walked away from the front desk and settled into one of the plush chairs flanking the front door.

GROTH ARRIVED at the hotel at precisely 8:05 a.m.

Remo spotted the German immediately. He was a barrel-chested man in his early seventies. Old age hadn't even considered sneaking up on Dieter Groth. At first glance, Remo guessed that it was afraid to.

Groth's features were severe, his face darkly tanned. He wore a short-sleeved dress shirt, untucked, and a pair of pleated white pants.

"Guten Tag, Herr Groth," the young desk clerk said nervously as his employer approached across the lobby. *"Wie geht es Ihnen?"* He seemed uncomfortable with the German words.

It didn't matter. Groth didn't seem to even hear him as he collected the morning mail from the desk clerk without a word. The boy seemed relieved to not be singled out for attention. Groth left him alone, walking down the employees' corridor next to the desk.

At that moment, the regular morning desk clerk arrived, ten minutes late for his shift. He was calling out excuses in Spanish the instant he stepped through the door.

The night clerk was so eager to chastise his fellow employee for his tardiness that he failed to notice that the hotel guest who had been sitting by the door waiting for the arrival of Señor Groth for nearly four hours was nowhere to be seen.

GROTH DROPPED THE MAIL to his desk with a loud slap.

"Hot," he murmured, flapping his arms uncomfortably. "I hate this damned heat."

He turned to the wall where the air conditioner

controls were located. He hadn't taken a single step before noticing something with his peripheral vision. He wheeled around.

"Good morning, starshine." Remo smiled. He was standing inside the closed office door.

It was impossible. Groth had shut and locked the door. He should have heard someone enter behind him. Were they asleep at the front desk? Heads would roll for this.

"I'm looking for directions," Remo said.

Groth scowled. "Front desk," he grunted, jabbing a thumb at the door. He sat down behind his own desk. When he looked up, he was agitated to see that Remo was still there.

"Kempten sent me," Remo said. He smiled tightly.

The look that passed over Groth's face was both subtle and telling. He knew. Old Kempten was dead and Dieter Groth already knew.

In the next instant, Groth was lunging for his desk drawer. He ripped it open, jamming his hand down atop the Luger pistol he stored there for emergencies.

Even before Groth opened the drawer, Remo was slipping behind the desk. As the German's fingers found the gun butt, Remo slapped his palm against the face of the drawer. It flew shut, with Groth's hand still inside. Wrist bones were instantly crushed.

The German tried to howl in pain. Before he could, Remo's hand snaked out and grabbed a spot on his neck. Though Groth tried desperately to scream, all that issued from the hotel proprietor's throat was a pathetic croak.

"I'm looking for Four, sweetheart," Remo pressed. "Where is it?" He eased the pressure on Groth's bull neck.

"Argentina," the German gasped. Sweat had broken out on his tanned forehead. The blinding pain in his shattered wrist was almost more than he could bear.

"Where?" Remo pushed.

Whatever Dieter Groth might have said was lost forever.

At the precise moment his thick lips were parting, the door to the office burst open. As Remo and Groth turned, a young woman leaped into the small room, brandishing a handgun.

Dieter Groth looked for a moment as if he had seen his salvation. The relief was short-lived.

Groth's eyes grew wide as the gun leveled on him. A crackling explosion filled the small room. A single bullet struck Dieter Groth's forehead with a satisfying thwack.

The German's dark eyes blinked once in bewilderment and then rolled back in his head, closing forever. The soft hiss of startled air from his slack mouth petered to silence.

"Dammit!" Remo snapped, dropping the dead Nazi onto the desk. Groth hit with a fat thud. The

German immediately began oozing blood onto the Hotel Cabeza de Ternera's morning mail.

"Do not move!" the woman threatened. She had twisted on the ball of one foot. Her smoking gun was now aimed at Remo.

"Not very bloody likely," Remo growled. Her eyes couldn't even begin to process his movements.

Remo flew across the room, snatching the gun from her hand. He flung it to the office floor.

"Who the hell are you?" he demanded.

She was trying to come to terms with what had just happened. Her beautiful face was shocked, but she quickly pulled herself together.

"I might ask you the same thing," she sniffed haughtily. Slender fingers pushed her blond bangs away from her eyes.

"Lady, you're this close to getting tossed out that window." He jerked a thumb over his shoulder.

"We are on the ground floor," she said defiantly.

"Believe me, I can make it feel like the twentieth."

Her lips tightened as she studied Remo's cruel face. She finally seemed to decide that he wasn't making an idle threat. The woman put her hands on her hips contemptuously.

"I am Heidi Stolpe," she declared imperiously.

"German?" Remo asked, surprised.

"I am of German ancestry, yes," she replied. The admission seemed distasteful to her.

"That accent isn't German."

"It is Spanish," she said. "I have spent much time here in South America."

"I bet," Remo said, annoyed. "Okay, spill it. Why'd you aerate Countess von Zeppelin over there?"

Heidi sneered as she looked over at the body of Dieter Groth. "I make no apologies for my actions," she said, eyes hooded. "He was a Nazi. His kind deserve to die."

Remo closed his eyes. "Oh, great," he muttered. "A Nazi-hunter."

Heidi puffed out her chest. "I am proud of that fact," she stated firmly.

"Bully for you," Remo said. "And in principle, you're not going to get much of an argument from me. But couldn't you have waited another two minutes before you plugged him?"

"He avoided punishment for his crimes for more than fifty years," Heidi said boldly.

She obviously had decided that Remo was no longer a threat. At least not to her. Proud chin raised high, she marched over to the corner of the room to retrieve her gun. Stooping, she tossed the weapon into the handbag that was draped around her neck.

"Another *minute* would have done it," Remo said to himself with a morose sigh. He dropped back against the wall, staring bitterly at the body of Dieter Groth.

"What is it you wanted from him?" Heidi asked, coming back over to the door. She seemed barely interested. Her azure eyes didn't even look upon the man she had just shot in cold blood.

"Nothing," Remo said, shaking his head. Even as he was saying it, a thought suddenly occurred to him. "Hey, you said you spent a lot of time down here," he said, looking up.

"Most of my life," she admitted.

"Ever hear of a place called Four? It's supposed to be a village or town or something."

Heidi considered for a moment. "The Spanish word is *quatro*," she advised him.

"No," Remo explained. "This isn't Spanish. I guess it wouldn't even be in German. It's just the Roman numeral IV."

"And this is the name of a village?" she asked dubiously.

"According to him, it's in Argentina." Remo nodded to Groth's body.

She shook her head. "I do not know of this place."

"From what I've heard, it's brimming over with semiretired fascists," Remo said slyly. "A Nazi-hunter could have a field day there."

Heidi frowned. "This is true?"

"Absolutely."

He could see he had piqued her interest.

"And you are certain Nazi war criminals live there?" Heidi asked.

"It'd be like shooting fish in a barrel."

Heidi seemed to reach some inner decision. "I

have contacts in the area. I will ask around for you and return here in an hour. You have a room at the hotel?''

"I *did,*" Remo said. "It might not be a great idea to stick around here after your Ozark Annie act." He indicated Groth's body.

"Perhaps not," she agreed. "Do you know the Old City?"

"I'm new in town," Remo said.

Heidi gave him a few precise directions. "Meet me at the Artigas statue in the plaza at nine-thirty. What is your name, by the way?"

"Remo."

"Is that Spanish?"

"It's actually sort of like the name-game version of the Junior Jumble," he replied.

She peered deeply into his eyes, looking for any hint of sarcasm. Finding none, she nodded once. "Nine-thirty," she repeated." With that, she fled the office.

"Why do I feel like I'd be better off *without* any help?" Remo asked the body of Dieter Groth once she was gone.

Leaving the dead German to ponder the answer to his question, Remo slid silently from the room.

FORTUNATELY FOR REMO, the Hotel Cabeza de Ternera staff was fearful of their domineering German boss. The body of Dieter Groth would be left undisturbed for hours.

Remo managed to pry the Master of Sinanju away from the television and, through the generous application of gratuities, was able to pack up Chiun's trunks and check out of the hotel in less than twenty minutes. In another twenty, the old Korean's luggage was stashed in a less opulent hotel and the two Masters of Sinanju were walking the busy streets of Montevideo.

The city had truly earned its reputation as one of the most beautiful in Latin America. Its tree-lined streets were wide, and the business and residential sections were planned at a time when city planning actually meant something. The buildings were a mixture of both old and new architectural styles.

The Old City that Heidi spoke of was on a small peninsula that had been the city's original location. At the heart of this section was the Plaza Constitucion—the original square of Montevideo. The square was bracketed by the city hall and cathedral, the city's oldest buildings.

In the square was a statue of the national hero General Jose Artigas, leader of the people of the Banda Oriental, which later became Uruguay.

As they approached the statue, Chiun cast a withering gaze up and down the immortalized figure of Artigas.

"Soldiers," he sniffed unhappily. "It is beyond my comprehension why the people of any nation would revere a simple peasant with a boom stick."

"What would *you* prefer?" Remo asked, suspecting what the answer would be.

"I would prefer that the citizenry appreciate the pivotal role an assassin plays in the development of their society. Namely me."

"That's all well and good, Little Father," Remo said, "but when people think of assassins, they don't automatically think of you."

"They should," the Master of Sinanju said haughtily.

"That's not the point," Remo objected. "They *don't*. And I'm not sure the public would rally behind a statue for John Wilkes Booth in the Mall in Washington."

"If not an assassin, perhaps the honor should be given to one who brings joy to the hearts of men the world over."

"That would be you again, right?" Remo deadpanned.

"No," Chiun said. "Though it would be right to honor one such as myself, your beloved lunatic Smith insists we toil in anonymity. Therefore, we are not known to the masses. But there *is* one who brings joy to all in every nation we have ventured to in recent months. I speak of none other than the brilliant comic Rowan Atkinson."

"You're kidding," Remo said flatly. This was the Englishman whose television show Chiun had been watching incessantly for the past three months. "You want a statue to a British TV comic?"

"It does not have to be too large." He looked up disdainfully at the statue of Jose Artigas. "As long as it is bigger than this eyesore, that will suffice."

"Good luck," Remo snorted.

"I will mention it to Smith."

"I'm sure he'll get right on it."

"Do you really think so?" Chiun asked.

Fortunately Remo didn't have to answer. He spied Heidi Stolpe coming toward them down the path near the statue.

She was dressed in a green sleeveless T-shirt and baggy khaki pants. Black military boots were laced up around her ankles. A knapsack was slung over her shoulder. Her short blond hair bounced perkily as she strode toward them.

Remo and Chiun walked over to meet her.

Heidi's face was flushed.

"I do not know what to make of what I have learned," she said. Her voice was excited. "Hello," she added, smiling at Chiun. The Master of Sinanju tipped his head in response.

"You know where Four is?" Remo asked.

She shook her head. "I am not certain. I have checked with contacts I have in the area about associates of Dieter Groth. There is one name that a few seemed to know. A man by the name of Adolf Kluge." She peered at Remo, trying to see if the name sparked any recognition.

Remo shrugged. "Don't know him."

She nodded. "One man I spoke to said this Kluge

could be found in a village in the lower Andes in Argentina. He didn't know the name of the village, but he knew how to get there. When I checked my maps of the area, I found that there was no such place officially listed.'' She dropped her knapsack to her feet. Crouching, she rummaged around inside it, eventually producing a hastily sketched map. She handed it to Remo. ''This is where he said it would be.''

Remo studied the roads and landmarks. There was a circle around a few bottomless triangles, which Remo assumed represented the Andes. In it, Heidi had written ''IV?''

''That could be it,'' Remo said, nodding. ''You want to check it out?'' he asked Chiun.

''Our new lodgings have no television,'' Chiun said with a bored shrug.

''Thanks,'' Remo said to Heidi as he pocketed the map. He and Chiun started to walk away from the Artigas statue.

Heidi ran around in front of them, propping a hand against Remo's chest.

''I am going, too,'' she insisted.

''Sorry,'' Remo said. ''Too dangerous.'' He skipped around her outstretched arm and continued walking.

Heidi kept pace with them.

''I know the area better than you. I could get there first and warn them,'' she said quickly.

Remo stopped. "Now, why would a Nazi-hunter want to do that?" he asked wearily.

"I would not want to, but you could force me to do it," Heidi said defiantly. "If you do not let me come."

"I don't have time for nonsense," Remo said. He waggled a warning finger at Heidi. "If you get shot, it's your business. Don't come bleeding to me."

"I will be fine," she said excitedly. "My jeep is parked around the block."

There was a bounce in her step as she slung her knapsack back over her shoulder. She took the lead. Remo and Chiun followed a few yards behind her. Heidi was humming a Spanish-accented version of an old German lullaby.

"Where did you find this one?" Chiun asked quietly.

"She's the one who shot Groth," Remo explained.

Chiun appraised Heidi's back. "She killed a mere hour ago and is able to sing?" he said. "This female has a heart of stone." There was admiration in his squeaky voice.

Heidi had begun singing softly as they strolled out onto the sidewalk.

"You wouldn't know it to listen to her," Remo snarled. "If she was any damned perkier, I'd kill her myself."

They followed the singing murderess down the busy streets of Uruguay's capital to Heidi's parked jeep.

9

Veit Rauch did not like the Numbers. He had been assigned three of them at his shack near the bottom of the lonely mountainside road that led up to the IV village.

The only route by land into the village, theirs was the first line of defense against intruders. It should, therefore, have been the most heavily manned area within the IV perimeter. Instead, there were only the four of them.

While Veit sat on his stool in the small shed, the three Numbers stood at attention along the road.

Numbers. That's what they were called around the village. They didn't have names; they had assigned digits. They were the blond-haired, blue-eyed creations of the late Dr. Erich von Breslau and his team of neo-Nazi geneticists.

The eggs of a violently unwilling host had been "harvested" by von Breslau. The woman, of course, had been sacrificed to a greater cause.

Through some genetic tinkering that Rauch could not begin to understand, a strand of perfect Aryan DNA had been produced in a laboratory. It combined the flawless traits of a dozen male volunteers. This genetic information was injected into the many egg cells, and the whole mélange was introduced into the bodies of local peasant women whose families had been well compensated for their nine-month inconvenience. The result was the Numbers—hundreds of identical soldiers programmed to blindly serve the leaders of IV.

It was discovered after the birth of the first infants that there had been some unseen flaw in the DNA cocktail. Von Breslau's monsters were born incapable of speech.

Not long after this failed experiment, Adolf Kluge had assumed his post as head of IV. The genetics lab was closed down and its research was halted. Proof of IV's sorry flirtation with manufactured perfection, the Numbers were kept alive as workhorses.

Rauch looked at the three men lined up along the road. He found them particularly unnerving in those instances when they happened to blink in unison. They could not even rightly be termed freaks of nature, Rauch realized, for nature had little to do with their creation.

They stood—each one interchangeable with the next—as monuments to failure. Rauch vowed that if there was any trouble, *they* would bear the brunt of it.

Rauch frowned as he considered the events of the past few months. It was disgusting that IV had come to this. Rauch was the grandson of an important Gestapo officer. The IV village had always been an unassailable bastion against the perverted thinking of the modern world. It had never seen any kind of trouble since his grandfather's day.

But there had been so many deaths in recent months. Some of the dead were people Rauch knew. IV was at the center of an ever tightening noose. And in the darkest corners of Rauch's mind, he wondered if any of them could survive.

There was a small black phone on the narrow shelf near Rauch's elbow. It squawked suddenly, causing him to jump.

He hadn't realized he had been so self-absorbed.

Rauch glanced at the Numbers. They hadn't seen his display of nerves. Not that it mattered. The brutish mutes would not have been able to tell anyone even if they had. He picked up the phone.

"Rauch," he barked.

The whining voice of Kluge's assistant, Herman, came on the line.

"There has been an incident in Uruguay."

"Yes?" Rauch said evenly.

"One of our contacts was found dead."

His heart skipped a beat. "Is it them?" Rauch asked.

"Not likely," Herman said. "Groth was shot to death, and the men we expect do not use weapons. Still, he is a direct link to us. Remain alert."

The line went dead. Rauch's frown deepened.

Getting up from his stool, he stepped out onto the road.

There was no wind today. The lush green scenery that stretched out around them was a painted canvas remarkable only in the diversity of tone. There were greens in these low hills unseen anywhere else in nature.

The mountains loomed high to his right. There were only two types of peaks from Rauch's vantage point. Tall and taller. To his left, down a short incline, the mountain road snaked a sharp U-turn, disappearing into the forest. Beyond the visible stretch of road was a wide-open field, and beyond that, still more mountains.

Though it was a breathtaking vista, Rauch barely saw it.

He was fingering his swastika collar pin as he stepped over to the three Numbers.

"Stay alert," Rauch ordered in a growl, repeating the command he had been given.

It was unnecessary. The men did not even turn his way. They continued staring intently down to the point where the road cut sharply down around an island of foliage.

"Freaks," Rauch muttered.

He turned around and was heading back for the shack when he heard something new echoing against the slowly rising hills. Rauch paused, listening intently.

The sound grew louder.

An automobile engine!

He glanced down the incline to the lower half of the road just as the jeep broke into view.

The vehicle drove swiftly up the steady incline, engine working overtime. As it approached on the lower level, Rauch could see only the driver. There were no passengers.

When the jeep passed on the road beneath, Kluge could clearly make out the face behind the wheel. It was a woman. And there was something about her features that seemed strangely familiar.

The car disappeared behind the stabbing strip of trees and overgrown shrubs. Back near the shack, the Numbers were already aiming their guns down the road. Ready to shoot the incoming car the instant it broke cover.

It never did.

The engine continued to whine, but the car didn't drive forward. It remained hidden behind the copse of trees.

"What is she doing?" Rauch hissed nervously.

"Maybe she had to make a pit stop," suggested a voice at Rauch's elbow.

He wheeled around.

Remo was leaning against the guard shack, a placid smile decorating his hard features.

"There is no need to be vulgar," the Master of Sinanju admonished. He stood next to Remo, dressed in an orange kimono with red piping. A pair of fiery red dragons reared on their hind legs across the front of the flowing garment.

"They are here!" Rauch screamed, stumbling back to the trio of men who still stared down the road. "Shoot them!"

The three blond men spun toward Rauch. Six perfect blue eyes registered surprise when they saw the two men standing by the shed. Almost at once, three pale fingers tensed on triggers.

Rauch dove out of the way as the men opened fire. He skidded on his belly down the incline to the lower road.

A hail of bullets erupted around Remo and Chiun, ripping chunks of wood from the shack and spitting white splinters back atop the deep green plants.

"Wait a minute," Remo said unhappily as he danced around the incoming lead. "Those are the same three guys from the airport. Something's screwy here."

"Yes," Chiun agreed quickly. "While you chatter on like a stupid monkey, we are being shot at." With that, the Master of Sinanju raced across the road to the three men.

"That's news?" Remo griped. He ran after his teacher.

Chiun was first into the group of men. Dodging their blazing rifle barrels, the old Korean danced in between the two nearest men. Grabbing handfuls of blond hair in his long, tapering fingers, Chiun brought the heads together with a supersonic crack.

Perfect Aryan brains spit from perfect Aryan ears and nostrils in perfect little driblets.

As Chiun was releasing his inert bundles, Remo was flying to the third and final triplet.

The last man was spinning in place, desperate to locate his suddenly missing targets. His blue eyes had only just alighted on the smears of gray puree on the road and the placid kimono-clad figure standing above them when he felt a tap on his shoulder. He wheeled.

Remo stood beside him, his cruel features fixed in stone. "Check-out time, Goldilocks," he said.

The surviving Number saw a thick-wristed hand flutter up before his face, index finger and pinkie extended. Briefly, in the uncomplicated center of his genetically engineered brain, the last Number wondered what this man was doing. Then his survival instinct kicked in. Unfortunately, in that infinitesimally short period of time during which he was raising his rifle, Remo's hand was already shooting forward.

The blond man felt an unbelievable, blinding pressure at his eyes. Twin supernovas exploded, each bearing the distinctive swirl patterns of his attacker's fingerprints.

And then the entire universe collapsed back into ethereal nothingness.

REMO ALLOWED the body to fall from his extended fingers. There were no eyes visible in the blood-lined sockets, yet not a trace of ocular fluid or gore was visible on Remo's hand. It was as if the eyes had simply evaporated.

Remo turned from the body.

"I better go get the other one," he said.

Before he had taken a single step toward the ridge down which Veit Rauch had slid, he heard a gunshot. Exchanging tight glances, both Masters of Sinanju raced over to the hill that looked down onto the lower half of the road.

Veit Rauch's twisted body lay on the ground. Above him, gun in hand, stood Heidi Stolpe. When Remo and Chiun broke into view on the hill, Heidi twisted and crouched, aiming her gun up at them with cool professionalism. When she saw who was looking down at her, she relaxed.

"Is it safe?" she called up.

"That depends on who you plan to shoot next," Remo shouted down to her.

Heidi took this as a yes. She ran back up the road, disappearing behind the cluster of trees. A moment later, her jeep pulled into view around the far turn and headed up the hill, stopping at the bodies of the three Numbers.

As he and Chiun climbed into the vehicle, Remo said, "You must be putting your ammo dealer's kids through college."

"Does he always feel compelled to talk even when it is not necessary?" she asked Chiun.

In the back of the jeep, Chiun nodded somberly.

"*And* he has no sense of humor," the old Korean confided. "I spend half my time shushing him and the other half explaining the punch lines to jokes. He is not a bad son, mind you, just dour. And a chatterbox. And he sometimes eats with his mouth open."

"Look, can we just get going?" Remo begged from the passenger's seat.

"He's your son?" Heidi asked, ignoring Remo. She suddenly seemed very interested.

"That's it," Remo announced, throwing his hands up in exasperation. "I'm walking." He reached for the door handle.

"Oh." Heidi glanced at Remo. "Oh, I'm sorry," she mumbled quickly, turning back to the wheel. She seemed upset with herself for becoming distracted.

She slipped the jeep in gear. But even as she eased around the bodies of the failed neo-Nazi experiment for perfection, her eyes strayed to the rearview mirror and the wizened figure in the back seat. There was something infinitely sad in the depths of her azure eyes.

The jeep continued up the winding mountain road.

ADOLF KLUGE WATCHED the jeep proceed on one of the many video monitors that lined the curving wall in the special rear room of the ancient temple.

The treetop surveillance camera tracked the vehicle as far as it could before the system automatically switched over to the next camera. The surveillance had been arranged so that once a vehicle entered the protected IV perimeter, it was never out of sight.

The jeep was moving fast.

This was it, Kluge thought. This was how IV would end.

He still couldn't completely believe that it would happen. Even though he had seen what these men could do, it was impossible to conceive that these two unexceptional-appearing men would overwhelm IV's defenses.

And yet Kluge would not have evacuated the village if he truly believed the village could survive otherwise.

Many of the monitors displayed the empty homes of the abandoned village. In streets and near the mouth of the fortress, his army of men waited patiently.

Kluge spun his chair around. Herman sat over near the radio equipment.

"Tell them they are almost here," Kluge commanded.

Herman obediently radioed the orders down to the troops.

Kluge had turned his attention back to the intruders. "Let us see if we cannot stop them before they get here," he muttered. But his voice lacked conviction.

Face somber, he flipped several silver toggle switches at a broad control panel before him. Once finished, his hand strayed to a single button, index finger hovering in place.

Eyes alert, Adolf Kluge watched the progress of the jeep.

"STOP THE JEEP," Remo ordered.

They were racing along the steep mountain road.

"What?" Heidi asked. "Why?"

"Stop!" Remo snapped.

Face registering her confusion, Heidi slowed to a stop. The mountain stretched up on their left. A wooded slope dropped off to their right, overshadowed by a nearby hill.

"You feel them, Little Father?"

"Of course," Chiun replied. "There are many of them."

"Too many to go through?"

"For *us,* no," the Master of Sinanju said flatly.

Remo looked at Heidi. From the way they spoke, she felt as if she was holding them back somehow. Her expression made it clear she didn't enjoy being treated as a handicap.

"What is it?" she asked, peeved.

"Wait here."

Remo got out of the jeep. Standing on the road, he felt around under his seat. Producing a tire iron, he held it out for Heidi's inspection.

"So?" she said with a look of perplexed annoyance.

"Watch."

Remo flipped the tire iron up the road. It soared two dozen yards before it finally struck the ground. The instant it hit, a huge flash of white and orange belched from the earth. The accompanying violent explosion rattled the road beneath them. The jeep was rocked on its shocks as the windshield was pelted with dirt and gravel.

Heidi sucked in a sharp breath as the unexpected flash of light flared and diminished.

"Land mines," Heidi breathed, once the commotion had died down. A huge smoking crater filled the road.

"The exploding kind," Remo agreed. "Looks like we'll have to hoof it after all."

"It is a lovely day for a walk," the Master of Sinanju said. He stepped down from the jeep onto the debris-scattered road.

Heidi shut off the engine. She was clearly confused. "How do we get through without setting them off?" she asked, trotting to catch up with the two departing figures.

"...WITHOUT SETTING THEM OFF?"

Heidi's voice sounded tinny on the small speakers.

"Damn," Adolf Kluge snapped. "How did they know?" His hand withdrew from the minefield's remote arming system.

Herman shook his head. "They could not possibly," he said. "We planted them only this morning."

"They *know*, Herman," Kluge snarled. He peered at Heidi more closely. The image was not clear. "Does she look like anyone to you?" he asked.

Herman shook his head. "Possibly the Numbers," he said.

Kluge nodded. "Of course. A perfect Aryan woman," he said, "siding with our attackers. A fitting irony for those who write the final history of Four."

He watched the three of them abandon the jeep and head away from the minefield. They went down the side of the hill, disappearing from the camera's range.

Kluge felt a tingle of excitement.

"Perhaps there is still hope," he said. He stood up, leaning over the board before him. With desperate hands, he remotely armed every mine in the road. When he was finished, he waited at the master control. "How long ago did they go down?" he demanded urgently.

"Twenty seconds. Perhaps thirty," Herman answered.

Kluge nodded. "They move quickly, but she will slow them up. Half a minute to the bottom, plus another minute to get in position..." Kluge was counting in his head. When he guessed a minute and a half had elapsed, he smiled nervously. "We will see if we can't surprise the men from Sinanju after all.''

With a sharp stab, he punched a single button. It was the one to detonate the entire field of mines.

THE TREE-DOTTED HILL sloped down sharply to a narrow strip of level land. This minigorge, which ran parallel to both the road on one side and to the upward slope of the adjacent hill on the other, was packed with pine needles and rotting leaves. Some of the boulders that had been displaced when the road was constructed had been rolled down into the ravine. There were many of these scattered like blocks after a child's tantrum. They stood in the way of Remo, Chiun and Heidi.

Remo assumed he would have to help Heidi through the rough terrain, but he was pleasantly surprised to find she was much more agile than he expected.

After abandoning the jeep, she had pulled a drab green coat on over her T-shirt, dragging her omnipresent knapsack over too. With her thumbs tucked into the backpack's shoulder straps, she was scaling the rocks like a professional mountaineer. Scampering up one side of a large rock, she would leap back down to the ravine floor.

For their part, Remo and Chiun appeared to float effortlessly up one side of a rock before gliding back down to the ground.

Chiun made the move look particularly graceful.

The hem of his kimono billowed like a gaily colored parachute as the material caught the small air pockets in the cramped valley.

"Are there any mines down here?" Heidi asked as she scampered up a rock face.

Remo's hands were stuffed in his pockets as he hopped down from a large boulder. "Hard to tell," he said casually.

Heidi, who until now had been in the lead, stopped abruptly. Remo stopped, as well.

"Don't you know?" she asked.

"It's a little trickier here," Remo admitted. "Given the terrain. Oddly enough, mines are much easier to detect in a car. I find that tires focus your senses."

"It is their hollowness," Chiun explained, passing the two of them. He scurried up another rock face. When the stone had been rolled down here, a massive tree was uprooted in its path. Long dead, it remained pinned beneath the huge rock. Enormous, gnarled roots clawed at the air.

"You think that's it?" Remo called up to him.

Chiun nodded. "The compressed air within reacts to the surface of the road. The normal sensory range is thus extended greatly."

"That's probably true," Remo admitted. "I never much thought of it."

"Fortunately for all of our sakes, you are not paid to think," the Master of Sinanju called. He disappeared over the far side of the high rock.

"Is he always so unpleasant?" Heidi asked.

"Naw," Remo said. "He's just showing off because he likes you. Let me give you a hand."

The rock Chiun had vanished over was the tallest so far. Remo was pleased to find that Heidi was not too proud to accept help when it was offered.

Remo held his hands out in an interlocking cuplike formation. Heidi placed one boot inside the U-shape and allowed Remo to boost her up to the rock.

He hopped up beside her.

They were walking to the other side of the great flat rock when Remo felt something reverberate up from the rock-and-leaf strewed ground. To his highly trained senses, it was a sudden snap—like a sheet pulled taut.

It came a split second before the explosion.

The ground beneath began to shake as in an earthquake. Belches of flame were briefly visible between the trunks and branches of trees as a black mushroom cloud poured into the crisp mountain air.

Heidi covered her face against the initial hail of pebbles. "The mines!" she shouted to Remo.

A few boulders ahead of them, the Master of Sinanju stopped dead. He shot a concerned look back to Remo.

"What the hell set them off?" Remo demanded.

The question died in his throat.

His senses had suddenly picked up something else. Even Heidi felt the new rumble through the rock. On the hill above them, she could see the tops of the farthest trees topple and vanish behind those closest to them. They were being flicked aside by some horrifying force.

It was like a clichéd movie scene in which some creature from a bygone age first makes its appearance. Except this terror was real.

An avalanche.

"Remo!" Chiun squeaked anxiously. Trees nearby rattled.

"Go!" Remo shouted back.

Chiun hesitated at first, too far away to offer assistance. All at once, he spun on a sandaled heel, his mouth a thin line. Rapidly he began bounding from rock to rock, distancing himself from the main area of collapse.

The trees nearest them ripped away. Like pencils in some massive sharpener, they were flung beneath the great rolling boulders. The mighty trunks were split to kindling and thrust into the ravenous maw of the avalanche.

When the mass of rock was nearly upon them, Remo snatched Heidi up around the waist. It would be difficult enough by himself. He didn't know if he could manage with extra baggage.

Remo didn't follow the Master of Sinanju. He was too far back. If he attempted to follow, Remo would be swept under the collapsing mountain of debris. Instead, he spun on his heel and—Heidi in tow—

headed directly into the incoming rush of stone and earth.

The first rock he encountered was only as large as a beach ball. It was rolling rapidly as Remo dropped one toe atop it. Using opposite force against the stone's forward momentum, Remo vaulted up and over. He landed on a larger, flatter stone that was being swept along at the fore of the advancing pile of churning rubble.

Fortunately Heidi was not fighting him. She remained limp beneath his arm, not wishing to distract him from his life-or-death ballet.

His next jump brought him to a toppled tree trunk. It was scraping down the hill at a terrifying speed.

Remo ran to the far end of the log, then rode it like a surfboard back down into the growing pile of debris.

Already in the valley, many of the rocks they had been climbing on earlier were covered by fresh stones.

When the lower end of the log they were on struck the swelling pile of debris, Remo jumped again. Both feet barely touched the surface of a dangerously splintering boulder before he sprang again. He landed on yet another stone.

The huge rock he had barely trodden on struck an even larger boulder at the bottom of the ravine and shattered. The pieces were instantly covered in a washing mass of dirt.

Remo leapfrogged a few more times, but found the going increasingly easier.

The avalanche was tapering off.

With a sigh of settling earth and a cloud of choking dust, the last of the largest chunks of earth and sections of broken road rolled into the ravine. Long after, tiny stones still toppled along the devastated path of the avalanche.

In all, it had taken no more than a minute.

Remo set Heidi down to the still-reverberating earth. He glanced back at the damage.

It looked as if the claw of a gigantic backhoe had swiped a huge chunk out of the side of the mountain. There was a single stripe of missing trees and rock running straight up to the road. The valley where they had been standing was buried.

Panting, Heidi looked at Remo. For all his exertions, he had not broken a sweat. He wore a deep scowl.

"Have I told you lately that I hate Nazis?" Remo grumbled.

As he spoke, Chiun bounded into view far ahead of them. He stood at the nearest visible part of the valley that had not been overrun by the avalanche. For an instant when he first saw Remo, the Master of Sinanju was visibly relieved.

"Remo, that was—" he suddenly considered his words, and his look of relief morphed into one of blasé acceptance "—adequate."

"Adequate, my ass," Remo griped. "That was

perfect. And how the hell did they do that without us stepping on the damned things?''

"They could be set to accept a radio signal.''

Remo turned away from Chiun, looking at Heidi.

"Thank you, Professor Science,'' he said.

"Do not ask if you do not wish to know,'' she said with a shrug. Readjusting the pack on her back, she struck off toward Chiun.

"No wonder everyone loves Germans,'' he muttered to himself. "They're so damned cuddly.''

Following Heidi, he began hiking across the fresh pile of stone rubble toward the waiting Master of Sinanju.

IT HAD BEEN forty-five minutes since Kluge had set off the field of land mines. The leader of IV had sat in front of the bank of video monitors the entire time, his anxiety level rising every minute.

"Has everyone reported in?'' he asked Herman.

"Yes, sir.''

"Even Theodor? You were not able to raise him.''

"It was a communications problem,'' Herman explained. "It has been corrected.''

Kluge nodded. He glanced at the monitor on which he had last seen his stalkers. A ragged V-shape crater was visible on the road. Beyond it sat the girl's parked jeep.

"They are dead, Adolf,'' Herman insisted.

"Possibly,'' Kluge said. There was a touch more optimism in his voice than there had been of late.

"I cannot imagine anyone surviving that," Herman said, indicating the minefield damage on the monitor.

Kluge snorted derisively. "In that case, I have the greater imagination." He bit his lip. "Still..."

Herman waited a moment before breaking the silence. "We could send the second unit down to sift the rubble," he suggested. Indeed, this was the third time he had floated the same idea in the past forty-five minutes.

Kluge nodded. "Yes," he said. "Yes, all right."

Herman wheeled around in his chair. He held his hand delicately over the slender microphone that was hooked around the back of his head and positioned it over his mouth.

"Christoph, come in."

Herman waited. There was no reply. He repeated the command. Again, his radio message was greeted by silence.

"More equipment failure," Herman griped.

He attempted to raise the IV soldier a third time. As he did so, Adolf Kluge switched his attention to the monitor screens.

The second unit was the designation given to the IV villager and his attendant group of Numbers who were at the next checkpoint up from that of the late Veit Rauch, only a few yards outside the periphery of the village.

When he called up the appropriate image on the

nearest monitor, the tree-mounted camera panned the designated scene.

Kluge's blood chilled to ice.

"Never mind, Herman," Kluge said woodenly.

Still trying to raise the second unit, Herman turned, confused. "Sir?" he said.

Kluge pointed at the monitor above the second unit's small guard station. Herman gaped at what appeared to be bodies lying around the road. When he looked closer, he saw a face that was clearly that of the man he had been trying to raise on the radio. The man's head was several feet away from his body.

"How—?" Herman asked, incredulous.

He never finished his question. At that moment, the sound of gunfire erupted outside the ancient stone temple.

THEY HAD FOLLOWED the ravine until it cut up by the upper guard shack. Remo and Chiun preceded Heidi up the hill. She was stunned by how easily they took out the dozen men stationed near the small shed.

The IV village sprouted out of the leveled mountaintop where the ruins of an ancient city had once stood. The priceless architecture of a culture long dead had been demolished for the comfort of the band of fugitive Nazis.

Looming far above the village was Estómago de Diablo—the name given to the huge old temple that was the focal point of the entire area. The massive stone structure stared down protectively over the orderly little houses from its separate mountain peak.

"Dollars to doughnuts the head guy's in there," Remo said, pointing to the temple.

Focused on the temple, they ran toward the first line of neat Bavarian-style houses...

...and into a hail of machine-gun fire.

"Crappity crap-crap-crap," Remo groused.

As a cluster of frantic IV soldiers ran toward them down the street—shooting madly—the three of them quickly ducked down an alley. Bullets ripped against the wall nearest them.

Remo quickly plucked Heidi from the path. Kicking open the door of the nearest house, he tossed her to the floor. "Stay put," he commanded, slamming the door tightly shut.

Remo and Chiun whirled on the soldiers.

The men ran into view at the mouth of the alley. Remo recognized their shared face immediately; he'd encountered the same face at the airport, as well as at the first two guard shacks.

"Not him again," Remo complained.

"Do not get distracted," Chiun warned the instant before the men opened fire.

Chiun leaped high to the left, Remo to the right. Hitting the eaves of the roofs with one foot, they pushed off and forward. They formed an invisible X as their paths nearly crossed in the air above the blazing gunfire.

The heads of the baffled soldiers slipped below them as both Masters of Sinanju flew over. Twisting in midair, they dropped down behind the startled IV troops.

Before the shock could even register, Remo and Chiun launched themselves forward.

A few guns fired feeble bursts of lead into the clear blue sky as Chiun ripped through the men. Diet-and-exercise-hardened fingernails clawed vicious strips through chest muscle and bone. Kneecaps shattered. Skulls collapsed.

Remo had torn into the crowd from the other side, spinning like a top on one foot, barely seeming to change position. As he swirled, an arm or foot would fly out of the twisting blur. In their wake, streaks of blood erupted from corrupted throats and chests.

In a matter of seconds, the attackers were dead.

"I'll get Heidi," Remo said quickly.

Racing back to the house where he had left her, he flung open the door. She was nowhere in sight. A quick search of the one-story structure found the house empty and the front door on the far side of the house ajar.

"Double crap," Remo complained. He ran back to meet Chiun. "Heidi's gone," he said, arriving back at the carnage in the alley.

"We cannot search for her now," Chiun stated.

Remo shook his head. "She can't say I didn't warn her," he agreed.

Together, they ran back out onto the tidy village road.

KLUGE HAD BECOME more animated as he watched the men from Sinanju slaughter his soldiers as easily as lesser mortals might step on an anthill. IV was still his home. He would do everything he could to preserve it.

"Have them pull back to the field," he ordered Herman.

"Is that wise?" Herman asked.

"Do it!" Kluge shouted. There was an angry spark in his eyes, a spark that had been absent ever since the dark days in Paris several months ago.

Herman obediently gave the order into his headset.

Kluge watched Remo and Chiun advance through the vacant streets of the village. Unseen by the Masters of Sinanju, the defenders of IV began backing along streets closer to the temple. On Kluge's order, they were retreating to the large open field with its trampled vegetable and flower gardens.

It seemed ridiculous. An entire army in retreat because of two unarmed men.

"Is the other system operational?"

Herman nodded. "Tested this morning."

"I want it ready to switch over to manual if automated tracking fails," Kluge warned.

"At your command, Herr Kluge."

Kluge saw that Herman was sweating. He had

been so calm during the whole time leading up to this crisis. Herman had never thought there *was* a crisis. The fool.

Kluge turned his attention back to the monitors. Remo and Chiun continued their relentless advance.

As he watched them move stealthily through the streets, his eyes strayed to a single red button on his control console. Unlabeled, it was covered by a clear plastic lid.

Unseen by Herman, Kluge flipped the plastic cover open.

And prayed.

"NOW, THERE'S SOMETHING you don't see every day," Remo commented. He nodded to the army of identical soldiers arranged in the field before the ancient stone fortress.

Although the men were lined up to fire, they didn't do so when Remo and Chiun cleared the last of the quaint little gingerbread houses.

"There is something else here," Chiun declared, concerned.

"Not more mines," Remo said. He had been stomping his foot occasionally to get a crude sonic reading of the land up ahead. As far as he could tell, there were no land mines.

The field was to their right. To their left, a stretch of rocky terrain dropped down after a few yards, only to come back into sight a little farther beyond. Continuing only briefly, it disappeared for good a short way farther on. Somewhere far below the last appearance of the rocky ridge was the road.

The army continued to stand down as they approached.

"Gee, you think it's a trap?" Remo asked sarcastically.

Chiun was peering at the uneven mound of stone to their left. Remo followed the elderly Korean's line of sight.

He immediately saw the thick metal barrel jutting from the stone. Beyond this was another. And a third, fourth and fifth. Each of the weird gun muzzles was aimed down the path. Directly at Remo and Chiun.

"Oh, great," was all Remo had time to say before the muzzles hidden in the rock flashed to life. All five of them exploded in a deafeningly violent, unified blast.

They weren't controlled by human hands, so Remo hadn't felt the telltale sign of men about to shoot. Before he had properly prepared for an attack, the air was suddenly alive with burning lead fragments.

More rounds screamed at him in that one instant than at any other single time in his life. His senses were strained to overloading as he flung himself to a protective outcropping of rock beside the road.

The outcropping did not shelter him for long. As soon as he had hunkered down behind the great black stones, the blond-haired IV soldiers in the field across the road broke their cease-fire. As one, they opened fire on Remo.

He slid down behind the rocks, pushing himself low behind a small lip. Bullets whizzed like angry hornets above his head, ricocheting off rocks and whizzing into the distance.

Remo was a sitting duck.

He didn't know where Chiun had gone to when the automated weapons had begun firing. Remo only hoped that the Master of Sinanju was faring better than him.

CHIUN HAD DONE much the same thing as Remo when the guns had begun their automatic firing. Unlike Remo, however, he had the fortune of landing in a crevice that was the sole blind spot of the nearest machine gun.

As the men in the field opened fire on Remo, Chiun quickly scampered around the far side of the large finger of rock behind which he had taken refuge.

He came out close to the nearest gun. It continued firing relentlessly, deafeningly down the path. But though it tracked from side to side with relative ease, it had more difficulty moving up and down.

Out on the road once more, Chiun ducked below the barrage of lead. He skittered crab-like to the left, coming up between the first two weapons.

They were altered versions of the GEC Minigun. Each was capable of firing 6000 rounds per minute.

The pockmarked road was testament to the effectiveness of the weapons.

Racing up alongside the automated guns, Chiun ducked in behind. With two slaps from one long-nailed hand, Chiun broke the heavy guns loose from their moorings. Two sharp kicks sent them spinning over in the direction of the small army.

The firing guns swept across the advancing mob of blond-haired men. Crumpling bodies spit streaks of crimson across the lush green field.

There was no defense against the remorseless attack of the automated guns. Some tried to run. Most didn't have the time to even consider the option. In seconds, the grisly deed was done.

As the bullet-riddled bodies fell, Chiun worked to disable the remaining three guns. By the time he had reduced them to pieces and returned to the road, the first two weapons had grown silent.

He climbed down to the path. The dying echoes of machine-gun fire sighed forlornly against the distant peaks of the Andes, fading to an eerie silence.

The entire IV army lay dead on the road. Not one man had survived the fierce gunfire.

Across the road from the nearest dozen bodies, Remo came out from his protective outcropping of rock. He ran up to meet the Master of Sinanju, his face growing more severe as he beheld the breadth of the carnage. He paused next to Chiun, looking up at the ancient temple.

"Let's finish this," he said, hollow of voice.

They turned to the huge stone fortress.

The road ended at a long stone bridge, a remarkable piece of ancient construction spanning the two peaks of the IV complex.

Remo and Chiun were nearly to the bridge when an odd expression crossed the face of the younger Master of Sinanju.

"Wait a sec," Remo said, stopping abruptly. His bare forearm barred Chiun's path.

Chiun frowned even as he stopped beside his pupil. "What is it?" he asked impatiently.

Remo squinted at the bridge, uncertainty clouding his features. "Didn't you feel—?"

He never finished the question.

A powerful rumble rose from beneath their feet. The vibrations were different from those of land mines or machine guns. This was something muffled and heavy.

And as both men watched, each one knowing now what Remo had heard, the bridge before them began to collapse.

The carefully buried charges tore huge slabs of the bridge away. The massive chunks of rock tumbled in slow motion to the ravine floor more than a half mile below.

The wide gap the crashing stone left behind was too great for even a Master of Sinanju to traverse.

ADOLF KLUGE removed his finger from the single red button. He turned to Herman.

"We should go," he said. His face was stone.

Herman seemed shell-shocked. He nodded numbly to the IV leader. Together, they left the monitor room, heading farther into the bowels of the ancient temple.

REMO RAN back to the village in order to find something to bridge the gap left by the collapsed bridge. He returned after a few moments with a long extension ladder.

Extending the ladder fully, Remo lowered it across the ravine.

Unmindful of the dizzying height, he and Chiun raced across the aluminum ladder and into the temple.

Remo was surprised when they encountered no resistance inside the huge, drafty fortress. He commented on this to the Master of Sinanju.

"This Kluge is wise," Chiun said knowingly as they raced through the cool stone corridors. "Fearful for his life, a prince would ordinarily surround himself with guards. He realized that his greatest safety lay in sending his entire legion against us."

"Fat lot of good it did him," Remo commented.

They found the monitor room, which had been abandoned. Remo immediately identified the pungent odor of nervous sweat.

"That way," he said, pointing to a narrow hallway off the large stone room.

He and Chiun ran through the cramped space and into a much larger chamber.

This had been the main sacrificial room for the priests of the ancient temple. A rock stairway led up the side of a huge pyramid-shaped stone structure in the center of the room. The sacrificial pit.

Obviously the previous occupants of the temple hadn't limited themselves to animal oblations. Cracked, brownish human skulls lined the ancient rock steps.

"I love what they've done with the place," Remo said dryly.

"Shh," Chiun hissed. He was listening intently to something distant.

Remo cocked an ear. He heard the sound, as well. It was very faint. And hollow.

Exchanging glances, Remo and Chiun flew side by side up the stairs to the sacrificial pit.

They found what they had expected at the top. There was a deep black hole in which the dead victims of the temple priests had been dumped. Far below—much farther than the floor of the chamber itself—could be seen the reflective glow of dull yellow light.

A steel ladder was attached to the interior stone wall of the pit. Obviously a new addition since the IV occupation of the village.

The noise they had both heard grew fainter as they climbed over the edge of the pit. Propping their hands against either metal side of the ladder, they slid down to the bottom of the pit.

The vertical shaft stabbed deep into the bowels of the mountain. The wide stone floor at the base was rimmed with shattered yellowed bones. Remo and Chiun touched softly to the floor amid the dusty, headless skeletons.

A horizontal shaft ran off from one side of the pit.

They followed the ancient escape route down a gradually declining tunnel. Emerging into sunlight a few moments later, they found themselves on a hollowed, level plateau, rimmed on nearly all sides by mountains. Only a narrow path appeared to lead down to the valley below.

But it was not the path that would have carried Adolf Kluge to safety.

The noise they had heard from inside was so indistinct by now as to be only a mocking memory. Remo's jaw clenched in helpless rage as his gaze settled on the well-tended and empty helipad that had been constructed on the plateau.

As the echoes of the helicopter's rotor blades faded, Remo became aware of another noise coming from behind them. He didn't even turn around as Heidi Stolpe burst, panting, from the mouth of the long tunnel.

"Where have you been?" he snarled. He was still staring up at the empty sky.

"Hiding," she said, breathless. She adjusted her

backpack. "There was a soldier in the house you threw me into. I barely escaped with my life."

"You're not the only one," Remo said.

Heidi also detected the faint sound of the helicopter. As she strained to hear, the sound was swallowed up by the mountains. Kluge was gone.

Wordlessly Remo wheeled back around to the tunnel's circular black mouth. As he did so, there was an angry rumble from within the dark cave.

The explosions came one right after another. The bombs had been placed midway up the length of the tunnel. As they were detonated from some remote location—presumably the helicopter—their force ripped apart the long rock cavern.

With a shudder of earth, the tunnel collapsed, sealing them outside the quickest route back to the IV village. A thick cloud of dust belched out in a massive mocking blast onto the elevated rock face on which they all stood.

"Perfect," Remo snapped.

It would take forever to climb back up the side of the cliff. The path was out of the question. The valley circled too far around the broad bases of several converging mountains. That route could take days.

And there was the matter of Heidi.

Remo looked dully at her.

"Um..." she said. She looked first to the path, then to the rocky cliff face.

Chiun had turned away in disgust. He was already

scaling the mountain face up toward the flat rear wall of the huge temple.

Heidi smiled wanly. "Could you...?" Sheepishly she pointed up toward Chiun.

Remo considered leaving her there. But his conscience got the better of him. "Let's go," Remo said with a deep sigh. Hefting Heidi up over his shoulder in a fireman's carry, he stepped over to the sheer rock face.

Trailing the Master of Sinanju, Remo began the tedious climb back up to the top of the mountain.

OVER THE COURSE of the next three days, Remo and Chiun searched for Adolf Kluge in vain. The trail was cold.

Heidi left for parts unknown. The Master of Sinanju eventually hunkered down in their hotel in Uruguay, refusing to involve himself in yet another wild-goose chase.

Smith had no luck finding the fugitive head of IV with the CURE computers. Eventually, he admitted defeat.

With great reluctance, Harold Smith ordered Remo and Chiun home.

10

When Keijo Suk accepted the money with a promise of more, he didn't know it was all the man had left in the world. He immediately deposited the large sum of cash in one of Berlin's many impressive Western banks.

If Suk had so chosen, he could have left it at that. The man who had given him the money had a desperate, hunted look about him. His clothes were disheveled, his hair unkempt. It looked as if he hadn't slept in days. Dark semicircles rimmed his watery blue eyes. If Suk had kept the cash without performing the requested service, he doubted the man would be able to do much to stop him. But the man had surprised him.

"You will not be able to take so much with you back to your country," he had said.

Suk only nodded. Already he had decided in his head which bank the money would go into.

"You will likely leave it here," the man continued.

Again, Suk silently agreed.

"If you attempt to keep the money without supplying me with that for which I have retained you, I will turn you over to the authorities of your country. I am certain they will want to know how you came to have so much in an illegal bank account.''

The look in the man's sleepless eyes convinced Suk that he was telling the truth.

Suk decided to abandon his plan to cheat the man of his money. Besides, he had been assured that there was much more to be had if he performed but one small service. When Suk returned for the balance, he wouldn't leave the West again. He would live like a king for the rest of his life.

But there was still the matter of the duty he had been hired to perform.

His flight from Berlin connected with another in Moscow. The plane he took from Russia carried him across the remainder of Europe and on into Asia. When he finally landed in the Democratic People's Republic of Korea, Keijo Suk was exhausted.

But Suk didn't have time to rest.

In Berlin he was the official representative of North Korea's Culture and Art Ministry. Allegedly sent to ''promote positive global understanding'' with the German people, Keijo Suk had in truth been sent to the West in order to form ties with the former Communists of the former East Germany who were vying for positions of power in the new, united Germany.

As a member of his nation's elite, Suk was allowed the privilege of owning a fine Western automobile. His Ford Taurus was waiting for him at the airport in Pyongyang.

When he drove out into the streets of the North Korean capital, Suk didn't head for his small apartment. He instead turned north, driving out of the city into the featureless, flat expanse that was the Korean countryside.

The official People's Highway was dotted with few cars—fewer still as he drove farther northwest. The traffic he met was largely people on foot or on bicycles.

Eventually the pedestrian traffic ended completely. He found himself on a long multilaned stretch of barren highway that appeared to go nowhere.

But Keijo Suk knew better than that. He knew precisely where this long road ended. He arrived at the rocky shores of the Korean west coast a little after sundown. The highway simply stopped dead, and a small footpath that seemed as old as the stars in the dark black canvas of the night sky angled down off the road. At the other end of the path, Suk spied bright square patches of yellow—the lights of a lonely fishing village.

Leaving his car on the highway, Suk skirted the edge of the village. He had no strong desire to draw unnecessary attention to himself.

A massive garbage heap overflowed onto the ground beyond the highway at the rear of the nearest houses. Though it was cold, rats cavorted freely through the piles of ordure.

Suk had to pull the tails of his dress shirt up around his mouth and nose in order to ward off the stench. The smell was so overpowering, his eyes watered. Unlike the rest of the population of North Korea, the people of this village ate well. The evidence was everywhere he stepped.

Scraping the muck from his shoes, Suk continued past the massive dump.

The village was positioned on the shore of West Korean Bay. Powerful gusts of early-winter wind whistled in off the churning black waters, stabbing frigid knives through layers of clothing. The only article appropriate for the weather was Suk's thick Western winter coat. It did him no good. He shivered madly as he walked stealthily forward.

The backs of the houses were plain wood with no windows. Suk crept past the homes, careful not to alert the occupants. His nervous heart was ringing in his ears.

The village ended in a small rise that led up to a solitary house. This dwelling was far more ornate than the rest. Parts of it seemed to have been constructed at vastly different periods of history. There was evidence of early Roman influence in the foundation, along with the practicality of ancient Greece. The frippery of the Renaissance, as well as that of Victorian architecture, was also present.

To Suk, the home was a garish mishmash of styles.

Checking first to see that he wasn't being followed, he made his anxious way up the path to the big, ugly house.

He found the front door unlocked.

Pushing open the door, Suk slipped inside, relieved to be able to shut out the persistent howling wind.

There was a light switch next to the door, but he dared not use it. Instead, he pulled a powerful flashlight from the pocket of his heavy down jacket.

As he shone the light around the interior of the first room, Keijo Suk's jaw nearly hit the floor.

Every spot his flashlight illuminated was filled with gold and jewels. It was more than a king's ransom, more than that of ten kings. In fact, enough treasure was crammed into this one room alone to ransom every ruler in the history of mankind.

Suk had developed a powerful love for material wealth since assuming his post in Berlin. That was his reason for being here. It was difficult for him to break the initial numbing trance this fabulous store of wealth had put him under.

After a few moments of slack-jawed gawking, Suk managed to pull himself together. He had a job to do. Stepping around the room, he began to search methodically through the bags of jewels, the golden statues and the gem-encrusted chests of heaping ingots.

IT TOOK HIM two solid hours of searching, but he finally found what he was after.

The lights in the village had winked out one by one. All had gone to bed for the night, never noticing the strange flashes of light that came from the house on the hill.

The object of Suk's search was propped up in a small room adjacent to the first. He had almost skipped searching this tiny chamber when his initial flashlight sweep failed to illuminate a single diamond.

The room looked to be some sort of library. There were huge leather-bound books, as well as a number of rolled parchment scrolls. The books were lined up on shelves while the scrolls were squirreled away in an ornate mahogany wall unit divided into tiny cubbyholes.

The object rested on a separate wall unit along the narrow distant wall. Suk recognized it immediately. It was exactly as the man in Germany had described it.

Suk had to step over a pair of large stone tablets that sat in the center of the floor. He pulled the object of his quest down from the shelf. Unbeknownst to him, Suk left a trail of freshly disturbed dust in its wake.

He picked his way back out into the outer room.

Across the room, flushed with triumph, Keijo Suk gave in to the urge to grab a handful of gold coins from an urn near the door. He couldn't help himself.

Like mints in a fancy restaurant, they sat there waiting to be taken.

Opening the door, Suk paused. He reached over and grabbed a few more handfuls of gold coins. Hands shaking, he stuffed the coins into the pockets of his coat. A few fell to the floor. Suk hardly noticed.

Giddy with success, Keijo Suk hurried back out into the frigid Korean night, slamming the door tightly behind him.

In the weak Asian moonlight, the three coins Suk had dropped glowed dully on the living-room floor of the Master of Sinanju.

11

The corridors of Folcroft Sanitarium were cloaked in chilly semidarkness as Remo Williams roamed up from the basement rooms in which he and Chiun had been staying since arriving back in the United States.

Ten days had passed since he had lost the elusive head of IV in the mountains of Argentina. Ten days of inactivity, ten days that Adolf Kluge would have used to burrow himself further and further away from the prying eyes of the world.

When he had returned to the top of the mountain, Remo found a computer area in one of the old temple rooms. Someone had hastily sifted through everything and boxed up and carted off whatever was deemed necessary. Everything else had been left.

The computers had been smashed to pieces, their hard drives destroyed.

Virtually.

They had been damaged, but apparently not enough. Smith was able to access a fraction of what was left on one of the hard drives. From this, the CURE director was able to reconstruct the entire structure of IV's finances.

Remo had never seen his employer appear quite as shocked as when Smith successfully broke the IV encoding system and uncovered the vast holdings of the neo-Nazi organization.

Smith had immediately set to work cutting the purse strings to IV. Some corporations he sold off; others he forced into bankruptcy. It took five whole days of work, but Smith had finally finished that afternoon. Wherever Kluge was hidden, he would not be able to access any IV funds.

Once the finances were out of the way, Smith was able to finally devote full attention to locating the head of IV. So far Smith had had no luck. And without a trail to follow, Remo was helpless to do anything.

Remo wandered off the elevator on the second floor of Folcroft's administrative wing.

Smith's outer office was empty. Mrs. Mikulka had gone home hours before. Remo walked through the secretary's drab little work area and pushed open the door to Harold Smith's slightly larger but no less drab office.

Smith glanced up from his work when Remo entered.

"Nothing yet," he said. He looked back down at the computer screen set into his desktop. Smith's weary eyes scanned back and forth along thin lines of text. The dull amber glow of the computer screen cast a demonic glow across the CURE director's pale, haggard features.

The Master of Sinanju sat cross-legged on the threadbare rug before Smith's desk. Crossing the room, Remo sank down into a lotus position before him.

"Did you sleep well?" Chiun asked.

"Not a wink," Remo replied.

"Sleeplessness does not a great assassin make," Chiun intoned. He was a pool of calm.

"Did you write that little aphorism for the next *Official Assassin's Newsletter?*" Remo deadpanned.

Chiun's brow furrowed. "Is there such a publication?"

Remo shook his head. "No," he sighed.

Chiun nodded. "I did not think there was, for no one contacted me. I sincerely hope that when there is, I will be the cover story of its premier issue."

"Speaking of grand delusions," Remo said, "any luck with either of your statue ideas?"

Chiun shook his head. "Lamentably, no," he said. "Emperor Smith has been far too busy with his current project. He has offered to take the matter under advisement."

As good as dead, Remo thought. Aloud, he said, "I'll put in a good word for you."

Chiun nodded. The two men fell silent. The only sound in the room was the incessant tapping of Smith's fingers as they struck against the high-tech surface of his desk.

Remo and Chiun sat in stony silence for more than two hours when the phone on Smith's desk suddenly squawked loudly. Smith had been deeply engrossed in the seemingly endless scrolling text on his computer screen. The ringing shook him from his work with a start.

It was Folcroft's outside line. Sanitarium business.

Smith reached for the receiver, at the same time looking at his watch. He frowned at the lateness of the hour.

"Smith," he said tartly. His features bunched into an unhappy mass as he attempted to discern what the speaker was saying. All at once, his eyes opened wide. He held the phone out to Chiun. "I believe it is for you."

Chiun scooped up the phone. Remo raised a quizzical eyebrow as the Master of Sinanju announced his formal title in archaic Korean.

"Who is it?" Remo mouthed.

"I do not know," Smith said with a frown. "However, I believe he was speaking rather frantically in Korean."

"Korean?" Remo said. Though his hearing was acute enough to have heard the speaker, he hadn't been interested enough to focus.

"They repeated 'Sinanju' several times. Is it possible that it is someone from Chiun's village?"

"I don't know," Remo admitted. His face registered intrigue.

He watched Chiun carefully. The Master of Sinanju's expression was unreadable. He tried to listen, but Chiun had pressed the receiver tightly against his shell-like ear. It was impossible for Remo to eavesdrop.

Smith cleared his throat. "Remo, I am not comfortable with the prospect that someone from Sinanju might have this number. There are security considerations."

Smith's admonishments were drowned out by the crashing of the handset onto the cradle of the phone. At the same time, a pained howl rose up from the very soul of the Master of Sinanju. It was a cry of both pain and rage.

Remo and Smith both wore wary expressions as they looked over at the elderly Korean.

"Oh, the dastards!" Chiun hissed. He was panting so hard Smith thought he might be having a heart attack.

"What is it?" Remo asked, concerned.

"Thieves! Scoundrels! Oh, the perfidy!" Chiun drummed his fist against his bony chest. He wheeled on Remo. "We must be off at once!" he cried.

"Off?" Remo said. "Off where?"

"To Korea, of course," Chiun snapped. "That this could happen after lo these many years. What is this world the gods have thrust down around one as trusting as I?"

"Chiun," Remo interjected, "I don't know what that was all about, but I am not going to Korea."

Chiun wheeled. An accusing nail stabbed the air between them.

"Betrayal?" Chiun cried in shock. "From my own son?"

"How can I betray you? Dammit, I don't even know what the hell you're upset about."

"The *treasure*," Chiun explained, seething. His hazel eyes were furious. "The vast stores of price-less tribute to generations of greatness that is the House of Sinanju have been swept from the floors of my home like driftwood in a ferocious monsoon." He gripped fistfuls of brocade kimono fabric. "I have been *robbed,* Remo!" he wailed.

Remo let the tension drain from his shoulders. "Is that all?" he said, relieved.

When he saw the sense of relief in his pupil's face, Chiun snapped back into outrage mode.

"How *dare* you be calm?!" he accused. A bony finger quivered at Remo. "The man you call father has been grossly violated. Thieves have pillaged my most prized possessions."

"That's too bad," Remo said. "Really. It's just that I thought there was something really wrong."

"'Really'?" Chiun cried. "'*Really*'?" His voice grew increasingly frenzied as he repeated the word.

Although it was long after midnight, Smith was concerned Chiun's screams would be overheard. He shot a cautious look at his closed office door.

"Please, Master Chiun," Smith begged.

The Master of Sinanju spun on him, his long robes twirling madly. "Stay out of this, white," Chiun menaced.

"Look," Remo said, attempting to be the voice of reason, "the treasure was stolen before. We got it back then, and I'm sure we'll get it back now. We can go to Sinanju as soon as we've cleared up this Four business."

"No," Chiun insisted, tugging at his tufts of wispy hair in frustration. "It *must* be now. Every day we dally allows the trail to grow ever colder."

Remo was determined. He was about to insist that they stay put when Smith broke into their conversation.

"If I may interject," the CURE director said.

Chiun twirled on him, eyes pinpricks of white-hot rage.

"I said mind your own business," he snapped.

"I only wanted to say that I have had little luck finding this Kluge. And, frankly, your presence here is drawing undue attention."

"You see," Chiun insisted, shifting gears so fast Remo swore he heard grinding. Though he spoke to Remo, he stabbed a bony finger at Smith. "The wisdom of a true emperor. Even Smith wishes us to go."

"If something comes up, I will contact you in Sinanju," Smith offered reasonably. "You still have a phone, correct?"

"The only one in the village," Chiun replied.

"Then it is settled," Smith said. Inwardly he was greatly relieved. He wasn't comfortable when Remo and Chiun stayed at Folcroft for extended periods of time.

"Don't I get any say in this?" Remo asked.

"No," said Smith and Chiun in unison.

Remo threw up his hands in defeat. "Fine," he said, exhaling loudly. "We'll go to Sinanju."

Whirling, Chiun raised a defiant hand as he marched over to the door. He flung it open grandly. "And woe to he who would pilfer the treasure of the most awesome house of assassins in the history of creation." He stormed outside.

"Yadda, yadda, yadda," Remo grumbled to Smith. His face held the look of a man totally devoid of enthusiasm.

Hands in his pockets, Remo followed Chiun reluctantly from the office.

12

Adolf Kluge was born in La Plata, the capital of the province of Buenos Aires in Argentina.

In spite of the fact that it was the country's national language, Kluge hadn't heard a word of Spanish spoken until he was nearly seven years old. By that time, he already knew that he was different from the people around him.

No. Not just different. Adolf Kluge was *better*.

Even before he could walk, the parents of young Adolf had taught their precious blue-eyed offspring that he was superior to all others. This—he would come to realize later in life—included them.

His proud Nazi parents had fled their homeland during the persecution that came in the wake of the Second World War. Wounded in the early days of the Polish incursion, his father had sat out the war as nothing more than an SS bureaucrat. If the brutality of the Nazi secret police force had never come to light, he might have been able to resume his anonymous life after the war. Unfortunately for the senior Kluge, his name turned up in several key files concerning the torture and deaths of dozens of suspected

Allied spies. He had been forced to flee to South America in order to escape prosecution.

The Nazis of Argentina were a close-knit group. They lived together, socialized only with their peers, married one another and raised their children in the old way. And, most of all, they kept the Nazi dream of global domination alive long after the world thought a stake had been driven through its evil heart.

Kluge was born in the early 1950s into a community fueled by bitter hatreds and a festering, impotent rage at the treatment it received from the outside world.

As the community of Nazi exiles grew, so did its members' desire for a place to call home. Germany was out of the question. None of them could ever go back. Not under the climate that dominated so much of world opinion.

It was more than ten full years after the fall of Berlin that IV village was established. As a boy, Kluge remembered driving up with his parents to see the homes under construction. To the little child who had seen his parents' beloved homeland only in old photographs, it was as if they had somehow magically driven across the Atlantic and into the mountains of Bavaria. The funds looted by Hitler's regime and held by Swiss bankers had been used to re-create a small scrap of Germany for that nation's most pitiful outcasts.

Adolf Kluge would never forget how his father

had stopped their car in the shade of the old stone fortress. As his mother stared in silence at the homes beyond the large open field, his father wept openly at the sight of the picturesque little houses.

Kluge would never forget the feeling of contempt his father's emotional outburst had raised in him. For, at the tender age of five, Adolf Kluge was as insufferably arrogant as he was intelligent.

Some people grew to rebel against that which they had been taught as children. Not Kluge. He fervently believed in the idea of the master race. He also fervently believed in his role as its eventual leader, a belief that became his driving ambition.

At the private German-only school he attended as a youth alongside the children of other refugee Nazis, he achieved the highest honors of any student in its history. He excelled at languages, mastering more than a dozen tongues by the time he graduated high school.

Kluge was sent to college abroad, studying in both England and the United States. The honors he received while away at school were such that, when his education was finally complete, he had left no doubt in the minds of his fellow villagers that he was the future of IV.

As the years peeled away, Kluge assumed a small position on the leadership council of the village. At that time, IV was still dominated by old-timers who thought that the vaunted Fourth Reich was on the verge of unfolding. Kluge knew that this was insanity. The old fools refused to admit to the political realities of an ever changing world. If IV was to survive, it would have to adapt.

Eventually and not unexpectedly, Adolf Kluge rose to his position as leader of IV. He was only the third in its history—the first from his generation.

At this point in his life, he no longer felt compelled to flaunt his superiority. Rather, he simply excelled at everything he put his mind to.

The life-styles of everyone in the village were enhanced because of Kluge's prudent investments. Unfortunately for the old surviving hard-liners, Adolf Kluge veered away from the principles of IV's founding.

Even though he was dedicated in spirit to the principles of Adolf Hitler, Kluge recognized the futility of trying to establish the Fourth Reich in the way IV's founders intended.

No one in the village seemed truly bothered by Kluge's leadership. Oh, they would scream and yell about the wrong-headed turn their nation of origin had taken, but they always returned to their cozy homes and warm meals. As long as their needs were met and their bellies were full, they didn't question the leadership of Adolf Kluge.

Until Nils Schatz.

One of the last of the original founders, Schatz had used stolen IV money to finance an invasion of Paris in a scheme that at its inception was doomed to fail. This maniac had brought the House of Sinanju down on all their heads.

Schatz was dead now, but his legacy lived on.

It was a waking nightmare.

The money was all gone. The bank accounts were empty. The stocks and bonds were inaccessible. The companies were all under investigation. All IV assets were frozen.

Kluge thought he had been careful to cover his tracks. He should have known. Given the timetable under which he had been forced to work, something must have been left.

To his knowledge, every last scrap of information in the village had been destroyed. But some small thing must have survived. And whoever the men from Sinanju were working for had used that single thread to unravel the entire IV financial fabric.

IV was destitute. As was its leader.

With the companies all gone, Kluge had only a paltry hundred thousand dollars at his disposal. It was his innate intelligence that made him open the lone bank account in Germany. But it was his supreme arrogance that told him to put so little into it. Now even that money was gone.

He had spent nearly every cent he had on a ridiculous dream. A bedtime story.

But, in the end, it was all he had.

Kluge sat alone in the back of the Berlin restaurant, lamenting the sad turn his fortunes had taken.

When he went abroad, he was used to dining in

PLAY BANGO! AND GET THREE FREE GIFTS!

It looks like BINGO, it plays like BINGO but it's FREE!

HOW TO PLAY:

1. With a coin, scratch the Caller Card to reveal your 5 lucky numbers and see that they match your Bango Card. Then check the claim chart to discover what we have for you — FREE BOOKS and a FREE GIFT. All yours, all free!

2. Send back the Bango card and you'll get hot-off-the-press Gold Eagle books, never before published! These books have a cover price of $4.99 each, but they are yours to keep absolutely free.

3. There's no catch. You're under no obligation to buy anything. We charge nothing — ZERO — for your first shipment. And you don't have to make any minimum number of purchases — not even one!

4. The fact is, thousands of readers enjoy receiving books by mail from the Gold Eagle Reader Service™ months before they are available in stores. They like the convenience of home delivery and they love our discount prices!

5. We hope that after receiving your free books you'll want to remain a subscriber. But the choice is yours — to continue or cancel, any time at all! So why not take us up on our invitation, with no risk of any kind. You'll be glad you did!

YOURS FREE!
This exciting mystery gift is yours free when you play BANGO!

only the finest eating establishments. The place he was in today was part of a fast-food chain brought over from America. The thick smell of grease made his gourmet stomach churn.

Kluge kept his breathing shallow as he tried not to think about his sorry fate, but of course he couldn't help but dwell on it.

It was desperation.

IV would have been insolvent years ago if not for his leadership. His labors had always guaranteed him a lavish life-style. That life-style had been taken away from him in a flash. He could never hope to reclaim it without great risk.

But *this* risk...

It was insanity. Utter, foolish insanity. Yet what choice did he have?

Kluge's heart skipped a beat as he saw a familiar face pass before the brightly painted window. Keijo Suk glanced in once as he passed by before continuing along the sidewalk.

A minute later, he was inside the restaurant. Walking briskly across the virtually empty dining area, Suk slid into the booth across from Kluge. His fat face was flushed.

"You were successful," Kluge said. He stared at the wrapped package the man had placed on the table between them.

Keijo Suk nodded. "It was much easier than I thought." The Korean grinned and pushed the bundle over to Kluge.

"That is because they were not there," Kluge said.

He loosened the twine Suk had used to tie the bundle and carefully unfolded the paper. It fell away, revealing a slab of ancient petrified wood.

It was in perfect condition. Much more so than the quarter that had been in his possession at the IV fortress.

Kluge ran his fingertips across the uneven surface, feeling every ridge of the carved wood.

In spite of his better instincts, he began to grow more confident. Why would Sinanju have saved this scrap of wood for so many years if it wasn't significant?

He thought of the stained-glass window back at the ancient temple. How many times had he looked at it and not seen the piece of wood in Siegfried's hand? How could he possibly have missed something so significant for so long?

Suk tapped his hand on the table, shaking Kluge from his trance.

"I would like my money now," the Korean said.

"I am sure you would." Kluge smiled.

Looking down, he carefully folded the paper back up around the block carving. He stashed the bundle in a black leather valise that sat on the bench next to him. When he looked back up at Suk, his eyes were hooded.

"I do not have the money," Kluge stated simply.

Suk was taken aback by the German's frankness.

"You do not have it *with* you." It was a statement, not a question.

Kluge shook his head. "I do not have it at all. I knew you would be greedy, Keijo. I did not have enough initially to split in half. If I had offered you half of that pittance up front and half after you gave the stolen object to me, you would have laughed in my face. Likewise, I knew that if I told you I had paid you everything up front you would have simply left with my money without performing the service for which you had been hired."

Keijo Suk shook his head in disbelief. "I have risked incurring the wrath of the Master of Sinanju for a scrap of firewood," he said, astonished.

"And a healthy sum of money," Kluge argued. "Eighty thousand is still a lot, Keijo."

"It was not *enough*," Suk snarled. He stood up, grabbing across the table for Kluge's valise.

As Suk snatched for the handle, Kluge locked his hand around the Korean's wrist. Twisting the fist around, the German thrust his other hand forward, fingers extended and rigid. They connected solidly with Suk's shoulder.

There was a crunch of bone and popping cartilage. Shocked air whooshed out of Suk's lungs.

Unable even to cry out in pain, the Asian dropped back into his seat. His lungs ached as he strained to refill them. He gulped for air, at the same time grabbing his injured shoulder with his good hand.

Kluge calmly retook his seat. He smiled grimly.

"I made a deal with you, Keijo, and I intend to keep it. I do not have the money now. But from what I have seen, this will allow me to pay you the balance in a few days." He nodded to the valise. "I will even compensate you for any medical expenses you might incur."

Suk shook his head in impotent rage.

"Of course," Kluge continued, "my generosity does not extend to anything the men from Sinanju might do to you. I am certain they frown on theft. It probably insults their honor or some other such nonsense."

Kluge collected his valise. He stood to go.

"When will I be paid?" Suk begged, his teeth clenched.

"Soon, Keijo. Soon. Although, if I have judged you correctly, I would say that you left the home of the Master of Sinanju with more than just the block carving." He patted the valise. "You are a greedy bastard, Keijo. That is what I like about you." He stepped from the table.

"My risks are my own," Suk called after him. He was nursing the pain in his shoulder.

Kluge paused. "When one has nothing else to lose, risk becomes a tool of survival," he agreed.

Adolf Kluge walked briskly away from the injured Korean. He crossed the linoleum floor of the sparsely filled restaurant and stepped out onto the crowded Berlin street.

13

Standing just inside the doorway, hands jammed firmly against his hips, Remo was more than just a little miffed.

"You mean to tell me you dragged my ass half-way around the world for a crummy handful of gold coins?" he demanded angrily.

"It is not the amount that is significant. It is what it represents," the Reigning Master of Sinanju explained.

They were in the packed living room of the Master's house in Sinanju. Bright sunlight shone through the tall windows, casting warming rays over only a fraction of five thousand years of accumulated tribute. The rest of the Sinanju treasure trove was stacked all around the house, like uneaten loaves of bread in an overproducing bakery.

Chiun was stooping to examine the gold coins that Keijo Suk had dropped in his haste to leave several days before.

"This is ridiculous," Remo complained. "You made me think they cleaned you out."

"Today it is a handful," Chiun said seriously. "Tomorrow it is another. Where will it end?"

"Judging from the pile of junk you have heaped around this dump, I'd say somewhere in the middle of the millionth century," Remo said.

Chiun paid him no heed. He collected the three coins from the floor. Never in circulation at any time in history, they had been minted specifically for Sinanju by a grateful employer. They bore the face of Cleopatra on one side and the symbol of Sinanju on the other. Each coin would have been priceless to a collector.

Chiun tossed the three coins into the copper urn next to the door. There were seven more jars stacked nearby, each brimming over with identical gold pieces.

"Ah-hah!" Chiun announced.

"What?" Remo asked, peeved. He was leaning on the door frame.

"See how the villain pauses." Chiun pointed at the footprints in the dust near the door. "He thinks whether he should steal from the glorious House of Sinanju, thus sealing his fate. An evil and stupid creature, he gives in to temptation." He indicated a mass of scuffed prints. "More hesitation. I have committed my base act of thievery, he thinks. If I must die, let me be cast into the Void for more than one handful of coins." Chiun raised an instructive finger. "He fills his pockets and then scurries off into the black of night, fearful even in his flight of the awesome vengeance to which he has condemned himself.''

Remo looked at the marks on the floor. To him, they looked like a mass of dirty footprints.

''If you say so,'' Remo said dubiously.

A fire burned in the great iron furnace in the cellar, heating a huge cauldron of water, which in turn warmed the chilly air within the house. This method of heat dispersal had not become popular in the West until the twentieth century. The Master's House had enjoyed this luxury since the time of Plato.

Chiun's caretaker and the man who had lit the fire in preparation for the Master of Sinanju's arrival was an aged villager named Pullyang. The man who had contacted Chiun at Folcroft, Pullyang stood near the archway that led into the next room. He rubbed his hands together nervously.

''Master, I believe the thief was here, as well,'' the anxious caretaker said, voice tremulous.

Chiun marched boldly across the room. Remo trailed him reluctantly, hands stuffed in his pockets.

Pullyang indicated an open door off of the next room. Remo and Chiun peered in around the frame. Crazed dust patterns swirled in the beams of hot yellow light that poured in through the lone window.

Remo knew the room to be a sort of library for the House of Sinanju. This was where nearly all the records of every past Master of Sinanju were kept.

When Remo had first seen the room years before, Chiun had promised him that one day the scrolls of

Remo's own masterhood would be placed in here beside the rest.

"Whoop-de-do," Remo had said.

Remo was not so glib today. He knew how much the histories of Sinanju meant to his teacher. The look of pain on Chiun's face was almost enough to make him forget his desire to get back to America in order to continue the search for Adolf Kluge.

Remo saw the streak of upset dust at the same time as the Master of Sinanju.

"Brigand!" Chiun cried when he realized what was missing. "Robber!" he shouted as he bounced over the debris field that was the floor. "Bandit!" he wailed, after he had made certain the ancient wood carving had not fallen to the sturdy old floor.

"What was it?" Remo asked, stepping gingerly into the room. He had to climb over a pair of stone slabs.

"A map to a treasure forever lost. A piece of a puzzle whose other fragments were scattered to the winds of history. An invaluable reminder of the folly of fools."

"It doesn't sound that bad," Remo offered encouragingly.

"Bad?" Chiun moaned. "It is terrible."

"I'd say you made out okay," Remo said. "A couple of gold coins and a useless puzzle piece. We should get a lock for the front door. Maybe an alarm system." As Chiun continued to stare at the vacant spot on the shelf, Remo turned to Pullyang. "Is there electricity in this rathole of a village?" he asked.

"Only in the Master's house," the caretaker ventured.

"See, Chiun," Remo said. "An alarm system would be easy. I bet Smith could fix you up real nice."

Chiun refused to be encouraged. His eyes never wavered from the barren spot on the shelf. Beside the marks in the dust, an ancient rusted battle helmet sat on the counter. A corroded falcon was locked in a perpetual struggle to take flight on the front of the headpiece.

The look on his teacher's face was so forlorn as he stared at the shelf Remo couldn't help but feel a welling sadness of his own.

Remo felt uncomfortable with someone else seeing Chiun in this inconsolable state. The old caretaker was hovering at the edge of the room, the mass of wrinkles around his aged eyes pinched to narrow slits.

"We can handle it from here," Remo whispered softly to Pullyang.

The aged caretaker wasn't certain if he should take the suggestion of the Master of Sinanju's white pupil.

"Master?" he asked.

Chiun didn't say a word. He raised a long-nailed hand, waving it dismissively. Pullyang bowed respectfully from the room. A moment later, the front door opened and closed.

The Master of Sinanju continued to stare morosely at the empty spot on the shelf.

This was not like Chiun. His angry reaction to the missing gold coins—*that* was Chiun. But by his own admission, the item stolen from this room had been worthless. Yet he seemed to grieve more for its loss than for the loss of his beloved gold. To Remo, it didn't make sense.

"Chiun?" Remo said gently. "If it means that much to you, to hell with Kluge. We'll go after whoever did this. I promise you'll get everything back."

Chiun at last looked up. There was still sadness in his eyes, but there was a sliver of pride, as well.

"You are a good son, Remo," Chiun said.

Remo felt his heart swell.

"Look, I know what this stuff means to you. It means something to me, too. It's our history."

Chiun nodded. "It is that," he said glumly. "More than you know. Come, Remo, sit down."

He indicated the two stone tablets on the floor. Remo obediently sank to a sitting position on the nearest slab. Chiun joined him on the other, arranging his orchid kimono hem neatly around his scissored knees. He settled easily into his role as instructor. Chiun closed his eyes, taking a deep steadying breath.

"You know, Remo, of Master Bal-Mung," Chiun began.

Remo nodded. "I know he's not on the A list," he said.

There had been several Masters of Sinanju in the long history of the ancient house of assassins who had in some way or another disgraced their ancestors. Most of them were stricken from the official history. Bal-Mung was one of the lucky ones. As part of his earliest lessons, Remo had learned Bal-Mung's name along with all of the other past Masters. However, he had learned nothing more. Until today, Bal-Mung had just been a name on a list with no connecting story.

"I have never told you the tale of Master Bal-Mung," Chiun began, "because it is a story that shames our House and all it represents."

It pained Chiun to even discuss this. In deference to his teacher, Remo resisted making a smart-alecky remark.

"What did he do?" Remo asked gently.

"Bal-Mung committed the most grievous of sins. He squandered his masterhood on a fool's search," Chiun said bitterly. "Before him, there were two other Masters called Bal-Mung. After the time of his disgrace, their names were changed in our records so as not to cause them the shame of being associated with such a one. Shame to you, Bal-Mung of the Fruitless Quest."

"He must have been pretty awful for someone to change the names of previous masters." Remo frowned.

"In truth, this was not so," Chiun lamented. "Until the time of his disgrace, Bal-Mung served his House and ancestors well. He was not on the level of the Great Wang, of course. But he was still not entirely inadequate."

Chiun's voice grew less inflected as he somberly related the painful tale of Bal-Mung's disgrace.

"This occurred in the Sinanju Year of the Fire Petals, by your Western reckoning prior to 500 A.D. It happened that at that time Bal-Mung the Waster of Precious Time was known as Bal-Mung the Good. Not Great, for that is a title bestowed only at death. But Good. Good is not bad, Remo, remember this.

"So Bal-Mung," Chiun continued, "who at that time was considered good, journeyed far from his home to toil in the employ of a great king. This king was named Siegfried and he did rule the people known as the Nibelungs. The king had conquered this race years before and had taken as his own their abundant treasure. This wealth was so vast that it was deemed worthy of a name. Called the Nibelungen Hoard, this store of riches and its possessor became known the world over. News of the Nibelungen Hoard spread even to these shores where Master Bal-Mung was resting between assignments. So taken was he with the stories he had been told, Bal-Mung did abandon his rest in order to venture to the land of the Nibelungs."

"He smelled the cash all the way from Korea," Remo interjected.

"I did say, Remo, that he was good," Chiun reminded him. "And so Bal-Mung and his servant did travel far across the great desolate mass of land to the west. For weeks they trekked through dangerous terrain. The people they met grew paler of skin and rounder of eye. The Master's servant was greatly afeared of these cloud-skinned men, afraid that his master had led him to the land of the dead, and that these were ghosts whose curse it was to walk the frigid land with eyes of an improper wideness. But Master Bal-Mung did allay the fears of his youthful companion. Sinanju had worked for whites for many years, having toiled in Greece and Rome. But to his servant, this was all new and so he continued on in fear.

"Eventually they did find the court of King Siegfried, and the Master did offer his services as protector of both sovereign and gold."

"I'll bet I know which one he was more interested in," Remo grumbled.

"The gold, of course," Chiun sniffed.

"No surprise there."

"And there should not be, for as I have told you, up until now Bal-Mung had demonstrated the qualities of a Master of Sinanju destined for posthumous greatness."

"So did he get the gig?" Remo asked.

"Of course," Chiun said. "The reputation of Sinanju had spread even to this barbaric part of the world. The king immediately retained Master Bal-

Mung as his royal protector. You have heard, no doubt, that Siegfried possessed a powerful sword, as well as a cloak of invisibility.''

"To tell you the truth, the only Siegfried I know was on 'Get Smart,'" Remo admitted sheepishly.

"Your lack of education aside," Chiun continued dryly, "history records that the Nibelungen king owned both of these items. History—as so often happens when it is recorded by whites—is wrong. The name of Siegfried's powerful sword is said even by those in the West to have been called Balmung. It is a distortion of the Master's name but not of his performance as defender of King Siegfried."

"I assume he was also Siegfried's cloak of invisibility?" Remo asked.

"That is true," Chiun confirmed. "At that time, the ability to shield oneself in darkness was long known to Sinanju. So the two things for which the greatness of Siegfried's rule are improperly credited are in fact rightly attributable to Sinanju. All hail the House of Sinanju."

"Okay, you've given me the background," Remo said. "But how did Bal-Mung the Good become Bal-Mung the Not-So-Good?"

"Master Bal-Mung did labor in the service of King Siegfried for many years. So many, in fact, that Siegfried did come to think of him as a friend."

"Whoops," Remo said. "I'll bet *that* cost him a pretty penny."

Chiun nodded. "It is a mistake to assume friendship in a royal assassin," Chiun agreed. "And it is right to take advantage when a king relaxes his guard. If only to instruct future kings on the folly of this presumption."

"Bal-Mung shafted him big-time, didn't he?" Remo said knowingly.

"It was agreed upon as a final tribute to the greatness that is Sinanju, that the entire wealth of the Nibelungen Hoard be bequeathed to Sinanju upon Siegfried's death. With the provision that the death come late in life and be of causes not unnatural."

"I presume Bal-Mung somehow got the shit end of the stick," Remo offered.

"Siegfried was murdered by a knave named Hagan at the behest of the Valkyrie Brunhild. There is his battle helmet," Chiun said, indicating with a sweep of his hand the shelf behind him on which sat the ancient rusted headgear and its attendant falcon. "Found near his slain body."

"So we forfeited the loot," Remo said.

Chiun seemed genuinely surprised. "Why should we have?"

"Well, it's pretty obvious. You said natural causes late in life. The guy was murdered."

"And for kings, there is no more natural a cause for death than treachery," Chiun said with bland surprise.

"Oh, boy," Remo said warily. He knew where this was heading. "What about late in life?" he challenged.

"There is no later point in anyone's life than the point of death," Chiun replied simply.

"Bulldookey," Remo said. "Bal-Mung lost the booty fair and square. Case closed."

"While I do not agree with your childishly silly reasoning, your conclusion is one that would have served Bal-Mung. Would that he had considered this a closed case. He would not have squandered years in search of the lost Nibelungen Hoard."

"Lost?" Remo asked. "When did it get lost?"

"Before his murder, Siegfried sent Bal-Mung off on a pointless journey to Gaul. While he was away, Siegfried hid the gold in a secret treasure cave beneath a mighty river, thought by many to be the Danube. The precise location was known only to Siegfried. It was said that those who had constructed the tunnel and moved the gold were executed in order to forever preserve the secret."

"I guess old Siegfried wasn't as big a dope as Bal-Mung thought he was," Remo said. "He stashed it away as an insurance policy."

"It did him no good," Chiun noted. "When the Master returned, he found the body of the Nibelungen king. Had Sinanju been at his side, his death would have been avoided. Bal-Mung spent the remainder of his masterhood in search of the Nibelungen Hoard. He never found it." Chiun hung his head as if this was a personal disgrace.

"So what about the thing that was stolen from

here? The puzzle piece—was it Siegfried's or Bal-Mung's?"

"It is believed that it was meant for Sinanju. Before his death, Siegfried commissioned a carver to make for him a four-piece map that detailed the resting place of the treasure. A quarter of this was found by Bal-Mung near the body of the king. It had fallen in water and was doubtless overlooked by his attacker."

"So where are the other three pieces?"

"Hagan—Siegfried's murderer—was believed to have one in his possession. One was thought to have been sent to the Burgundian king Gunther, who was brother-in-law to Siegfried. Another was said to have been passed down to Siegfried's own illegitimate son. None of this is known for certain, for each piece of the puzzle was guarded to the point of paranoia by its possessors. Each one coveted the prize. Several of the principal players vanished in their attempt to search for the Hoard themselves. Bal-Mung hunted for the Nibelungen Hoard for many years but never recovered it. He finally returned to Sinanju, where he died in disgrace."

"And no one could figure out from their own section where the dough was?"

Chiun shook his head. "Each piece of the map detailed only a portion of the Hoard's true location. It was designed in such a way that, without the other three, a single piece would be useless. When this room was constructed, the Sinanju piece was placed on that shelf as a reminder of the folly of Bal-Mung.'' Chiun's eyes were sorrowful as he looked at the barren shelf.

After hearing the story, Remo found it difficult to work up much enthusiasm for going after a scrap of wood. However, Chiun meant more to him than anyone else in the world. If it was important to Chiun, it was important to Remo.

"I'm sorry, Chiun," Remo said, "but I think it could be a lot worse. But my promise still goes. If you want to find whoever did this, you can count me in."

Chiun nodded. "It is important to preserve our history," he concluded. "Future generations should not forget the lesson of the foolish Bal-Mung."

"Okay," Remo said, getting to his feet. "I'll give Smith a call and see if he has any ideas."

Chiun rose to his feet as well, revealing the square of stone he had been sitting on. The Master of Sinanju began padding to the door.

Remo craned his neck around to look at the spot where Chiun had been sitting.

"There's been something I've meant to ask for a long time," Remo said suddenly. "What are these?"

He nodded at the two stone tablets on which they had been sitting. There was some kind of ancient writing burned into the surface of each. The tablets appeared to have been shattered at one time and fastened back together. Ancient fissures crisscrossed the stone.

Chiun shrugged. "They were of some significance to the Hebrews at one time. A Babylonian prince awarded them to the House as a bonus after a relatively easy assignment. More worthless junk. My grandfather used them as bookends." With that, Chiun left the room.

Remo peered at the inscriptions in the rock. There were five separate lines on each. Ten in all.

He remembered Charlton Heston smashing similar tablets in an old movie.

Not wishing to think about the possible significance of what he and Chiun had been using as stools, Remo quickly exited the Sinanju library.

14

A good night's sleep had done nothing for Smith's persistent headache. It had, however, beaten back the fatigue he had been feeling for more than two weeks.

He arrived at Folcroft late, coming in at the lazy hour of 7:00 a.m. He had just taken his seat behind his desk and was opening his drawer for the morning's first dose of aspirin when the blue phone rang.

He tucked the receiver between shoulder and ear. "Yes," he said crisply as he twisted the aspirin bottle cover.

"Only me, Smitty," Remo's voice announced. "Chiun and I need a little favor."

"What is it?" Smith asked. He tossed two pills back into his dry throat. Quickly he picked up a glass from his desk and swallowed a mouthful of tap water.

Remo hurriedly explained the Sinanju legend of Bal-Mung and the objects taken from Chiun's home. In conclusion, he said, "So I guess what we need to know is if there's some way you can track either the coins or the wood carving."

"That might be possible," Smith said. He turned

on his computer, quickly logging on. He continued to talk even as he typed. "Do you believe there might be a connection between this and Four?"

"Why should I?" Remo asked.

"I assumed that was the point of your call," Smith explained. "The story you have described is the *Nibelungenlied*. It is an epic German poem of around 1200 A.D."

"Chiun, you didn't tell me these people were German," Remo said off the phone.

"Forgive me, but I assumed in you a level of cultural erudition," Chiun's squeaky voice called from the distance. "Obviously an error on my part."

"I wouldn't get too full of myself," Remo grumbled. "That ain't exactly *Masterpiece Theatre* you've been watching to death lately."

"I found them," Smith interjected, drawing Remo's attention back to the phone.

"Everything?" Remo asked, surprised at the speed with which the CURE director had tracked the items.

"Just the coins," Smith said. "Following the German pattern, I thought to begin my search there. They were offered to a rare coin dealer in Berlin by a Korean cultural representative. The merchant was concerned that the coins might be stolen, so he brought in the authorities. When their authenticity was confirmed, the Korean was remanded to the custody of his embassy. With no explanation for how he came by them, he was sent back to North Korea to face disciplinary measures for their possession.''

''Where are the coins?''

''They are being sent along with him. The Korean government requested them for use in the trial. With the cultural official's diplomatic immunity, they were useless to the Germans as evidence.''

''What's his name and when does he arrive?'' Remo asked.

''Keijo Suk,'' Smith said. ''His plane lands in Pyongyang at three o'clock, your time.''

''Thanks, Smitty,'' Remo said. ''I owe you one.'' He hung up the phone. ''Did you get all that?'' he asked, turning to the Master of Sinanju.

''I did,'' Chiun said. He was standing impatiently near the front door, arms tucked inside the folds of his kimono sleeves. ''However, he did not mention the carving.''

''They probably didn't think too much about it,'' Remo reasoned. ''The coins would be more important to them. Anyway, it won't do any good to sit here and think about it. Let's shake a leg.''

Remo headed for the door. When he pulled on the handle he was surprised to find that he had yanked into the house someone who had been grabbing the knob from the other side. The intruder tumbled forward into him.

Remo grabbed the toppling stranger by the shoulders, setting her on her feet. He was about to demand that she identify herself when he realized he recognized her face.

"Hello, Remo," said Heidi Stolpe. She smiled guiltily.

"I DID NOT MISLEAD you completely," Heidi promised.

They were racing along the highway away from Sinanju in a government car Remo had liberated earlier that day from the Pyongyang airport parking lot. Remo was behind the wheel. Heidi sat beside him in the front. Chiun had positioned himself like royalty in the center of the rear seat.

"I *was* in South America in search of fugitive Nazis," she continued.

"But that was only part of it," Remo said angrily. Frozen mud fields whipped past the speeding car.

"Not at first," she insisted. "But eventually, yes. You see, I am a descendant of Gunther, whose sister Kriemhild was married to Siegfried."

"Your relatives must have the stupidest-looking headstones in Nibelung," Remo said. "Wherever the hell that is."

Heidi persisted. "I only recently became aware of the legend surrounding the treasure. My uncle died, and I inherited my family's castle in the Harz Mountains. In his personal belongings was Gunther's portion of the block carving. It has been in my family's possession for fifteen hundred years."

"This carving. It is in good condition?" Chiun asked from the back seat. He feigned disinterest.

"The map has survived intact," she said to him.

Remo could tell that Chiun was intrigued. However, the Master of Sinanju was playing it cool.

"Still," Chiun ventured, "with only two sections we are no nearer the gold."

"Not two sections," Heidi said excitedly. *"Three."*

"How is this possible?" Chiun asked with a frown.

"At the Four village in South America," Heidi explained. "While the two of you were chasing after Kluge through the tunnels, I searched through the things he left behind. One of the sections of the carving had been packed in a box but not taken with him. I suppose he did not think it crucial to whatever future he has planned for his group."

"Wait a minute," Remo said. "While we were risking our necks, you were on some frigging scavenger hunt?"

"I do not have to explain myself to you," Heidi sniffed.

"Damned lucky for you," Remo replied angrily.

"How did you know Kluge would have a map section?" Chiun asked, steering them back to the most important topic.

"I did not mention that?" she asked, surprised. "According to what I have learned, he is a direct descendant of Siegfried. The block has been in his family for as long as we have owned our respective sections.''

"You used us," Remo said. "You knew about Kluge all along. You used us to get yourself safely into the village."

"There is still the final quarter," Chiun insisted, pointedly ignoring Remo. "Which, according to rumor, fell into the hands of the murderer Hagen."

"That piece will be difficult," Heidi said thoughtfully. "Through my uncle's records, I traced both Siegfried's and Hagen's descendants. The last of the family of Hagan died out around the time the Nazis came to power. His land and possessions were confiscated by order of Hitler. If there *was* a fourth surviving piece, it was lost back then."

Chiun sank back into his seat. The glimmer of hope threatened to fade from his hazel eyes.

"Then we, too, are lost," he lamented.

"Not necessarily," Heidi stressed. "We have three out of four sections. It is possible that we could piece together enough of the map to locate the treasure."

"I suppose I don't have to remind you, Chiun, that she was in Sinanju to steal our piece of the map," Remo called over his shoulder.

Chiun stroked his thread of beard pensively. "She is enterprising," the Master of Sinanju offered. "It is an attractive trait. What did you have in mind, daughter of Gunther?"

"Whatever we recover will be split ninety/ten."

"That would be acceptable," Chiun nodded.

Heidi seemed surprised. "I did not think you would agree to such an arrangement. According to my family record, the House of Sinanju is quite greedy."

"Give him a minute," Remo warned.

Chiun waved a magnanimous hand. "Ours is a reputation undeserved," Chiun proclaimed. "You have done much work. You have earned your ten percent."

"Bingo." Remo grinned.

"*What?*" Heidi demanded.

"It is a large sum, surely," Chiun said, considering. "Perhaps I should allow you only five. What do you think, Remo?"

"Don't get me in the middle of this," Remo said.

Heidi was livid. Her porcelain skin had flushed red. "If anyone is getting five percent, it is you," she challenged.

"Are you mad, girl?" Chiun asked, shocked. "You did not believe I would allow you to steal nine-tenths of my money?"

"*Your* money?"

Chiun grew indignant. "The treasure is the rightful property of the House of Sinanju. If I so desired, I could keep the entire amount myself."

"Without my half of the map, your quarter is useless," Heidi reminded him.

"And without my quarter, your half is useless," Chiun countered.

Heidi fumed. "Seventy/thirty," she said eventually. "The seventy goes to me," she added quickly.

"That is ludicrous," Chiun huffed. "Sixty/forty. In the favor of Sinanju."

"No," Heidi insisted stubbornly.

"As an impartial observer who doesn't give a wet fart in a windbreaker about the gold, why not split it fifty/fifty?" Remo suggested.

"Outrageous," Chiun snapped.

"Out of the question," Heidi sniffed.

"In that case, you're both going to walk away with diddly. Just like your ancestors."

"That treasure is Sinanju property," Chiun fumed.

"You forfeited it when Siegfried was murdered," Heidi countered stubbornly.

"Are you deranged, woman? That is when it *became* Sinanju property."

"Siegfried only hid the Hoard because he did not trust your ancestor Bal-Mung," Heidi snarled hotly.

"Lies!" Chiun shrieked. Hands knotted in fists of furious bone. "Stop the car, Remo. I will not travel another inch with one who dares sully the name of my beloved ancestor."

"First off, I am not stopping. Secondly you weren't too charitable to him back at your house," Remo reminded him.

In Korean, Chiun snapped, "*I* may say what I want about my family. *She* may not."

"All right, all right!" Heidi snapped, angry that

she couldn't understand what Chiun was saying. "I will agree to a fifty/fifty split."

"Sixty/forty," Chiun said quickly.

"Fifty/fifty," Heidi repeated firmly.

In the back seat, Chiun huffed as he considered the offer. At long last he broke his silence.

"Though my heart breaks to cast away that which is so obviously mine, I fear I am at your mercy, devil woman. Fifty/fifty. And may you choke on your ill-gotten prize."

The Master of Sinanju settled back into the rear seat.

"Then we have a deal," Heidi said, exhaling in relief. "Where is your quarter of the map?"

"Here's where it gets tricky," Remo said, smiling.

"Why?" Heidi asked suspiciously. It was as if a light suddenly snapped on in her head. She spun around in her seat. "You *do* have it, do you not?" she asked Chiun.

"That would be not," Remo said.

"You are joking," she accused.

"Nope," said Remo happily. "That's why we're here. Somebody stole our section."

"I cannot believe this," she said, twisting back around. "Stop the car."

"Lady, I didn't do it for him—I'm sure as hell not doing it for you," Remo promised evenly.

"This is beyond duplicity," she said, astonished.

"It is no wonder Siegfried did not trust Bal-Mung. You are a family of liars. Stop this car!"

"I have memorized the map," Chiun said softly.

Though she had been growing more enraged with each passing second until this point, Heidi instantly became calm. She peered cautiously at the Master of Sinanju.

"Is this true?" she questioned suspiciously.

Chiun gently tapped the parchment skin of his temple with the tip of a tapered fingernail.

"Every detail of our map section is forever burned into my memory," he said pleasantly.

Heidi looked at Remo questioningly. Remo paid her no attention as he looked out over the hood of the speeding car. Finally she turned back to the Master of Sinanju.

"How good is your memory?" she asked.

Chiun didn't respond to the insulting question. He merely stared out at the frozen paddies as the car soared down the empty highway.

15

Keijo Suk could not believe how quickly he had been apprehended. He had always trusted in the basic dishonesty of every Western store owner. Unfortunately he had found the last honest merchant in the hemisphere.

The coin dealer had called Suk back to his shop twice before turning him over to the authorities. Suk had thought the man was working up the courage to purchase the coins he had stolen from the Master of Sinanju's house. In retrospect, he realized that the man was checking on their authenticity. Without proof of ownership of the heretofore unknown variety of coin, it was determined that Suk was quite obviously a thief. The only question was how he had managed to sneak into and out of Egypt with his stolen prize. Never mind the fact that while there he had discovered and looted an unknown yet apparently flawlessly preserved tomb.

Suk realized how useless it would be to explain where he had gotten the coins. He had decided to merely sit quietly and take whatever punishment was given, hoping that he would not encounter the Master of Sinanju.

In truth, Suk doubted the Master of Sinanju would ever find out about the theft. There was so much treasure in that rambling house that the infamous assassin could not possibly miss a few coins and a simple chunk of wood. Also it was known in his native land that the Sinanju Master spent much of his time in the decadent West where he had been commissioned to train a white in the ancient arts of his village. It was likely that he would not return for months. Perhaps years.

Reasoning thusly, Keijo Suk had managed to calm himself somewhat as the German authorities turned him over to the North Korean consulate in Berlin. Even the torn cartilage and fractured bone in his shoulder had begun to feel better.

His embassy had shipped him off to North Korea, where he would be placed under arrest the moment his plane landed.

The official government aircraft had just touched down at the airport in Pyongyang. As it taxied slowly to a stop, Suk made a final appeal to whatever gods might still listen to a thieving Communist that the Master of Sinanju would never learn of what he had done.

REMO PARKED THE CAR in the same spot from which he had stolen it that morning.

The Korean soldiers who patrolled the airport

gave them a wide berth. Although it would have been more than reasonable to question an odd group like theirs, the reputations of both Masters of Sinanju preceded them. They were allowed to move across the parking lot with impunity, just as they had been after landing earlier that day.

But this time Heidi was with them. A thought suddenly occurred to Remo.

"How did you get in here, by the way?" Remo asked. He was looking at her very pale skin and obviously non-Korean features.

"Anything is possible with the proper bribes," Heidi said. She clearly didn't wish to discuss it further.

"Whatever." Remo shrugged.

Remo left the others and went inside the terminal to ask about the flight from Germany. He learned that it had landed only a few minutes before.

Coming back outside, Remo led their party out through the restricted chain-link fence onto the tarmac. The soldiers on duty made an effort to look wherever Remo and Chiun were not.

A boarding ramp had just been secured at the side of the government aircraft, and the first of the passengers was beginning to deplane. Keijo Suk was led out in manacles in the company of a pair of North Korean police officials.

The Korean cultural officer needed only one glance at the pale purple kimono on the old man who waited for him at the bottom of the ramp. His eyes grew wide in fright.

"Ahhhhh!" screamed Keijo Suk. He turned around and, shoving his captors roughly aside, raced back up the stairs, disappearing inside the plane.

Recognizing the flight instinct of a guilty man, Remo and Chiun each hopped up onto a railing of the ramp. They ran up, jumping onto the platform at the top. They followed Suk inside. Heidi was forced to push her way past the irate passengers. The men who had been escorting Suk stayed far behind in the doorway, fearful of the Master of Sinanju and his protégé.

Inside, Chiun found Suk cowering on the floor behind the last three coach seats. He cradled his injured shoulder with his shackled hands.

"Thief!" the Master of Sinanju charged, eyes furious.

Chiun grabbed Suk by the front of his jacket and dragged the terrified man to his feet. Suk was sweating profusely.

"Don't kill him yet, Little Father," Remo warned, running up behind Chiun.

"Yes!" screamed Suk. "Please! Do not kill me yet!"

"Tell what you know, thief!" Chiun ordered. As incentive, he slapped Keijo Suk back and forth across his tear-soaked face.

"I know that I have stolen from the Glorious House of Sinanju and that I must be made to pay for my actions," Suk blubbered. He held his hurt shoulder away from Chiun.

"And so you will," Chiun hissed.

"But must that payment be in blood?" Suk pleaded.

"Of course," Chiun replied, as if Suk were an imbecile.

"Everything is negotiable," Heidi Stolpe volunteered in German. She was standing behind Remo.

"Silence, wench," Chiun menaced.

Suk looked up at her, a spark of hope in his eyes. "Yes," he said, also in German. "She is correct, Master."

"She is a woman and is therefore incapable of correctness. You are dealing with me," Chiun warned. "Where is my property?"

"The men who escorted me here have the coins," Suk answered.

"Remo," Chiun snapped. He jerked his head toward the men who still stood back near the door.

Remo went dutifully, if somewhat reluctantly, over to the door. One of the men held a small package—about the size of a cigar box. He willingly handed it over to Remo.

"Wait here," Remo ordered. He jogged back to Chiun. "Here it is," he said. His tone was painfully uninterested.

Chiun ripped the box from his hands. Tearing it open, he fussed over the coins inside. They were wrapped in two long tubes of cellophane.

"Is this all?" he asked, knowing full well that it was.

"Oh, yes," Suk said pleadingly. "They are all there."

"Very well," Chiun said. Snapping the box shut, he handed it to Remo. "Where is the other item?"

"Other item?" Suk said. He was frightened beyond reason.

"The wood carving," Remo interjected.

"Oh, *that*. I no longer have it."

"What!" Chiun bellowed.

The old man picked up Suk as if he weighed no more than a packet of complimentary cashews. Kimono sleeves snapping, he hurled Suk against the bulkhead of the plane. Suk slammed full force against the wall. He slid painfully into a window seat.

Chiun was on him again. Yanking the whimpering man to his feet once more, the Master of Sinanju flung Suk to the other side of the plane. As he slammed against the far wall, the nearest Plexiglas window cracked beneath Suk's elbow. His bone fared no better.

Suk shrieked in pain. He scampered back against the wall as Chiun again approached him.

"I know who has it," Suk begged, cradling his arm.

"Who?" Chiun demanded.

"A man. A German," Suk panted. "Adolf Kluge."

"Kluge?" Remo asked, coming up behind Chiun. For the first time, this wasted trip began to interest him.

"Kluge?" Chiun demanded of the air. "Who is this fiend who springs up at my every turn?" As he asked the question, he shook Keijo Suk so violently the thief's molars rattled.

"I do not know," Suk whined. "He approached me a year ago for business reasons. He wished for me to broker a deal between our government and one of his companies. Only last week did he ask me to steal the piece of wood."

"Where can we find him?" Remo asked.

"I do not know," Suk breathed. "He always called me. He was going to contact me once more when he—" he looked down, ashamed "—when he collected the balance owed me for taking the carving."

"So, Kluge expected to come into some cash," Remo said.

"What?" Heidi asked. She hadn't understood a word of what had just been said until Remo's last comment in English. "What has Kluge to do with this?"

"He's the one who has our quarter," Remo explained.

"Not for long," Chiun said. He spun back to Suk.

"Mercy," the thief begged. He was on his knees, sobbing uncontrollably.

Chiun's lip curled as he regarded the pathetic fig-

ure before him. "You will have it though you did
not earn it," he intoned.

A tight hand drew back and fired forward, slamming against Suk's chest. The thief's eyes sprang
wide as his fragile heart exploded inside his chest
cavity. Suk dropped forward onto the carpeted aisle
of the plane, his mouth leaking a puddle of deep red.

Chiun pulled the box of taped coins from Remo.
Wheeling, he marched up to Suk's waiting Korean
entourage.

"You," Chiun said, pointing to one man. "Take
these to my village. My caretaker will be there to
collect these." A cautionary nail found a spot on the
man's throat. "And be warned, I know *precisely*
how many are there."

The official cast an eye to the body of Suk. He
was unaware that he had begun nodding enthusiastically.

"Yes, Master of Sinanju. At once, Master of Sinanju."

He took the box in quivering hands, racing out the
door and down the stairs. A moment later, Remo
spied him out the window, running for all he was
worth across the cold tarmac.

"And you," Chiun said to the other. "Remove
this carrion from the Master of Sinanju's plane." He
indicated the body of Keijo Suk.

"At once, Master of Sinanju," the government
agent said.

As the agent hustled down the aisle and hefted the

corpse awkwardly to his shoulders, Remo sidled up to Chiun.

"*Your* plane?" he asked.

"It is the least they can do, considering my ordeal," Chiun said. "After all, it was a representative of this despicable regime who violated the sanctity of the Master's House." Thus justified, he marched past Remo and took his usual seat over the left wing of the plane.

"I hope the despicable regime agrees with you," Remo muttered, shaking his head.

He ushered a confused Heidi Stolpe back down the aisle. The guard came past in the other direction carrying the body of the late Keijo Suk.

16

Adolf Kluge hated living hand to mouth. As head of IV, he was accustomed to an opulent life-style. Now he was reduced to begging for every meal.

When he had taken over the stewardship of IV, one of his first acts had been to sever the organization's ties with Germany's neo-Nazi underground. He considered the years of money that had been lavished on these groups by his predecessors to be money completely wasted.

But Kluge was not without some vision. He had somehow planned for a day where he might be in the situation he found himself in now. It must have been on some instinctive level, for he certainly never truly expected it to happen. Lucky for him, his instincts had been correct.

Kluge had wisely not cut IV's ties with *every* neo-Nazi group. The ones that remained—while not eager to part with their money—were loyal to the cause and, therefore, loyal to Adolf Kluge. They shared what little they had with him.

It was only right. After all, at one time it had been Kluge's money.

Feeling the lightness of his wallet every step of the way, Adolf Kluge stepped into the lobby of Berlin's Unser Fanatischer Bank. Trying to preserve the sense of arrogance he had displayed his entire life, Kluge marched boldly over to the receptionist's desk.

"Please inform Mr. Riefenstahl that I wish to see him," he said officiously.

The woman was aware that Kluge was a large depositor at Unser Fanatischer. She immediately dialed the interoffice number of the bank manager, unaware of the hard times that had recently befallen Herr Kluge.

She found out soon enough.

When Riefenstahl answered the phone, the receptionist informed him of Kluge's request. There was a great deal of talking from the other end of the line—much more than there would have been a few short weeks before.

The receptionist grew nervous. Embarrassed, she tried to avoid eye contact with Kluge who stood— growing ever angrier—before her highly polished half-shell desk.

The bank manager was actually trying to avoid him! A far cry from the way the man had always fawned over Kluge when the IV leader controlled accounts in the millions.

It was more than Adolf Kluge could bear. Lunging across the desk, he ripped the phone from the startled receptionist's hand.

"Listen to me, you fat Prussian pig," Kluge hissed. He was so angry, his words launched spittle into the receiver. "I need access to my safe-deposit box. And unless you want me to turn you over to the national banking commission, I would suggest you drag your greasy carcass down here now!" He slammed the phone into the cradle.

Huffing and puffing and running as if the building were on fire, Otto Riefenstahl appeared down the lobby staircase twelve seconds later.

"Herr Kluge," he begged obsequiously. "Forgive the error. I was led to understand that you were someone else." As he mopped his forehead with a sopping handkerchief, he shot an appropriately dissatisfied look at the receptionist.

"My safe-deposit box," Kluge said, jaw clenched tightly. His eyes shot fiery daggers at the portly bank manager.

"Of course." The man smiled nervously.

Riefenstahl waddled rapidly away from the desk. Kluge followed, hands clasped behind his back, fingers clenching and unclenching anxiously.

They detoured around the teller windows, heading through a doorway at the end of the long row of glass-enclosed booths. A long hallway lined with several offices led to yet another door—this one polished steel. Riefenstahl used a special key from a chain hooked to his ample midsection to gain admittance into the room.

A short hallway led to a bare archway. This

opened into a large inner room. The bank's safe-deposit boxes were lined up along three of the four walls. There were hundreds of simple metal doors, each with two slots designed for two separate keys.

It was always cool in here, even in the summer. In winter, it was worse. Kluge shivered as they passed the rows of identical boxes and walked over to the larger cabinets that lined the narrowest wall. These were as big and plain as high-school lockers.

"Which was it, Herr Kluge?" Riefenstahl asked nervously.

"*Achtzig,*" Kluge said.

"Ah, yes."

Riefenstahl went to the eightieth locker and inserted his master key into the right slot. Kluge inserted his own key from the chain he had taken from his pocket.

They turned the keys simultaneously. The locks popped obediently. Kluge pulled down on the handle, and the door sprang open, revealing a large metal box.

"Let me know when you are finished," Riefenstahl said.

When Kluge said nothing more to him, the grateful bank manager hurried from the chilly room.

Once Riefenstahl was gone, Kluge hefted the large box from the bottom of the locker. Bearing it ahead of him like a sacred relic, he placed it on one of several tables that were arranged around the center of the floor. Inserting the same key he had used on the safe deposit box door, Kluge opened the lock on the top of the large box.

There was not much inside. Just a dusty collection of useless things his father had been proud of. Things that Kluge had never really bothered with since assuming his position as head of IV.

His family's lineage had been lovingly recorded and preserved. Not that Kluge had ever believed that he was a direct descendant of the *Nibelungenlied* protagonist Siegfried. The entire history had been recopied sometime at the end of the last century. The pages of the book in which the Kluge family tree had been written were yellowed with age.

Kluge had only recently begun to lend credence to the old stories. Encountering the Sinanju Masters had been the catalyst. If *they* were real, then perhaps his father's fanciful stories were true, as well.

Looking down on those pages, he only wished that someone had had the sense of history to save the original manuscripts from which this one book had been compiled. They would have been priceless.

Kluge placed the book to one side.

Aside from the lone manuscript, there was a folded Nazi flag tucked into a corner of the box. A memento of his late father's war days. There was other assorted junk—the Iron Cross, old letters. Kluge went instinctively to the two letters that were written and signed by Hitler himself. He had always sought these two out, even as a boy. He examined their dog-eared edges for a moment before putting them aside.

It was a paltry pile of useless junk.

The item Kluge had been looking for was at the bottom. Atop it, half-tucked into a yellowed envelope, was an old photograph.

Kluge picked up the envelope. Pulling the photo out, he examined it carefully.

He was disappointed to find that it was not as he hoped it would be. Most of the details of the map were clear; however, there had been an unintentional blurring in the lower right-hand corner of the picture.

He cursed himself inwardly for not being certain the box containing the IV section of the map had been spirited away with the rest of his personal belongings. There had been so much planning at the end, and—truth be told—even though he imagined early on that the village was doomed, he had never expected that the men from Sinanju would find a way to bankrupt the secret Nazi group. He had always thought to set up IV elsewhere. Now that his businesses were gone and he was forced to resort to archaeological sleuthing, all he had to go on was a blurry old photograph.

Well, not *all*, he realized.

The final item in the box was in an old black felt bag, which Kluge lifted gently from the bottom of the metal container. Unknotting the dingy cord at the neck of the bag, Kluge slipped a flat square object from inside.

Kluge examined the details of his family's section of the Siegfried block carving. It was in excellent shape. Better shape, in fact, than the IV square.

That piece of the puzzle—now missing—had been collected by his father during the height of Nazi Germany's power. The descendants of Hagan's family were weak. And, as an odd quirk of fate would have it, they had found themselves at that unfortunate time in history to be of a particular religious sect that was not in line with the progressive reforms of the fascist government.

After they were dead, Kluge's father had pillaged their belongings. His search had turned up not only the block carving, but also the stained-glass windows which would eventually be installed at the South American fortress of IV.

Kluge supposed he owed the Hagan family a favor. If not for the picture of Siegfried holding a piece of the block in that window, he might never have realized the significance of the sections already in his possession.

Kluge quickly slipped the block, as well as the picture of the missing piece, inside the cloth bag. Replacing the other items inside the safe-deposit box, he secured the lid. He put the container back inside the locker, shutting the door tightly.

After he locked the door, he collected the black bag from the table.

Though the Hagan block was no longer in his possession, he did have a photograph of it. That, along with his family's section and the Sinanju section so thoughtfully provided by Keijo Suk, had already given him a fairly strong idea where the treasure might be hidden.

But he needed to know for certain. There was one section left. And Adolf Kluge knew where it would be.

He hurried from the room, not bothering to tell the obese bank manager Riefenstahl that he was through.

17

The North Korean government was surprisingly generous in loaning its plane to the Master of Sinanju and his party. Provided, of course, that the Master of Sinanju not blame the actions of Keijo Suk on the North Korean government.

Via the pilot's radio, Chiun had flatly stated that there would be no provisions. Government authorities had said that this was good, too, and told the pilot to do as he was told.

The jet had been cheerily refueled and allowed to take off from Pyongyang airport without delay. To Remo's delight and Chiun's dismay, there were no British situation comedies being played on the plane.

The long flight back to Germany was uneventful.

As the plane finally began its descent over Berlin, Remo looked out the window at the rapidly growing rooftops.

"It feels like we just left here," he griped.

"I will not complain," Heidi said in her soft Spanish accent. "I spend far too little time here."

"Do not talk of spending, swindler," Chiun accused from the seat behind them.

"Is he going to start again?" Heidi asked Remo.

"One thing you should know about him," Remo explained. "He may quiet down for a continent or two, but he never really stops."

"Really, Remo, I do not know why you would converse with this flimflammer," Chiun called over the top of the seat. "We merely agreed to do business with her—we do not have to be nice to her. Look on her as you would a rat catcher or the Rooty Rotor man."

"This is *your* deal, Little Father," Remo reminded him. "At this point I'm just going along to zap Kluge."

"Remember that when we find the gold," Chiun cautioned. With that, the Master of Sinanju fell silent.

Remo rolled his eyes. "*If* we find it," he muttered.

"We have three-quarters of the map," Heidi reminded him. "Success may be in our grasp." She nodded serenely. "It is as it was intended to be."

"How so?" Remo asked, bored. He was looking out the window for the regimented runway lines of Tegel Airport.

"Siegfried was actually quite clever," Heidi said. "According to my family records, which date back to the time the carving was made, Siegfried wished that the money be divided equitably at the time of his passing. His son would have a segment, as well as each of our ancestors. At the time of his death, the location of the fourth piece would be revealed and the three interested parties would be able to find the Hoard. We could then divide it in thirds.''

Behind them, Chiun snorted. "Poppycock," he volunteered.

Heidi pressed ahead. "With our two factions united, we need only bring aboard the descendant of Siegfried. If he is willing, we could all be much richer by morning.''

"Wait a minute," Remo said, spinning away from the window. "You're not talking about cutting a deal with Kluge?''

"If necessary," Heidi admitted.

"Any separate deals you make will come out of your fifty percent," Chiun piped in.

"Think of another option," Remo told Heidi.

She shrugged. "We do not *necessarily* need to make a deal," she suggested. "As long as we acquire his portion of the block carving.''

"No deals," Remo said firmly. He turned back to the small window. The airport runway was racing rapidly up to meet them.

Heidi sighed. "As you wish. It is a shame, however. We have come so far to fulfill the wishes of an ancient hero. This quest was intended by Siegfried to be a group effort by those deserving of the treasure.''

"I deserve it all," called the Master of Sinanju's squeaky voice.

The Korean jet touched down with a heavy jounce and a shriek of tires.

As HE WAITED in the car, Hirn Zeitzler touched the small flesh-colored bandage on his nose with delicate fingertips.

It still hurt, but nowhere near as much as it had when his nose rings had been ripped out.

That was two weeks ago.

Two weeks since the killer with the dead eyes had assaulted Hirn and his neo-Nazi friends in the Schweinebraten Bier Hall in Juterbog. Two weeks since the same man had killed Gus Holloway and Kempten Olmutz-Hohenzollerkirchen. Two weeks since the deaths of Nazi sympathizers had stopped.

The assassin was obviously gone.

And with his departure, those who had been lucky enough to survive his attacks had woven tales of great heroism in which they played the dual role of both victim and hero.

Hirn's nose had been shredded so badly that it had required more than forty stitches to piece it back together. He had spent much of the past two weeks in great pain and with his proboscis swathed lavishly in gauze bandages. However, any discomfort he may have felt was not enough to stop Hirn from claiming that he was one of the ones who had stopped the assassin in his tracks.

Since the attacks by the killer had ceased after his encounter with Hirn, he felt safe making this boast.

Of course, he had had the good sense to wait a week and a half before bringing it up among the neo-Nazi beer-hall circuit. After all, Hirn wasn't completely stupid. The last thing he wanted was to invite the angry return of the man who had liberated him of not only his nose rings, but also of much of the cartilaginous ridge between his nasal hemispheres.

Once he had begun weaving his tall tales, it had taken just under two days for Hirn to actually begin believing his own stories concerning his deadly encounter with the mysterious assassin.

As they waited in the car, Hirn and his skinhead companions whiled away the time laughing and cursing as they recounted the story to one another. Each of the men managed to embellish the account further.

One of the other two—a youth named Erwin—had already gotten the remnants of his nose pierced. A silver swastika dangled on a chain from out the cluster of deep red furrows where his skin had been pieced together.

"Did that hurt?" Hirn asked, pointing to the chain. At the moment, he had no strong desire to have anyone poke anything through his nose.

"Not as much as it hurt for that American!" Erwin said with a raucous laugh.

Though they hadn't a clue what he meant, the other skinheads laughed uproariously.

The air inside the vehicle was fetid, the interiors

of the windows covered with a thick fog of condensation. Their laughter carried to the sidewalk outside.

Eventually, and with much difficulty, they got control of themselves. Eyes watering, they took long drinks from cans of thick German beer.

"Is he coming?" Erwin asked after he was through swilling his beer. He scratched the tip of his nose.

Hirn could not yet bring himself to do that. He was afraid his nose would come loose under his fingers.

"What time is it?" he asked.

As if on cue, the rear door of the vehicle popped open. The trio of skinheads searched through the pile of trash on the seats and floor for their guns. Only Erwin found his. From the passenger's-side seat, he pushed the gun toward the figure who was climbing in the rear of the car next to Hirn Zeitzler.

As Erwin did so, Adolf Kluge grabbed the gun in his left hand, at the same time launching forward with his right. The rabbit punch connected with Erwin's quilt-work nose.

Howling in pain, Erwin released the gun. He grabbed at his nose, which had begun to spring several major leaks, none of which at the customary openings.

Kluge settled in beside Hirn, tossing Erwin's gun to the mountain of discarded cans in the footwell.

"I do not have time for your stupidity," Kluge warned.

"Heil Hitler," Hirn said proudly. He slurred the words.

Kluge ignored him. "We must hurry," he said to Hirn.

Erwin cried anew as a fresh seam opened up along the bridge of his nose.

"Shut him up," Kluge hissed to the man behind the wheel.

The other skinhead in the front seat did his best to quiet Erwin. It seemed to help, for it gave the bleeding neo-Nazi someone against whom he could vent his anger.

As the two men in the front seat got into a slapping fight, Kluge concentrated on Hirn.

"You have contacted your men?" the IV leader asked.

"Yes, sir," Hirn enthused drunkenly.

"How many?"

"Almost one hundred," Hirn said.

"How many?" Kluge repeated, more angry this time.

Hirn glanced up at Erwin. He was still bleeding as he fought with the driver. His hands were slick with blood.

"Fifty-eight," Hirn admitted. "But I called one hundred," he added quickly. "More than one hundred. But this was all that agreed to go. You must understand, Herr Kluge, the failure in Paris over the summer weakened the movement. No one has the belly for it. And the American killer who was slaughtering our men did even more damage. The three of us stopped him too late."

"You did not stop him at all, idiot!" Kluge snapped. "Save your tales of glory for the fools with whom you spend your drunken nights."

Hirn was like a chastised dog before his furious master. He grew very quiet, staring nervously at the head of IV.

"Fifty-eight," Kluge complained to himself. He shook his head. "It will have to do." He turned to Hirn. "You have rented the vehicles?"

"I had my men do it this morning."

"Good. See to it that all of your men show up at the designated rendezvous. I want fifty-eight there, Hirn. Not fifty-six. Not fifty-seven. It is going to be difficult enough with so few. Is that understood?"

Hirn looked at Erwin. The bleeding was slowing, but he was still a bloodstained mess.

"Yes, sir," Hirn said enthusiastically.

"Fine," Kluge said. "Now, before we can leave on this expedition, I need one last thing."

"Sir?"

Blue eyes washed in gray fixed on the young skinhead.

"I need you to steal a block of wood."

THE STOLPE FAMILY castle was a huge old-world edifice resting on a jagged slab of rock in the Harz Mountains in the Niedersachsen region of north-central Germany. It sprawled morosely across the craggy mountain peak in hideous contrast to the beautiful early-winter countryside through which they had just passed.

As they drove up the winding black road to the castle's front entrance, Remo noted the only thing that might have made the scene complete would have been a dose of crackling lightning and a couple of howling wolves.

"I don't want to sound rude or anything," Remo said as they passed beneath the rusted portcullis and into the spacious inner courtyard, "but this has got to be the crummiest castle I've ever seen."

"It has been in my family for generations," Heidi countered, a faraway look in her azure eyes.

Remo could tell by her tone that she didn't disagree with his assessment. Following Heidi's instructions, he took the smooth path that skirted the inner battlements. Remo parked their rented car near the massive stone entrance to the tall, circular donjon.

"What is that?" the Master of Sinanju asked in disgust as they exited the car. He pointed to a deep furrow that had been carved along the exterior wall of the inner tower.

Heidi's cheeks flushed. Remo was surprised that the woman who had been so brave and ruthless in South America and Korea could be embarrassed.

"My uncle's idea. He was the last Stolpe to live here. It is supposed to be a moat."

"A moat?" Chiun asked. "At the interior? Tell

me, girl, why was your uncle not committed to an asylum? This defacement is obviously the work of a deranged mind."

Again Heidi didn't argue.

"He thought that this was the image of a castle people would like. You see, we are forced in better weather to rent out to tourists," she said sadly.

Remo couldn't help but feel sorry for her. "That's a shame," he said, consolingly.

"A shame?" Chiun scoffed. "It is a crime. A fine home like this should never be turned over to fat American hamburger eaters and their squealing offspring."

"I agree." Heidi nodded. "And it will not be again if we are successful. Come, the carving is in here."

She led them up the half-dozen steep steps and through the rounded door frame of the old dungeon wing.

"This building predates the time of Otto the Great," Heidi remarked as she led them through a narrow corridor.

Chiun snorted.

"Did I say something wrong again?" Heidi asked warily.

"It's just that Otto wasn't so great as far as we're concerned," Remo said. "He used us to help him beat back the Magyars and enslave the Poles and the Bohemians, but then he got all caught up with the

Church of Rome. Which," he said to Chiun, "I don't think is all that bad an idea."

"Spoken like one who was raised by virginal wimple wearers," Chiun commented.

"The nuns weren't so bad," Remo said defensively.

"Go on," Chiun said, striking his chest. "Defend them if you feel you must. Each ungrateful word twists the knife further into your poor old father's ailing heart."

"Put a sock in it, Tallulah Bankhead," Remo suggested.

The corridor ended at a narrow staircase. This led down into the old dungeon of the castle. At the bottom of the stairs, a replica of an old-fashioned wooden door was slightly ajar. Flickering torchlight, as well as hushed voices, came from within the room beyond. There was the sound of metal scraping against rock.

"There should not be anyone here," Heidi whispered.

Remo pressed his fingers to his lips. He and Chiun slipped down the staircase, making no more noise than a pair of thousand-year-old spirits. Heidi followed on tiptoes.

The voices grew louder as they neared the open door.

"How am *I* supposed to know?" someone said in German. "He said it was behind one of these."

"I checked those already," insisted another.

Remo—who was the only member of their group not fluent in German—stuck his head around the door frame. He caught sight of three figures inside one of the dungeon cells. Their actions were illuminated by a burning torch that had been jammed into a metal hoop in the wall.

Remo was surprised to find he recognized the trio of skinheads. Each of the three men he had met at the Schweinebraten Bier Hall carried a crowbar that he was jamming into the large fissures between the stones of the cell wall.

"Wait here," Remo whispered to Heidi.

Curious, he sauntered into the room along with the Master of Sinanju. The men in the cell were so engrossed in their work that they didn't notice their visitors.

Remo paused near the rusted bars of the cell. He leaned against the open door.

"Hey, fellas," Remo said brightly. "What are you doing nosing around in here?"

The trio of skinheads nearly jumped out of their skins. As soon as they saw who it was who had spoken to them, their initial surprise rocketed into the stratosphere of abject terror.

Three separate hands flashed instinctively for three separate noses.

"Good," Remo said, stepping into the cell. "We don't have to get reacquainted. What are you doing here?"

The cell was small. Too small for much maneuvering. In spite of that, Erwin's fear of the terrifying Nazi killer got the better of him. As Remo approached, he took his crowbar in a double-handed grip and swung it fiercely at Remo's head. At least, that was Erwin's hastily hatched plan.

However, at the point where the crowbar should have made contact with Remo's face, something went desperately wrong. Remo's head was no longer where it was supposed to be.

Even as his eyes were registering the dull afterimage of Remo ducking out of the way of his mighty swing, Erwin's momentum was carrying the heavy crowbar in a wide arc. The bar whizzed around the cell, slamming with a loud finality into the forehead of the third skinhead. The man dropped like an undercooked strudel to the damp stone floor of the cell.

Erwin's brain was trying to register what his body had just done. He stared dumbly down at the corpse of his friend. So amazed was he by what had transpired that he didn't feel the crowbar being plucked from his hands. He only briefly became aware of the metal rod as it was bent over the back of his skull. Then he was no longer aware of anything.

Remo tossed the twisted crowbar onto Erwin's body.

"So much for Larry and Curly," he said dryly. Remo turned to the surviving skinhead.

"We were sent to find a block of wood," Hirn blurted out. His hand was still over his bandaged nose.

"This was what they were after," Heidi Stolpe said, excited. She stepped past Chiun and made her way into the cell.

Heidi tugged at a rusted manacle that was secured to the wall. It pulled away easily, along with the facade of the rock beneath. A hollow behind revealed the contours of yet another section of the Siegfried carving. Heidi took out the wooden block, handling it with great reverence.

"Whoever they are working for must know at least part of my family's history to know of this hiding place," she said, examining the block.

"Of course," Remo said sarcastically. "Isn't everyone in on this dink-ass treasure hunt of yours?"

Heidi and Chiun weren't listening to him. The Master of Sinanju had padded into the cell behind Heidi. Both of them were observing the carvings in the surface of the ancient petrified wood. They quickly left, arguing about the true location of a river.

Remo turned his attention back to the lone skinhead.

"Who sent you?" he asked Hirn.

"What?" Hirn asked, startled. He had been watching Chiun and Heidi bicker.

"If you're hard of hearing, I can match your ears to your nose." He reached for the sides of Hirn's head.

"Kluge! His name is Kluge. *Adolf* Kluge."

Remo's bloodless lips thinned to invisibility. Hirn

recognized the predator's glint in his eyes. The skinhead again pressed a hand over his injured nose. His free hand he placed over an ear. He was forced to jam the other ear protectively into his shoulder.

"Where is he?" Remo asked.

"What?" Hirn yelled.

"Oh, for heaven's sake." Remo slapped the skinhead's hands away from his face. "Kluge," he repeated. "Where?"

"At an inn," Hirn said, nervously rubbing his smarting hands. "Waiting for us. It's in the Black Forest." He gave Remo the name of the lodge. "I can take you there," he offered lamely.

"Thanks," Remo said, "I already have a guide."

He launched a hard finger deep into Hirn Zeitzler's broad forehead. Surprisingly, the neo-Nazi's brain must have performed some function in life, for when it ceased to operate, so too did Hirn Zeitzler.

As the skinhead was collapsing atop his neo-Nazi comrades, Remo was already heading up the dungeon stairs.

His cruel face held the promise of violent death.

18

He sat alone on the terrace. Waiting.

The late-afternoon air was cold. Adolf Kluge watched his breath escape in tiny puffs of steam.

He checked his watch.

Late.

Hirn should have been here hours ago. It was a simple matter. The only way Kluge could have made it simpler would have been to take them by the hand and lead them to the block carving himself. These skinhead creatures were moronic.

He would have sent one of the Numbers, but there were precious few of them left. Some were here. He had sent more with his aide, Herman, to help with the South American relocation of the IV villagers. Most of the genetically engineered men were dead. To Kluge's knowledge, only one was unaccounted for. He was the last of the four-man team Kluge had sent to Berlin weeks ago to intercept the two Masters of Sinanju at the airport. Presumably that one had ended up like his companions. All dead.

All thanks to the men from Sinanju.

Kluge glanced at his watch again. Barely fifteen seconds had elapsed since the last time he checked.

All the planning he had done would come to naught if Hirn failed to get the final piece of the ancient puzzle. The skinhead's friends were already camped in the woods up the road from the Pension Kirchmann. Only thirty-eight of them had shown up. In truth, that was more than Kluge had expected. He had augmented the band of skinheads with a few of the surviving Numbers from the IV village.

Kluge had the vehicles and the men. If the gold was in the right place, he would have that, too. But only if Hirn came down from whatever drug- or alcohol-induced stupor he was in today and brought Kluge the one thing he needed to make the whole plan come together.

Somewhere in the forest nearby, an animal snorted.

Kluge had never spent much time in this area of Germany, but in spite of his newness to the region he knew one thing: this part of the Black Forest had been appropriately named.

Staring into the woods from his terrace at the rear of the inn was like staring into the great abyss.

The trees were ghastly, gnarled aberrations. As old, it seemed, as time itself. Kluge tried to see between the nearest ones, attempting to find whatever animal had made the noise. It was probably just a local dog.

He leaned forward, looking intently, but saw nothing.

The first snow had not yet fallen. It would have helped to have something light as background. Even just a dusting of powdery crystals would have reflected some light.

Whatever had made the noise, it was probably long gone now. Kluge settled back into his chair.

His head hadn't touched the fanned wooden back of the handmade chair when Kluge felt a sudden, intense pressure around his throat.

It was as if all of the veins and muscles of his neck had somehow impossibly animated themselves and had wrapped snakelike around his throat. He felt the blood clog in his head. His eyes watered and bulged as he grabbed at the constricting force at his throat.

Instead of finding a neck, Kluge felt a hand.

Woozily he followed the hand to an abnormally thick wrist. As his vision swirled around him, his spinning gaze somehow located the person at the other end of the hand.

Adolf Kluge found himself staring into the eyes of the Angel of Death.

"The gold rush is over, Kluge," Remo said tightly.

Kluge gasped for breath, but none could pass beyond Remo's clenching fingers. He pulled at Remo's hand, but to no avail. It was as powerful as a vise.

At the moment when he was about to black out, the strong grip relaxed slightly.

"Wait a minute," Remo said, peering intently at Adolf Kluge. "I know you."

Kluge sucked down a pained lungful of air. His head began to clear.

"Yes," Kluge rasped, nodding. He found the effort difficult with Remo's hand still clasped around his throat.

"From Paris, right? You claimed to be a British secret agent. You're the one who whacked Smith."

"Yes," Kluge panted. "I helped you stop Schatz."

"Helped, my ass," Remo said, remembering the neo-Nazi takeover of Paris. "He was a renegade from Four. The only reason you wanted to stop him was to cover your tracks. It didn't do any good. I'm here now. And you're checking out."

Remo increased the pressure on Kluge's neck once more.

A frantic voice shrieked suddenly from the corner of the inn. The Master of Sinanju had just come running into view near the well-tended shrubberies.

"Unhand him!" Chiun shouted desperately. Kimono sleeves flapped as he raced up along the rear of the building beneath the dining-room windows. Heidi trailed behind him.

Remo and the Master of Sinanju had gone in opposite directions when they arrived at the Pension

Kirchmann. Remo had been lucky enough to stumble on Kluge first.

Chiun vaulted up over the low hedge that rimmed the terrace. He landed next to Remo and the seated Kluge.

"I'm not letting him go, Chiun," Remo warned evenly.

"Remo, your village needs that treasure," Chiun cried.

"That bunch of ingrates has so much loot they could eat it, wear it and smoke it for a hundred years and not make a dent in it," Remo retorted. He continued strangling Kluge.

Heidi Stolpe rounded the terrace and ran up the rear stairs. Sliding to a stop, she watched the drama unfold, helpless to do anything to stop Remo.

Chiun's tone grew soft. "Do it for me," he pleaded.

Remo's hand relaxed. He looked at Kluge's bright red bullfrog features. He glanced at the Master of Sinanju. The man who had given him everything in life. He hesitated.

"Smith's orders were clear, Little Father," Remo said.

"Pah! Smith's orders," Chiun mocked. "This gold will be with us long after Smith has issued his last demented decree."

Remo's grip had slackened to the point where Adolf Kluge was able to suck in a huge gulp of air. The IV leader wheezed painfully.

"Gold doesn't matter to me. Never has."

"It matters to *me*," Chiun insisted, eyes imploring. "Therefore it should matter to you."

Chiun had tossed down his trump card. Toying with Remo's affection for him. Remo knew that the wily Korean was only playing with his emotions. Unfortunately Chiun was right. Even though he was motivated purely by greed, it would hurt Chiun if Remo killed Kluge. For this reason alone, Remo couldn't bring himself to complete the act.

With great reluctance, he released his grip on the gasping IV leader.

Kluge hacked and wheezed alternately, dragging cold, ragged mouthfuls of air down into his oxygen-deprived lungs.

Chiun smiled. "You are a good son," he said proudly.

"No," Remo answered solemnly. His eyes were flint. "That's a load of baloney. You wanted to make mc feel guilty, and it worked. End of story."

Chiun was taken aback by Remo's candor. "You were being rash. Sinanju *needs* that gold."

Remo shook his head sadly.

"I'm not buying it anymore, Chiun," he said. "*You* want the gold. Now you'll get it. The almighty buck has always been the love of your life. Maybe it'd be good for you to remember that that's what got Bal-Mung into trouble."

Remo turned abruptly away from the silenced Chiun. Marching past Heidi, he began walking alone across the vast, darkening lawn behind the rambling, old-fashioned inn.

He didn't look back.

HOUR FED INTO HOUR.

Night had taken firm hold of the ancient forest around the Pension Kirchmann. Elongated rectangles of amber light stabbed across the black lawn from the inn's brightly lit rear windows, marred only by the crisscross pattern of the painted wooden strips separating each pane.

Heidi Stolpe pulled her woolen coat more tightly around her shoulders as she crossed the sprawling lawn. Her years spent in South America had spoiled her. She wasn't used to such cold weather. And winter was only just beginning.

She found Remo sitting in the dead autumn grass, his back propped against the trunk of a huge European ash.

Remo's arms were crossed stiffly. He stared angrily at another nearby tree. If looks alone could fell a tree, the one Remo was scowling at would have already been halfway to the lumber mill.

Heidi stared at him for a long time. When he realized she wasn't going to go away, he finally looked up.

"What do you want?" he asked, flat of voice.

"I only wished to see that you were all right," she said gently. "Your father said you would be."

"You mean Daddy Warbucks stopped wheeling

and dealing long enough to think of me?'' Remo said, feigning shock.

"Do not be overly harsh with him, Remo. He is not a young man. Appreciate him for who he is." She paused, as if considering whether she should speak further. At long last, she continued. "I never knew my father," she whispered, staring wistfully into the forest.

"He isn't my biological father, Heidi," Remo said.

Her smile held an odd sadness. "I am not blind," she said softly. "But biology cannot be everything, can it?"

There was something deeply troubling in the way she said it, as if her life held some sorrowful burden that was almost too great for her to bear.

Her sadness touched him.

For a time years ago, Remo had searched for his biological parents. But when he learned the truth of the two strangers whose DNA he carried, he found that they could never replace the man he had come to know as his spiritual father. And here was Heidi— virtually a stranger to him—defending Chiun. Remo's heart went out to her.

"I'll get over it," he murmured.

Heidi smiled once more. She hugged herself for warmth. "Aren't you cold?" she asked, changing the subject.

He had worn nothing but a thin T-shirt since she met him. It had to be below freezing out here.

"No," Remo said simply.

She nodded. "I suppose I should get back inside. Before they cut me out of the deal altogether."

"How's it going?" Remo asked.

"Kluge wanted to divide it into thirds. He argued that this was how it was historically supposed to be."

"Chiun didn't go along with that," Remo said firmly.

"Not in the least." She laughed. "He still maintains that the deal we made is the one that supersedes all others."

"The one where he gets fifty percent," Remo said knowingly.

"Yes," Heidi said. "I eventually agreed to split my fifty percent evenly with Kluge, if only to get all of this over with. That seemed to satisfy them both."

"For now."

She agreed. From the way she stared off toward the bright lights of the inn, Remo could tell she was thinking about the future. "Kluge has trucks and men to haul the treasure. I think it is for this reason as much as any that Chiun is allowing him to live."

"You haven't known him long, but you know him well," Remo said with a shrewd smirk.

"He and I are very much alike. I am desperate to keep my family's property from falling into bankruptcy. It is a far worse thing, Remo, to have had money and lost it than to never have had it in the first place. We were nobles at one time. With the Nibelungen Hoard, we will be again.''

"I don't know what the big fuss is about gold,'' Remo grumbled. "It's just like any other metal.''

She squatted, patting him gently on the shoulder. "Tell that to the landlord when the rent is due,'' she said plaintively.

Remo felt an odd tingle of electricity from her touch. There was an air of mystery about her that he hadn't noticed before. Her concern for his relationship with Chiun and the way she shielded the secrets in her past—it was almost as if there was a strange connection between the two of them.

Remo had no time to act on these newfound stirrings before she was gone.

Heidi's hand brushed away from his shoulder. She turned abruptly on her heel. Marching briskly, she headed back across the frozen yard toward the sprawling old inn.

THE LIGHTS BURNED well after midnight as Chiun, Kluge and Heidi labored over all the details of the expedition.

Kluge thought that he should be compensated for the use of his people and equipment. Chiun agreed and told him to see Heidi. Heidi said that this was out of the question since she had already cut her share of the take in half. She suggested that the cost of mounting the expedition was offset by his dishonesty in stealing the Sinanju piece of the carving.

Chiun agreed with all of this, provided it didn't cost him anything.

It was approaching 12:30 a.m. when Kluge finally agreed to absorb the cost of the trucks and supplies.

The three of them then set about recording the terms of their contract on paper to allay any confusion as to precisely what terms had been agreed upon. This started the whole negotiating process anew.

At one point, Remo stuck his head in the door to the inn's library where the trio was negotiating. He announced that he was turning in for the night. No one—not even Heidi—seemed to notice he was there.

It was approaching two in the morning when their meeting at last broke up. Each of the interested parties went to bed with a version of the contract, handwritten by the Master of Sinanju himself in Korean, English and German.

The ink was still wet on his copy of the contract as Adolf Kluge made his weary way up to his bedroom. He shut the door behind him with a soft click.

Alone, Kluge massaged his aching throat as he stepped over to his suitcase.

Folding the seven sheets of paper carefully, he tucked the contract in his meager luggage. He dared not throw it away. Not yet. Kluge would keep up the act until it was no longer necessary.

Kluge had memorized the details of the Sinanju and Siegfried family sections of the map. Likewise, he had committed to memory all that was visible in the photograph of the Hagan piece. He had then destroyed all three.

Chiun claimed to know all that was on the Sinanju piece.

Heidi had the full Hagan segment.

But only Kluge had seen the Siegfried quarter.

Apparently, the Nibelung king had told the carver to put something extra on the piece he had intended for himself. It was probably an incentive for the others to not stumble blindly into the treasure trove, even if they somehow managed to find it without the missing piece.

It was King Siegfried's revenge from beyond the grave.

And since Kluge was the only one who knew what was on that quarter, he was the only one of them who would be truly safe when they opened the age-old chamber.

Kluge would sign as many contracts as they wanted him to sign. He would argue passionately for each bargaining point as if it truly mattered to him.

But it did not.

With what he had learned from the piece of the carving in his family's safe-deposit box, he had all the bargaining chips he would ever need.

Tomorrow they would find Siegfried's gold.

And then Chiun, Remo and Heidi would die.

19

The shabby convoy was lined along the ancient road that snaked through the thickest forests of Schwarzwald, eventually leading to the shores of the famous Danube River.

The sallow sky held the promise of snow, though no meteorologist had forecast it. The swollen white clouds vied with gray, pressing down like a gloomy canopy to the gnarled treetops.

It was 6:00 a.m. The Master of Sinanju went from truck to truck, inspecting tires and checking equipment. He found Remo leaning against one of the rear trucks.

"I would have thought this sort of thing would be beneath you," Remo commented as Chiun tugged at one of the bungee cords on the supply truck.

Chiun regarded him with flinty eyes. "*I* do what I must," he said.

"I've noticed that about you," Remo said, nodding. There was no malice in his tone.

At that moment, Heidi walked into view around the truck, nearly plowing into Remo.

"Oh—" she seemed surprised to see him "—good morning, Remo. Are you going with us?"

Remo shook his head. "Naw. I'm sitting this one out."

Heidi nodded her understanding. Her face was flushed as it had been the previous day at her family's castle. This time, however, it was not from embarrassment, but excitement.

She and Chiun began the long trek up to the lead car. It was the one Remo had rented on their return to Germany the previous day. Since he didn't intend to leave the inn until they returned, he would have no use for it.

As Chiun and Heidi walked beside the trucks full of skinheads, Remo trailed distantly behind them. He noted that there were a few of the blond-haired mutes from the IV village mixed in with the rest. Remo couldn't help but think of the vast number of them that had been mowed down by Kluge's machine guns beneath the shadow of the old stone fortress.

There were fifteen trucks lined up behind Remo's rental car. Chiun commented to Heidi that they would likely not be enough.

Kluge was seated behind the wheel of the rental car. Chiun climbed into the back. Heidi debated for a moment whether she should join the Master of Sinanju but finally decided against it. She sat in the front beside Kluge.

The head of IV started the car's engine. Behind him, the other fifteen vehicles rumbled to life.

Before the car could drive off, Remo tapped on the rear window. Kluge powered it down from the front.

"Little Father?" Remo called in softly.

Chiun's hazel eyes were focussed on the road ahead.

"Yes."

Remo smiled tightly. "Good luck."

The Master of Sinanju nodded crisply. The window rolled back up with a smooth hum.

Kluge waved his arm out his own window in a circular fashion. With a crunch of gravel, the convoy began moving forward down the long road. The last of the trucks pulled away a minute later.

Standing alone on the desolate country road, Remo could only watch them go.

NEWS OF THE EXPEDITION to find the lost treasure of the Nibelungs reached the hands of the German chancellor by fax at nine o'clock that morning.

It was the sort of crank note that would have been filed and forgotten under ordinary circumstances. The thing that made this fax different from the rest was the signature. At the bottom of the page where there would ordinarily have been a name, a Roman numeral had been sketched in large, careful letters. It was the number IV.

His assistant had brought it to him at once.

The chancellor's pudgy fingers shook as he scanned the few short lines of text. Swirls of sweat had dampened the curled fax paper by the time he placed it on his desk.

This was a crisis far greater than that of a few short months before. The neo-Nazi takeover of Paris had been an embarrassing reminder of Germany's unsavory past.

But this...

This could spell financial ruin for one of the greatest economies in the West. Perhaps, if the legends were true, it could even send the world into a spiraling depression, the likes of which had not been seen since 1929.

And the Great Depression was what had given rise to Adolf Hitler. After the turmoil of the German national elections less than two short months before, anything was possible. The chancellor shuddered at the thought.

The rough details were all there in the letter.

Siegfried and Hagan. Something about a long-lost map to the Hoard, alleged to have belonged to the two players in the *Nibelungenlied.*

All backed up by the mark of IV.

That was what confirmed it to the chancellor.

He had been aware of IV for years as it hovered at the edge of legitimate society. But until now, the actions of the secret organization had always benefitted the economy of Germany.

But this came too close on the heels of the Paris

incident. If IV had finally decided to make its move to destabilize the German mark, what better way to do it than by flooding the gold market? That much of the priceless metal dumped at once would surely devalue gold prices to the point of worthlessness.

IV's holdings were already on shaky ground as it was. Vast sums of cash had been exchanged over the past few weeks. Companies thought strong were collapsing before their stockholders' eyes. Others were being sold off for bargain-basement prices. The result was a growing uncertainty in the stock market in Frankfurt.

As those reports had come in, the chancellor had thought that IV was dying. Either internally, or due to some unseen external force. He now realized he had been mistaken.

He now saw that it was most certainly part of some grand strategy by the shadowy neo-Nazi organization to make one last grab at power.

And it would destroy Germany to do it.

The chancellor pressed the button on his desk intercom.

"Yes, Chancellor?" asked his concerned assistant. It was the same nervous man who had brought the fax to the German leader.

"Get me the head of the Federal Border Police," the chancellor intoned. His voice was grave.

20

Within the confines of his modest Folcroft office, Smith watched the uncertainty unfolding in the German market with a look of pinched displeasure.

Always an erratic business, it was difficult now to gauge precisely why the market was slipping. But there was no doubt that it was.

It was very slight at the moment. The overall market had lost only five percent of its value since trading had begun that morning. The London market had reacted to the trend, dropping by a few points, as well.

It was a ripple effect that was barely registering. Trading on Wall Street had begun only an hour before, and the European markets had yet to have anything more than a minor influence on the Dow Jones. It appeared that it did not yet matter to anyone of consequence.

Except Harold W. Smith.

Smith had been watching the markets carefully ever since he had begun dumping shares of IV companies onto the German trading floors. There had been a gradual downward trend in Frankfurt about two weeks before. This had brought a minor adjustment all around the world. Wall Street had caught on to the trend. As a result, the Dow had dipped by about thirty points before adjusting to the hit caused by the liquidation of the secret organization's vast holdings. Barely a hiccup. Afterward the markets had rebounded and had pressed bullishly upward. It had been smooth sailing ever since.

Until now.

Something was causing a downswing in European trading. And it was originating in Germany.

Utilizing a program he had created during the stock-market upheavals of the late eighties, Smith accessed the private computer lines of one of Germany's largest brokerage firms. Not wasting time with the transactions themselves, Smith went immediately to the top. Typing rapidly, he accessed the company president's morning E-mail.

He found that it was all pretty dry stuff.

There were concise digests of the previous night's activities on Japan's Hang Seng Stock Exchange. A note had been sent from the lawyer of the company president's soon-to-be ex-wife. As Smith watched his screen another electronic letter materialized—this one from the man's mistress.

He chose not to be voyeuristic.

Abandoning the personal note, Smith scanned quickly through the rest of the mail. He was about to deem his search a failure and move on when he found something startling nestled comfortably between a pair of interoffice memos. Smith blinked in surprise, for a moment forgetting the dull, constant ache in his head.

IV.

The Roman numeral leaped out at him, mocking him from beneath the neat rows of letters lined up on his high-tech computer screen.

Smith scanned the electronic note. With each line, his eyes grew wider behind his rimless glasses.

After he was finished reading, he backed out of the system and dived quickly into the E-mail of some of the other large Frankfurt brokerage firms.

The same note had been sent to each. At the bottom of every letter was the same legend: "IV."

Smith was acutely aware of his headache now. It pounded in sharp, furious bursts at the back of his skull as he exited the last of the German stock-market computers.

He had thought he had finished them. They had no funds. Smith had been so very careful in his market manipulations. Certainly some unlucky investors had experienced losses, but he had averted a major downward turn with his deft handling of the IV accounts.

Now it might all have been for naught.

On another level, it concerned Smith that so many powerful men in Germany had been aware of IV for years and kept silent. It didn't reflect well on a nation trying to crawl out from under its fifty-year-old past.

Obviously the news contained in the E-mail had not yet exploded on the European trading floors. But it had leaked out. And the hesitation in the day's market was the result.

The reluctance to accept the fanciful tale at face value was probably the only thing that had saved the world market from collapse. But if the rumors contained in the memo proved true, the panic would be worldwide. For in the end, the stock market would react however the stock market chose to react. Smith would be helpless to avert a total meltdown.

But for now, there was still cause for hope. By the sound of his last phone conversation with the CURE director, Remo was already in the thick of things.

The future of the world's economic stability—and, by extension, civilization itself—was in the hands of CURE's enforcement arm. Harold Smith only hoped that Remo was up to the challenge.

21

Remo sat on his private, second-story balcony at the vine-covered side of the Pension Kirchmann. The empty road leading into the Black Forest snaked off around a tree-shrouded bend far away. There had been no traffic on the desolate path since Chiun's caravan had left eight hours ago.

All Remo could do was wait.

On the floor of the balcony before his chair were several handfuls of small stones. Until an hour before, they had rested in a large decorative clay pot near the black-painted wrought-iron railing.

Remo had dumped the stones out where they could be easily reached. Bored, he would occasionally flick one with the toe of his loafer. The trunk of a tree at the side of the yard had borne the brunt of the deadly missiles.

The resulting clap as each stone hit and burrowed inside the tree was enough to draw a few increasingly curious guests from the warmth of the lodge. Two swore they had heard gunshots. Suspicious eyes strayed in Remo's direction.

Whenever they looked up from the lawn, Remo

would shrug his confusion and pretend to search the treetops. Each time they would eventually give up and return to the inn. The last time they had gone inside was barely two minutes before.

Remo was pulling another rock into firing position when the room phone squawked at his elbow. Not wanting to get up from his chair, he had placed it on the cheap metal table next to him. Remo hefted the phone to his ear, at the same time snapping his toe into the next stone in line.

The rock took off like a shot. It moved in a blur, cracking audibly into the thick black tree trunk.

There was a shouted voice from below.

"Remo?" asked the puzzled voice of Dr. Harold W. Smith. Since lifting the receiver, Remo had failed to speak.

"Just a minute, Smitty," Remo whispered, leaning forward.

A group of lumpy Germans and Continental tourists came bustling into view below him. They were pointing at the woods and chattering excitedly to one another.

Two of them were dressed in khaki clothing. These took off through the underbrush. There was crashing and shouting as they stumbled and panted out of sight.

Their labors had a comforting effect on Remo.

"Yeah, Smitty," he said. "How'd you track me down?"

In the distance, the hunters still labored through the woods.

"Your credit card," Smith explained quickly. "Are you and Chiun still searching for the Nibelungen Hoard?"

"It's always right to the chase with you, isn't it?" Remo said. He toed another rock into place. With a sharp kick, he launched it into the forest. There was renewed shouting as the stone struck a tree much farther in.

"Remo, I *need* to know," Smith demanded urgently.

"I'm not," Remo replied. "Chiun is."

"He is not with you?"

"Nope."

"Have you any idea where he has gone?"

"Into the Black Forest," Remo said. "Which isn't really all forest. Did you know that?"

"Yes," Smith said tersely.

"Really? 'Cause I didn't."

"Remo, I have come across information that indicates that Four is also in search of the Hoard. They plan to disrupt the economy of Germany by dumping the treasure onto the market all at once."

"So what?" Remo said. "I thought America was supposed to be all worried about Germany's big-shot new economy. I say let 'em wreck it."

"It is not that simple," Smith said. "There is an interconnectedness among economies in the modern age. And Germany's is one of the most complex of the Western world. If it topples, it could bring the rest down with it.''

''Again,'' Remo said, ''so what?''

''It could be the dawn of a new Dark Ages.''

''Sinanju survived the first Dark Ages,'' Remo countered. ''In fact, Chiun would probably be happy if the world economy collapsed. There'd be a whole slew of regional despots vying for our attention. It'd be an assassin's feeding frenzy.''

Remo could hear Smith taking patient, calming breaths. He heard the rattle of one of Smith's pill bottles. The CURE director had just downed a few more baby aspirins.

''Remo,'' he said levelly, after the pills had gone down, ''please be serious. Things could very well be as you say. If the world economy collapses, the type of people who would stand to benefit the most are those least suited to lead. We have encountered men from Four twice before. I cannot believe that you would want the likes of them leading the world. And I find it less likely that you would want to work for them.''

Remo frowned. ''You got that right.''

Smith persisted. ''Chiun, on the other hand, would have no such reservations. If he chose to throw in with Four, there would be an inevitable rift between the two of you.''

''Where were you yesterday?'' Remo muttered.

''What do you mean?'' Smith asked.

''I mean it's already too late. Chiun took off this

morning into the Black Forest with Adolf Kluge's band of merry Nazis to find the lost pile of gold.''

"You actually *met* Kluge?" Smith asked, shocked.

"So did you, Smitty," Remo said. "He's the guy who cracked you over the noggin in Paris. He's teamed up with Chiun and that girl we met in South America. They're going to divvy up the prize when they find it."

Smith was attempting to absorb this information.

"You cannot allow that to happen," Smith urged. His lemony voice was tight with concern.

"Too late," Remo said. "The ink's already dry."

"You have to stop them, Remo," Smith insisted.

"Chiun wouldn't listen," Remo explained, sighing. "He'd just be ticked at me for keeping him from his precious gold."

"Remo, I am ordering you to find Adolf Kluge and kill him." The serious treatment Smith was giving this was evident by his choice of words. Ordinarily he would substitute a euphemism for the distasteful *kill*.

"Hold that thought," Remo said all at once.

He heard a rumble of engines in the distance. For an instant, he thought Chiun was returning. He soon realized, however, that the sound was coming from the wrong direction. As he spoke to Smith, a line of drab blue official-looking trucks pulled slowly into view on the road in front of the inn. They headed off in the direction Chiun had taken.

"Hey, Smitty," Remo asked, "are they sending the army into the forest?"

"One moment," Smith said. Remo heard the drumming of Smith's fingers against his desktop. A moment later, he returned. "That would be the Federal Border Police," he said. "A letter was sent to the chancellor of Germany this morning identical to the ones E-mailed to the major brokerage houses in Frankfurt."

"Whoa," Remo said. "What letters?"

"I did not mention them?" Smith said. He sounded annoyed at his own forgetfulness. He went on to tell Remo about the notes that told of IV's plan to dump the Nibelung gold onto the German market.

"That doesn't make much sense," Remo said afterward. "Wouldn't they want the element of surprise?"

"Perhaps their arrogance is such that they don't feel concerned," Smith suggested.

"Maybe," Remo hedged. He didn't sound convinced. Brow furrowed, he watched the large column of trucks continue to roll forward into the forest. "Do you know what time those E-mails came in?" he asked.

"The first went to the chancellor at 9:00 a.m. The others were sent out shortly thereafter."

"That isn't right," Remo said, confused. "They left hours before that."

"Perhaps Kluge left a representative behind," Smith suggested. There was uncertainty in his voice.

"To rat him out?" Remo said skeptically.

"I will not pretend to understand the thoughts of a madman, Remo," Smith said. "I only know that if there is any truth to the legends surrounding the Nibelungen Hoard, Kluge would have enough raw capital to reestablish Four, as well as to ruin Germany's—and possibly the world's—economy. It is imperative that you stop him. Whatever the cost to your relationship with the Master of Sinanju."

"Cost." Remo laughed bitterly. "That's what this all comes down to." He sighed. "I'll see what I can do," he said finally. Standing, Remo hung up the phone.

With a half-dozen sharp kicks, he launched the last of the stones on the balcony in a final flurry. They impacted against the trunk of the already damaged tree, one right after the other. The last one to enter pushed the others forward roughly. The stones dumped from the far side of the tree as if from a primitive slot machine, dropping to the forest floor. All that was left in their wake was a clean, four-inch-wide hole straight through the trunk.

The men in the woods came tumbling out of the underbrush a few minutes later, scratched and panting. When they looked up at Remo's balcony, as they had several times after the loud noise, they saw that the strange American tourist was gone.

COLONEL FRIEDRICH HEINE bounced unhappily in the passenger's seat of the shiny blue jeep at the head of the long line of border police jeeps and trucks. He viewed the countryside through hooded, washed-out green eyes.

It was as if the ancient, gnarled trees around him were menaces over which to cast a suspicious glare.

Heine was the commanding officer of the Federal Border Police regarding the matter dubbed "Siegfried's Revenge" by Berlin. The broad details of the situation had been explained to Colonel Heine by the German chancellor himself.

It was a tricky affair.

During the crisis in Paris a few months before, Heine had been in command of a detachment of border police sent to prevent civilian Germans who were sympathetic to the Nazis in France from swarming across the Rhine into the neighboring country. His job had been complicated by the fact that many of the men beneath him were in agreement with the evil cadre that had taken control of the French capital.

This morning, the chancellor had informed him that a shadow organization called IV had been responsible for the incident in France. The same group, it was explained to Colonel Heine, was now threatening to destabilize the government of unified Germany. Heine was to locate them in the Black Forest and stop them at all costs.

The colonel's job would be complicated by the

fact that many of the men who were ready to switch allegiance a few months ago were still under his command. If they learned the true nature of their mission and what this group IV represented, they would most likely abandon that mission to join their enemy. Colonel Heine might find himself a lone patriot battling this new neo-Nazi menace.

Heine would never think to join the rest. The grandson of a Catholic death-camp survivor, he detested the Nazis and all they represented. This had contributed in a very large way to the chancellor's decision to put Heine in command. For, if it became necessary, Colonel Friedrich Heine would not hesitate to shoot his own men if their loyalties swayed.

The convoy had passed a lonely inn about a kilometer back and the colonel's jeep had just rounded the most recent desolate turn in the winding road when a strange chatter from the rear trucks began to filter up from the radio. The men of his force were yelling some nonsense about someone running up alongside the convoy.

"How fast are we going?" Heine asked.

"Forty kilometers per hour, sir," his driver replied.

Too fast for anyone to follow on foot. His men were obviously in a joking mood. Heine hoped that they hadn't already learned about IV.

Heine was about to instruct his driver to advise the men to hold down their chatter when the door near the man suddenly sprang open. A hand reached in and plucked the driver from his seat, tugging him out and flinging him upward. Heine became aware of a sudden weight on the roof of the jeep, even as a strange intruder slipped into the now vacant driver's seat. The man slowed the jeep to a stop.

Taking the cue from their leader, the column of vehicles whined to a stop, as well. The colonel's driver scampered down from the roof, his boots denting the hood in his haste.

Behind them came angry shouts. Doors opened. Feet clomped up the narrow forest road. At the direction of the colonel's young driver, the jeep was surrounded by armed soldiers in a matter of seconds. Rifles leveled menacingly.

From the driver's seat, Remo looked out at the dozens of men. He yawned.

"Let me guess. You're on a picnic and they're here to interrogate the ants," Remo said to the colonel.

"You are not German," Heine accused.

"No way, sweetheart. Could never get used to all that black shoe polish."

"Leave now," said Heine. "And I will not file charges."

Remo was aware that the colonel was surreptitiously reaching for the gun at his hip holster. Heine suddenly pulled the weapon loose. He swung it around to Remo, only to have it pulled from his hand before he had even found his target. Remo placed the gun beneath the driver's seat.

Heine seethed. "I suppose you are with Four?" he said.

"You know about them?" Remo asked.

Heine nodded. "I have been sent to stop you."

"Sorry," Remo said. "I'm not Four." He quickly appraised the colonel. "Give me your hand," he announced.

The intruder had already disarmed him with ease. Heine thought it pointless to resist. Scowling, he stretched his hand out to Remo.

Remo took hold of the fleshy area between the colonel's thumb and forefinger. He squeezed.

The pain was so intense and came so quickly that it took the colonel's breath away. He could not even scream.

"Are *you* with Four?" Remo asked, easing back on the pressure.

"What?" Heine demanded. "No. No, of course not. My orders are to obliterate them."

Remo knew he was telling the truth. He released the colonel's hand. Heine immediately jammed the injured part of his hand into his mouth.

"Sorry, pal," Remo said. "Just had to make sure."

"Who are you?" Heine garbled past a mouthful of thumb.

"All you need to know is that I'm on your side."

Colonel Heine examined Remo with the same suspicious eyes he had been using earlier on the trees of the Black Forest. He seemed to reach some internal conclusion.

"It is nice to know someone is," the colonel harrumphed, pulling his hand from his mouth. Heine rolled down the window of his jeep. "Get these men back in their trucks," he ordered his driver.

After a moment of convincing, the surprised driver did as he was told. Reluctantly the men began lowering their rifles. Heine got the distinct impression that some of them had hoped to catch him in the cross fire. Repayment for his failure to join the fascist cause of a few short months ago. Slowly the troops began trudging back down the road to their waiting vehicles.

"You realize a lot of those guys were ready to shoot you, too," Remo commented as he started the jeep.

"They are more loyal to the ghosts of the past," Colonel Heine said somberly.

Remo frowned deeply. "There's been a lot of that going around lately," he said. He stomped down on the accelerator.

With a lurch, the police convoy began to roll once more down the ancient, curving road.

22

The ragtag convoy led by Adolf Kluge passed through the gentle lower slopes of the Black Forest, avoiding the high mountains of the Baden-Württemberg region. These large dark peaks loomed like giant sentinels along the distant horizon.

Above the frosted mountaintops, the heavy gray clouds of early morning had grown more swollen with every passing hour. However, they had failed as yet to produce a single flake of winter snow.

As the lead vehicle broke into a wide clear patch in the middle of the forest, the Master of Sinanju cast a glance at the distant mountains.

From the rear seat, his squeaky voice intoned:

"'Twas as much as twelve huge wagons in four
whole nights and days,
Could travel from the mountain down to the salt
sea bay,
Though to and fro each wagon thrice journeyed
every day.''

"The *Nibelungenlied*," Heidi said, nodding. The look of flushed exuberance had not left her face since morning.

Beside her in the front seat, Adolf Kluge was silent. The farther into this primitive portion of Germany they had traveled, the more convinced he had become of the authenticity of the legends. As he watched the mountains rise up through the desolate clearing, he felt a flutter of excitement in the pit of his stomach.

"If that is so," Kluge said thoughtfully, "we do not have as many vehicles as we will need."

"The wagons used were as the poem describes," Chiun said knowingly. "I will be surprised if the conveyances with which this expedition is equipped are able to hold even a third of what Siegfried's carts transported."

Heidi was thinking aloud. "So it was three trips a day for twelve wagons?"

"That is correct," Chiun said.

"For four days," Kluge added. "That would be 144 wagonloads."

"And if Chiun is right, we will have three times as many loads as that."

Kluge nodded. "Which makes 432," he said.

Heidi's cheeks grew more flushed as her mind attempted to encompass that much treasure. Try as she might, she couldn't begin to imagine so much wealth in a single place.

"That is a lot of gold," she said breathlessly.

They continued on for a few miles more before the Master of Sinanju ordered Kluge to halt.

The lead car slowed to a stop. Behind it, the trucks of the expedition stopped, as well. Their engines idled briefly before growing silent.

Chiun, Kluge and Heidi climbed from the rental car. The surviving Numbers from the IV village along with the handful of skinheads got down from their trucks.

"Tell your pinhead army to remain where they are," the Master of Sinanju commanded.

Kluge did as he was told.

The skinheads and the rest stayed back by the trucks. They were stretching their arms high in the air and twisting their spines, trying to relieve some of the muscle strain the long ride had inflicted on them. Only the identical blond-haired men seemed interested in what was going on up by the lead car. They stayed back where they were told, sullenly staring at Kluge and Heidi.

"I find those genetic freaks unnerving," Kluge complained as he tore his eyes away from the unflinching gaze of the Numbers.

Heidi, who had been eyeing the Aryan men with a look bordering on sympathy, shot a nasty glare at Kluge. Whatever her dark thoughts, she kept them to herself.

"Why have we stopped?" she asked, turning to Chiun.

"It is no secret to any of us," he said. "We all know that we are close now to the Sinanju Hoard."

"The *Nibelungen* Hoard," Kluge corrected flatly.

"Do not quibble, thief," Chiun cautioned. He marched over to a nearby copse of trees.

The Master of Sinanju used the sharpened edge of one long fingernail to sheer a slender branch from a small tree. With a flurry of fingers, he stripped any small sticks or nubbins from the black bark. Coming back over to Heidi and Kluge, Chiun used the heel of his sandal to kick up a sandbox-size area of dirt in the frozen mud at the shoulder of the road. With the thin end of the three-foot-long stick, he drew out a perfect square, cutting it into four large sections. He began sketching in one of the quarters.

"I act now in good faith," Chiun said as he drew. "Behold, the segment of the map discovered by my ancestor Bal-Mung beneath the body of the slain Nibelung king."

Heidi was the only one there seeing the Sinanju section of the map for the first time. As Kluge looked on, bored, she appeared to be studying every detail of the map as Chiun formed it in the powdery earth.

"There!" Chiun said, finishing with a flourish. He had sketched in a portion of a long river. "I give you the Sinanju legacy of a long-dead king."

There was a pause from those assembled, as if they were uncertain how to respond to such histrionics. The mood was broken by a dull, lifeless clapping of hands. Heidi and Chiun looked at Kluge.

"I am sorry," he said, sarcastically. He stopped his flat applause. "Is not that what we were meant to do?" His smile was all condescension. "That is not as impressive as you would like it to seem,'' Kluge said, nodding to the etching in the dirt. ''After all, I have already seen it.''

Chiun was indignant. ''Only due to your act of thievery, Hun,'' he sniffed.

Heidi didn't wish for this posturing to go any further. She injected herself between Chiun and Kluge.

''I will go next,'' she offered.

Heidi took the stick from Chiun and quickly began filling in one of the three empty squares. Some of the lines met up with those of the Master of Sinanju. Chiun watched with interest while she worked. When she finished, she handed the stick over to Kluge.

''Here,'' she said.

Holding the stick lightly in his hand, Kluge looked down upon the half of the map that was sketched out in the cold dirt of the Black Forest.

''Very nice,'' he said, nodding. He indicated a corner of Heidi's section with the end of the stick. ''That portion was not visible in my photograph.''

''What do you mean?'' Heidi asked blandly.

''This is not your family portion of the map,'' he explained. ''It is the Hagan piece, which I kept for years on my mantel at the Four village. Presumably you stole it when you stormed the fortress.'' He smiled.

''Enough, brigand ancestor of a deceitful king!'' Chiun snapped. His eyes were fire.

Kluge considered only for a second. With an outward dispassion that belied his inner fear of the wrath of the Master of Sinanju, he squatted down next to the nearest empty grid. He hastily sketched out his family portion of the map.

When he was finished, Kluge—still on his haunches—handed the stick up to Heidi.

"It is your turn. Again." He smiled tightly.

Heidi didn't hesitate. She pulled the stick away from Kluge. In the final quarter of the larger square, she drew for them the last piece of the Siegfried map.

Chiun examined the section she had drawn, making certain that its lines matched the ones in the piece they had retrieved from Heidi's ancestral home. They did.

In the dirt before them, staring back at them from across the ages, was the entire map to the Nibelungen Hoard. Incomplete for more than fifteen hundred years, its assembled pieces now gave them clear directions to the great treasure.

"I have maps of the area," Kluge said, excitedly, pushing himself to a standing position. "We can use them to find the location."

The IV leader began striding to the car, but Chiun stopped him with a hand on his shoulder.

"That will not be necessary," the Master of Sinanju said. "My ancestor compiled many maps in his years of feckless wandering in these woods." Chiun nodded to the map they had all drawn. His voice was filled with a grand solemnity. "This place is known to me."

REMO WAS PEEVED. He made this clear to Colonel Heine.

"I don't know why I'm even going," he complained. "I mean, it's got nothing to do with me."

"Perhaps—" Heine began meekly.

Remo interrupted. "It's just another dippy million-year-old legend he's somehow gotten me dragged into," he griped as he steered the border police jeep down the long forest road. "I tell him I'll help him find his block of wood and his gold coins. Fine. Everything should be hunky-dory afterwards, right? Wrong. No sooner do we find them, along with the guy we've been looking for for the last three months, than he goes running off with the bastard on some half-assed treasure hunt. And he gets mad at *me*." Remo's voice approached a level of incredulity that left Colonel Heine nodding in nervous, sympathetic confusion.

"I have found only recently that loyalties are not what they should be," Heine said through clenched teeth. He was holding on to the seat with both hands as Remo's foot stayed clamped heavily to the accelerator. The forest whizzed by.

"Tell me about it," Remo continued. "You've got a heck of a bunch back there," he commented, nodding to the trailing line of trucks. "If I were you, I'd sleep with one eye open and a frigging howitzer under my pillow."

"There is a danger that they might join the enemy," Heine admitted. "If that happens and we fail, the army will be called in. Although I would not trust that the army will not join them, as well.''

Remo shook his head. He wondered again whether or not he should let Chiun go this one alone. After all, the Master of Sinanju had only the neo-Nazis, the border police and possibly the German army to contend with. It'd serve him right to work up a sweat over this one.

They came tearing around a corner near a pile of toppled boulders. A fork suddenly appeared in the road ahead of them. Remo barely lifted one foot off the gas pedal as the other one was stomping down on the brake.

The jeep spun out on the shoulder, completing two full circles on the dusty road. At the nadir of the first screeching circle, Colonel Heine saw the rapidly approaching shape of the nearest trailing truck. It, too, had slammed on its brakes. Plumes of dust poured up from beneath its locked wheels.

Heine closed his eyes and waited for the truck to plow into them. As he did so, he was vaguely aware of the driver's-side door opening and closing. He felt the jeep grow lighter.

When a few tense seconds had passed without the sound of a crushing impact, Heine opened one eye. The jeep was rocking to a gentle stop near an old-fashioned wooden signpost. Colorful characters and black German words marked the three destinations beyond them.

Remo was crouching at the fork.

With a sigh of relief, Heine opened his second

eye. He climbed out of the jeep on wobbly legs, walking up to join Remo. Looking back once, he saw the troop truck had stopped a hair away from the parked jeep.

"They took the left fork," Remo said. He nodded as if to some obvious marks in the road. Heine saw nothing but a few grooves in the sandy shoulder.

"Can you get some helicopters in here?" Remo asked, standing. "With a few eyes in the sky, we could get this thing over with in less than an hour."

Heine shook his head. "The chancellor does not wish to alert them," he said, panting. His mind still reeled from his brush with death a minute before.

"I wish we were closer to Berlin," Remo complained. "One visit'd get the air force out here like a shot. Heck, kidnap the presidential pastry chef and you could probably get that pork hog to surrender to France." He spun from Heine. "Let's go."

"Do you wish me to drive?" Colonel Heine said with weak hopefulness.

"Naw," Remo said. "We've screwed around enough. I think we're going to have to start picking up the pace."

He headed back to the jeep. Heine followed reluctantly.

23

In spite of the cold weather, they found the digging easy. The nearness of the small stream kept the ground where they worked much damper than the rest of the forest floor.

The skinheads were caked with slippery brown mud. They grumbled among themselves with each shovelful of rich, cold earth they overturned.

The pile of displaced slimy sod had grown large over the past two hours. The Master of Sinanju remained at a cautious distance, ever aware of even the slightest dollop of mud that might fly his way. Whenever a skinhead would overshoot the pile and send a speck of dirt near Chiun's brilliant yellow kimono, the Master of Sinanju would let out a horrified shriek.

Once, when a clod of dirt came perilously close to his brocade robe, Chiun had stomped over to the diggers and wrenched the shovel from the perpetrator's hands, clanging the young man over the head with the flat end of the metal spade. After that, both the skinhead and his companions had made an extra effort to keep the mud within the designated area.

Kluge had brought three small folding stools from the rental car, one for each of them. Chiun had refused the seat, preferring instead to stand as close as possible to the deepening hole. Heidi paced back and forth between the line of stools and Chiun. Only Adolf Kluge opted to sit.

Kluge was sitting there now, hands folded patiently across his precisely crossed knees. The only outward hint of any inner agitation the IV leader might have felt was at his mouth. Kluge's tongue darted forward with unswerving regularity, dampening his lower lip. It was a nervous habit he had picked up years before.

"Pah!" Chiun complained, spinning from the massive mound of jiggling mud. "It is too deep."

"That is the correct spot according to the map," Heidi said nodding. Arms crossed, she chewed one thumbnail anxiously as she watched lumps of mud fly up from the hole.

"Fifteen hundred years is a long time," Kluge suggested. He pointed at the marks in the surrounding uneven forest floor. "It appears as though the river ran directly through this area at one time. Surely sediment would have collected, covering it more deeply."

"But if the river was here, how did they build it to begin with?" Heidi asked.

"That which you call engineering was not invented for the convenience of this century," Chiun said impatiently. "Such a feat would not have been impossible. It would also explain the difficulty my ancestor had in finding the Hoard.''

''I hope we have better luck than him,'' Heidi said. She continued to stare into the wide hole at the muddy riverbank.

The men dug for another half hour. Kluge was about to suggest that they should redraw the map, this time with more care, when a sharp clang emanated from the deep hole. It was followed by another.

Kluge got to his feet.

''There is something here!'' one of the skinheads called from within the deep pit.

Kluge and Heidi looked at each other, neither of them certain what to do next. Heidi seemed genuinely surprised.

The Master of Sinanju was first to react. He flounced to the edge of the hole, looking in his jaundiced kimono like a huge yellow bird that had just spied a particularly succulent worm. He stopped at the muddy edge of the pit.

Only five skinheads could fit in the hole at one time. The area they had excavated was more than ten feet deep. The men inside were looking up from the bottom, their bodies coated with thick black mud.

''See?'' one of the skinheads said.

He handed his shovel to one of the others and got to his soiled knees. With the palms of his filthy hands, he wiped away a pile of thick, gloppy mud, revealing a flat surface underneath. The men were standing atop what appeared to be a buried strip of sidewalk.

Kluge and Heidi came up behind Chiun.

"Clear off the rest!" the Master of Sinanju boomed. His eyes sparkled brightly.

The men did as they were told. More shovelfuls of mud had to be removed to clear the stone to its edges. It was found to be rectangular in shape.

Some of the blond-haired men brought buckets from one of the trucks. As the last of the dirt was hauled out, water was brought from the nearby stream. Lowering the pails into the hole, they washed the surface of the chiseled granite.

"I cannot read it," Kluge said. He strained to look down at the ancient letters. They appeared to be nothing more than a series of indecipherable slashes. He glanced at the Master of Sinanju for help.

Chiun's eyes had narrowed to narrow slits, swallowing up any small spark of hope in his hazel orbs. His mouth was a thin, furious line.

"Accursed fiend," Chiun hissed. There was far more menace in the softness of his tone than in a thousand screaming voices. "He dares mock the House of Sinanju from across the ages." His rage suddenly boiled over. "Villain! Cur! Fraud! Lying Hun *thief!*"

Like a crazed Olympic diver, Chiun flew down into the hole. A swirling, frenzied yellow tempest, he swatted vicious, angry hands at the skinheads still gathered below. The slime-coated men scurried up the muddy banks in fear.

Mindless of the grime, Chiun dropped to his knees atop the stone. It was as large as a big door. He pried slender fingers around its smooth edge.

"What does it say?" Kluge asked in wonder as he watched the aged Korean tear at the stone.

"I believe those are runic characters," Heidi said. Her eyes narrowed as she attempted to read what was visible around Chiun. They looked like random cat scratches. "I am not entirely unfamiliar with this. Those are bitter runes. They are intended to bring down evils upon enemies."

Kluge glanced from the scampering form of Chiun to Heidi. "This is not the storing place of the Nibelungen Hoard?" he asked. He could not mask his disappointment.

Heidi smiled tightly. "I am afraid not," she said.

In the pit, the Master of Sinanju had pried up the massive flat stone, heaving it to one side. There was nothing beneath but a pile of mud-swamped rocks.

"Aiieee!" Chiun screamed.

His hand flew toward one of the short sides of the stone. There was a sound like a thunderclap. As Kluge watched, the flat rock split in two long halves. Before the pieces had even fallen to the bottom of the pit, Chiun's pipestem legs shot out in two quick jabs. The halves split in half again, falling into smaller pieces. Chiun fired his tiny fists forward into the quarters, cracking the chunks of stone into ever smaller fragments. All the while, he screamed his anger and frustration at the mud walls of the deep, slick pit.

Kluge backed slowly away from the hole. Witnessing the awesome sight of the wizened Asian shattering a two-ton slab of rock as if it were made of glass, Kluge felt almost a little grateful that he hadn't been able to follow through on his plan to kill the Master of Sinanju. This lasted only as long as it took him to realize that the wealth he so coveted was not there. Without that money, there would be no reestablishing IV. The fifty-year-old ultrasecret Nazi organization was finished.

And along with it, Adolf Kluge.

This realization was only just beginning to sink in when Kluge spied the first figure creeping through the underbrush on the other side of the river.

He stiffened. Made an effort *not* to stare.

Kluge tried not to let the man know he had spotted him as he casually began to scan the surrounding flora.

There was another. And another.

Creeping forward, they were attempting to stay hidden in the winter woods. The men were all armed.

In the pit behind him, the Master of Sinanju continued to pound away at the diminishing chunks of rock. Dust and pebbles flew up out of the hole as if from some insane sculptor's underground studio. The tiny Korean's screams had grown less fierce with every passing second.

Kluge hardly noticed Chiun's tantrum any longer. Keeping his arms close to his sides and his movements subdued, he walked with forced casualness over to Heidi.

She was in the process of gathering up Kluge's three collapsible stools from where they had been propped on the forest floor. They were draped over her forearm as Kluge stepped up to her.

"We are being watched," he said in a measured tone.

She had been lost in thought, obviously thinking of the amount of gold she had lost.

"What?" she asked, perturbed. She handed the stools off to a waiting skinhead. "What are you talking about?"

Her answer exploded from across the small river. The first gunshot ripped through the torpid silence of the ancient forest.

The bullet caught the skinhead beside them square in the chest. The young man wheeled around, flinging the three stools into the air as he did so. They flew through the air, landing in a tangle of bushes near the heap of displaced mud.

The dead skinhead fell to the forest floor as the next bullet tore from the tangle of low plants across the river.

Kluge threw himself to the ground. His elbow slammed against a flat rock. He ignored the shooting pain in his arm as he half crawled, half pushed himself along the damp forest surface to the protection of a cluster of thick pine trees.

All around him, Kluge's mud-soaked neo-Nazi followers had drawn weapons. Ducking for cover themselves, they had begun to shoot blindly at their concealed attackers.

Gunfire erupted all around.

The men who had ambushed them were in no hurry to advance. They stayed at a distance, firing with care into the cluster of neo-Nazis. From his vantage point behind the trees, Kluge could see that the first man he had noticed wore the uniform of the German Federal Border Police. He skulked on the other side of the small tributary, popping into view every few seconds with a blast of automatic-weapon fire.

A volley of bullets ripped into the soft trunk of the tree above him, sending splinters of pulpy wood down onto Kluge's sandy hair.

Kluge glanced frantically the other way. Through the overgrown forest, he could barely glimpse his parked convoy of trucks. As he watched, the lead car began rolling off down the road. It was joined a moment later by several of the trucks. The Numbers were fleeing.

He was so shocked that he began to climb to his feet. A fresh hail of bullets made him reconsider. Dropping back to his belly, Adolf Kluge began crawling slowly through the tangle of bushes toward the road.

He got only a few feet before his injured elbow fell atop the toe of a boot. Kluge had no weapon. He rolled over onto his back, hands held up in surrender.

A group of men dressed in the drab uniforms of

the Federal Border Police fanned around him. They grabbed Adolf Kluge by the arms, pulling him to his feet.

As the firefight continued to rage over near the river, the men spirited Kluge to the waiting line of trucks.

THE DETACHMENT of Federal Border Police had split up at the river, hoping to ensnare the entire band of neo-Nazis within their widely cast net.

Remo was on the other side of the river when he heard the first gunshot. It was followed almost immediately by a sustained firefight. He turned to Colonel Friedrich Heine.

"Who told them to start shooting?" Remo demanded.

"They are not authorized," Colonel Heine said angrily.

Remo didn't wait for more of an explanation. He began running through the woods toward the sound of the guns.

He broke into a small clearing on the side of the river opposite the neo-Nazis. He saw the deep mud hole beside the small man-made hill of displaced earth. Tiny puffs of dust rose from within the pit.

Colonel Heine came running up behind Remo, desperately short of breath. The firefight was blazing, with swarms of angry lead projectiles whizzing around his head as Heine slammed up against the thick trunk of a bullet-riddled tree. He pulled out his side arm.

"You," he demanded, pointing at one of his men crouching in the nearby bushes. "Who gave the order to fire?"

The man shrugged. "It simply happened, sir," he said.

Heine shook his head to Remo, fiercely apologetic. "Not all of these men are pro-Nazi," he explained. "Some are like me. Although *I* was hoping for a peaceful resolution."

"That's shot to hell right about now," Remo snarled.

The skinheads were entrenched on the other side of the river. The border police had only managed to pick off a few of them early on. The rest were dug in behind trees and boulders, preserving ammunition by firing in short, directed bursts at their attackers.

The border police had lost the element of surprise. They were hunkered down across the river, unable to advance on the skinheads. The other half of Heine's men appeared to have vanished.

It was an equally matched standoff.

Remo didn't seek cover like the others. He stood in the open near the river, dodging the occasional bullet that flew his way. He frowned as he looked across the river. He didn't see the Master of Sinanju anywhere. Nor Kluge or Heidi, for that matter.

"Get down!" Heine insisted. He was amazed that Remo had not yet been shot.

Remo didn't appear to hear the colonel. He sighed even as he sidestepped a violent burst from a skinhead's Uzi. "Leave it to the only American here to have to clean up this mess," he grumbled.

Leaving Heine to splutter that he was committing suicide, Remo hopped onto a moss-slick stone that jutted up a foot out from the river's edge.

It wasn't far across. Though the water raced fast, it was more of an overgrown stream than a real river. Hopping from damp stone to damp stone, Remo bounded over to the other side in a few short leaps.

He landed in a clump of brown weeds.

Remo hadn't taken more than two steps up the bank before a wild-eyed skinhead came screaming at him from out of a heavy thicket. The man wielded a large hunting knife before him. The scream was apparently meant to distract his victim as he plunged the knife home.

Without even missing a single step, Remo snatched the skinhead by the wrist. With a quick, fluid motion, he redirected the knife back and around. The young man's hand traced an elaborate circle in the air as the blade whirred back toward the attacker. It buried itself up to the hilt in the startled skinhead's unmuscled abdomen.

Striding forward, Remo flung the doubled-over body into his wake. The skinhead toppled into the weeds and then rolled over, splashing into the racing water. He floated only a few feet downstream before his body snagged on a rock. The river splashed over and around his lifeless form.

Remo continued onward, his expression grave. He had yet to see Chiun anywhere.

Judging from the gunfire, there weren't as many men in the woods around him as had left the inn during the wee hours of the morning. Some must have escaped when the shooting began. Realizing he might have been too hasty killing his first attacker, Remo sought out another skinhead.

He found one crouching amid a tangle of bushes. The man was firing shots from his assault rifle in random bursts at the police across the river. The slender barrel of his West German Gewehr jutted out from a tangle of laurel.

Coming up from the man's blind side, Remo wrapped his fingers around the gun barrel and yanked hard. The startled skinhead popped out from the bushes, still hanging on to the other end of his weapon. He seemed shocked to find someone else attached to his gun barrel.

"Okay, *pfeffernusse*," Remo began, unmindful of the young man's surprised expression. "Do you—?"

A loud series of gunshots sounded across the river. A cluster of crimson stains erupted across the skinhead's chest and stomach. His eyes rolled back in their sockets as his head lolled to one side. The man fell back to the bushes, propped up by the thick branches. He didn't move again.

"Hey, watch it!" Remo shouted to the border police. Their response was even more gunfire. So far, none of it was directed at him.

Dropping the man's weapon angrily, Remo went off in search of another skinhead.

His yelling alerted those close by of his presence. As Remo walked in the direction of the mountain of mud, a pair of skinheads who had been waiting in ambush leaped out of the bushes before and behind him.

This time Remo was unable to get out a single word before the men were mowed down by the police.

"Dammit," Remo snapped as the pair of bodies fell.

This was obviously not going to work the way he planned. Taking a different tack, Remo dived into the bushes where his keen senses told him a cluster of neo-Nazis was hiding.

There were six of them.

Unfortunately they had witnessed the horrible deaths of the other men Remo had so far encountered. Not wanting to end up like their comrades, the men fled into the open as soon as Remo appeared before them. They were instantly fired upon by the border police and were slaughtered to a man.

"Dammit, dammit, dammit," Remo griped.

He heard a scuffling somewhere before and above him. A single, rapid heartbeat filtered down through the thick pine branches. Boots scraped along rough bark.

Remo took a few steps forward. He found a lone skinhead hiding in a tree above the spot where the six men had been hunkered down. The man was attempting to hold on to the tree trunk while at the same time angling his rifle down at the top of Remo's head.

Before the man could fire, Remo reached up and grabbed him by his loose shoelace. He pulled.

The skinhead came crashing out of the tree like a clumsy fat bird, collapsing to the forest floor amid a pile of broken branches. Pine needles continued to rain down on him as he shook his head in groggy confusion.

The flurry of activity around the tree started a new wave of gunfire from across the river. Luckily for Remo, they were behind the broad tree trunk, safe from the bullets of the Federal Border Police.

"Speaky the English?" Remo asked the skinhead.

"Yes," the man answered fearfully. He shook some of the needles out of his hair. Though his eyes stayed locked with Remo's, his hand searched for his dropped gun.

"The old Korean who was with Kluge. Where is he?"

"There," the man said, nodding out toward the hole.

Remo looked out at the mound of earth. He raised a skeptical eyebrow.

Even as he did so, the skinhead was grabbing up his gun from the ground. Still seated, he spun around with the weapon, aiming it at Remo's exposed belly.

In a move so swift that it was almost blinding, Remo used one hand to pull the gun away from the man. As he was tossing the weapon away, he used his free hand to pull the skinhead to his feet.

"I'll check, but you better not be lying," he warned. With that, Remo tossed the man out into the clearing. There was the expected burst of gunfire, followed by the sound of the dead skinhead dropping to the ground.

Remo hardly noticed the noise as he strode out into the wide opening. Both sides began to fire wildly—the skinheads at the closeness of the intruder, the border police in anticipation of more assured kills. Remo had to twist and turn spastically to dodge the lead volleys as he made his way across the clearing to the edge of the hole.

At the muddy rim, amid the hail of bullets, he looked down in surprise on a familiar tiny shape standing among the ruins of the unearthed stone marker.

"I gotta hand it to you. Money hasn't changed you one bit," Remo said from the edge of the pit. Bullets zinged like pesky flies around his head.

The Master of Sinanju looked up, his face cross. He stood ankle deep in a pile of chipped stone.

"The gold was not here," he snapped.

"I gathered as much."

"The scoundrel Siegfried left a carved note in runic berating thieves who would attempt to locate the Hoard without a proper map."

"I thought you had the whole map," Remo said.

Chiun tipped his head. "As did I," he said. He had been so intent on venting his anger and frustration against the stone marker that he had lost all reason. As he stood there now, however—coated with mud in the remnants of his own destructive rage—a thought seemed to pass visibly across his aged features. He looked up at Remo, head tipped in sudden confusion. "Is it possible that my partners have betrayed me?"

"Oh, I don't know," Remo replied sarcastically. "One was a Nazi who broke into your house and tried to have us killed about a zillion times. The other was a woman we knew pretty much nothing about except that she lied to us *and* tried to break into your house. Sounds like a decent enough bunch to me."

"Descendants of dastards," Chiun hissed.

"Look," Remo called down. He jumped to avoid a fresh batch of autofire, "the thing is, I'm kind of getting shot at up here. So if you're done working this vein, I'd suggest the two of us skedaddle."

Chiun nodded. Remo didn't see his legs tense beneath the hem of his mud-splattered kimono, but the Master of Sinanju was suddenly airborne. He appeared to float gracefully up from the bottom of the ten-foot-deep pit—the reverse film of a feather sinking to the ground. He landed on the muddy lip beside Remo. Bullets zipped relentlessly around them from every direction.

The instant he had landed, they were both running. Remo and Chiun took off for the protective cover of the forest.

"What have you started up here?" Chiun demanded as they ran through the driving storm of lead. His nose crinkled unhappily as he eyed the half-hidden skinheads.

"Don't blame me. This was your party, remember?"

"It was peaceful before your arrival," Chiun said.

They made it safely to the trees on the side of the clearing opposite the river. Once they were beyond the firing line, Chiun began glancing around the woods.

"Where is the thief and the harlot?" he demanded.

"I haven't seen them." Remo shrugged.

The look of pain that passed over the aged features of the Master of Sinanju was so great it was as if someone had reached into his body and plucked out his very soul.

His eyes held a look of horror Remo had never before seen. When he spoke, his voice was faraway.

"My money," Chiun croaked.

24

The rented car bounced crazily through the rough terrain beside the mighty Danube River.

The vehicle hadn't been built for this type of driving. Heidi knew this to be true even as she steered down into a broad gully in the middle of the unused road. The rear wheels caught briefly in a pool of muddy water before grabbing on to the sandy clay beneath.

The car lurched suddenly forward, clamoring madly up the far side of the shallow indentation. It bounced wildly as it flew back up onto the road. Heidi had to cling to the steering wheel for dear life.

Her head slammed against the roof of the car even as the vehicle settled back down onto its straining shock absorbers.

The stretch of road ahead of her seemed positively level compared to the area she had just passed through. Used only for access in the warmer months, the road was lucky to see a single government truck every few weeks. She aimed the car down the rugged straightaway, unmindful of the rocks and potholes that littered the path before her.

She had to be sure first. After that, everything would fall into line.

She couldn't believe how easy it had been. Kluge and the Master of Sinanju were so blinded by greed that they didn't notice her deception.

Indeed, how could they? They had taken her word that the quarter of the map she had drawn in the dirt had been real. They had never expected her to lie.

Chiun with his blind avarice. Kluge, just as greedy, yet masking his money lust in a blasé veneer.

It had been too easy.

Of course, the piece she and the men from Sinanju had retrieved from her family castle in the Harz Mountains was a forgery. It had been commissioned by one of her ancestors in the century after Siegfried's death. Her family had the bogus segment carved as a decoy for thieves.

She had destroyed the original copy months ago. Heidi had memorized the genuine quarter long before she had gone back to her family castle with the two Masters of Sinanju.

It was all a show. She had to make it look as if she didn't intend to cheat them. It had worked.

The speeding car struck a deep rut. The front right wheel grabbed at the road for a moment and the car began to slide to one side.

Heidi cut the wheel into the turn, stomping down harder on the accelerator. The car popped free of the pothole. Skidding in the dirt, she righted the car expertly.

Without a change in speed, she continued racing down the bumpy road.

"THAT IS NOT HIM!" Chiun screamed as the border police brought forward the tenth skinhead body. He swatted at the corpse with his long talons.

The police officer holding the body dragged it away. The others nearby were herding captured neo-Nazis into the backs of awaiting Federal Border Police trucks.

"I'm afraid it looks like he's gone, Little Father," Remo said. "Along with Heidi and a bunch of their men."

"And some of *my* men, it seems," Colonel Heine admitted.

"Woe is me," Chiun moaned to himself. He was staring over at the empty mud hole.

Remo ignored him. "What happened here?" he asked the colonel. He indicated the carnage around the small clearing with a nod.

"I am afraid my men were divided in their loyalties," Colonel Heine said, shamefaced. "Somehow word of our mission leaked to them before we even left our headquarters. They had been discussing the entire way here how they would proceed once we met up with our intended targets. Some apparently decided to throw in with the neo-Nazis."

"Leaked?" Remo asked. "How?"

"A mysterious letter was sent via electronic mail to our barracks this morning. I was not aware of it until now." Heine glanced at the police who were waiting near the trucks.

A few of the men around him seemed embarrassed. Though they hadn't joined the Nazis, neither had they betrayed their fellow border police—men who had every intention of joining the expedition they had been sent to apprehend.

"What is it with all these E-mails?" Remo asked no one in particular.

"Oh, my precious, precious gold," Chiun moaned pitifully.

Remo was still thinking aloud. "The chancellor gets one, telling him about Four's plan to wreck the economy. The top money guys get them, as well. Now you're telling me your men got them, too. It's like someone *wanted* to make sure this expedition was followed."

"Why would that be?" Heine asked.

Remo shrugged. "I don't know. But throw out enough bait, and you're bound to catch a fish."

"Is the answer not obvious?" Chiun lamented. "They wished to prevent me from claiming that which is mine."

Remo nodded reluctantly. "I guess it looks that way."

Heine changed the subject. "I have contacted the chancellor. On his order, reconnaissance planes are en route to the area. If they locate the missing trucks, they will inform us."

Remo frowned, pointing down the road. "Where does this lead?" he asked.

"The Danube, eventually," Heine said. "There are other roads that lead off of it along the way. They could have taken any one of them."

"Chiun, didn't you say the treasure was supposed to be buried under the Danube?"

"That was the legend," Chiun admitted.

"So why were you digging here?"

"The map indicated that this was the proper location. I assumed the *Nibelungenlied*'s mention of the Danube to be Siegfried's final mendacity. The river is, after all, not far from here." His face was clouded.

Remo crossed his arms. "So this Danube is pretty big, I take it?" he asked unhappily.

Heine nodded. "It is the second longest river in Europe," he said.

Remo sighed. "I suppose I should be happy it's not the longest," he said. He held out a hand to Heine. "Keys."

After a moment's hesitation, the colonel reluctantly pulled the keys to his jeep from his pocket. He had only had them back in his possession for under an hour. Heine dropped them into Remo's outstretched palm.

"Don't wait up," Remo said, trudging over to the jeep.

The Master of Sinanju walked behind him in his mud-splattered kimono. His cheerless expression never wavered.

HEIDI HAD SET UP her surveying equipment in the clearing a few dozen meters away from the raging

Danube River.

She had gone through the same procedure only a few short hours before back at the false site. Here, however, she was not merely putting on an act to fool the others.

She was far more careful this time as she peered through the eyepiece of the theodolite. Her fingers delicately adjusted the leveling screws.

Heidi had been genuinely surprised when they had discovered the stone carving at the other site. She expected the excavation to be futile. Actually she had *planned* it that way. Heidi had assumed that they would dig and dig until they finally gave up.

The more she thought about it, however, the more she realized that it should not have been totally unexpected. Her deviation from the map had been the logical turn it should have taken. It was the guess that someone might have made had they not been in possession of the entire map.

That had been the devious charm of the quartered block carving. Without even one piece, it would be impossible to extrapolate the rest of the map.

The runic writing on the other stone was Siegfried's final joke from beyond the grave. There were probably many other mocking stone carvings buried all around the area.

But not here.

Heidi wasn't having an easy time surveying. The reference points that would have been used originally were long gone. Even the geography of the region had changed over the past fifteen hundred years.

It was painstaking work.

In the end, Heidi was forced to use a mishmash of mathematics and geography to determine where the excavation should be. Even with the passage of fifteen centuries, there were enough clues for her to make a reasonably educated guess.

The spot was a minor declivity in a field a stone's throw away from the cold, churning water of the river.

Leaving her equipment and notebook behind, Heidi stepped gingerly across the small windswept meadow. She felt as if she was disturbing an old grave.

Using four broken twigs, she staked out a square around the spot. It was the best she could do for now without any help. All she could do in the meantime was wait.

Heidi looked down at the area she had marked off. It was approximately six feet by eight feet. Mottled frozen grass lay damply away from the river—a weed army toppled by the relentless wind.

That it could be here! Just below her boots!

As she looked down on the spot, Heidi suddenly noticed something in the tall, knotted grass. It had escaped her detection during the hour she had been surveying. There appeared to be a single solid line almost completely buried beneath the clumpy soil.

She dropped to her knees in the grass, feeling along the edge of the long section of stone.

Her heart tingled excitedly as she realized it was not naturally occurring. It was man-made.

She used her fingers to rip up divots of grass, flinging them away. Clawing along the rough edge of the buried chiseled rock, she uncovered a four-inch-wide strip. Her hands were shaking as she tore away the years of earthen buildup atop the stone boundary.

It stopped at a right angle. Heidi followed this shorter section of stone to another angle.

She worked furiously. Her hands were caked with black grime by the time she completed the square. When she was finished, the outline of an ancient stone boundary was clearly visible.

Heidi knelt—filthy and panting—in the grass before the sealed opening beyond which lay the fabled Nibelungen Hoard. Unmindful of the ferocious wind that whistled down the neck of her heavy woolen coat, she stared in awe, sweating from both exertion and excitement.

Her feeling of exhilaration was short-lived.

There was a sound behind her. A dull *clap-clap-clap*.

Unenthusiastic applause.

"Bravo," a voice shouted over the wind.

She recognized it instantly. She hadn't heard his approach over the fierce gusts of frigid air.

Heidi's shoulders sank in defeat. As she climbed to her feet, she began turning around, snaking a hand inside the unzipped front of her jacket.

"Uh-uh. Slowly," cautioned Adolf Kluge.

Heidi pulled her hand from her coat. Woodenly she did as she was told.

Kluge was there with a few of his skinhead henchmen. He had also brought with him a number of Federal Border Police. Out of respect for the service they had abandoned, the ex-police had taken the liberty of removing their official insignia. However, their guns were still plainly evident, and were aimed at Heidi.

One of the former police trotted over to her. He reached inside her coat, removing her handgun from her shoulder holster. He stuffed it into his belt.

"Did you intend to keep the treasure all to yourself?" Kluge asked with an evil smile.

"Didn't you?" she countered.

Kluge shrugged. "Of course," he said. "But at least I had sense enough to bring along a little help. I suppose you intended to dig it out all by yourself and then carry it away in your pockets?"

Heidi didn't respond.

Kluge appraised her for a long moment. Finally he pulled a shovel from the hands of one of his skinhead thugs. He threw it over to where Heidi stood. It fell near her feet, clanging on the stone lip that she had exposed.

"You have a few more hours to live," Kluge said magnanimously. "They may as well be productive. Dig."

Heidi considered refusing. However, that would surely encourage Adolf Kluge to shoot her that much sooner. She decided that if she stalled for time, she might yet be able to get out of this alive.

She picked up the shovel at her feet.

As a few skinheads came over to join her in the excavation, Heidi jammed the tip of the spade into the cold ground. She forced it in deep with the sole of her boot.

With no fanfare save the howling Danube wind, Heidi Stolpe turned over the first spadeful of earth that had entombed for centuries the fabled Nibelungen Hoard.

THE TALL PINES of the Black Forest roared past at breakneck speed. Though they were driving like a bat out of hell, Chiun recognized the blurry clutch of conifers that flew past the jeep for the third time.

They squealed around a corner on two wheels. Long black skid marks from their previous two journeys around the same corner marred the roadway.

"You are driving aimlessly," Chiun challenged Remo.

Remo was hunched behind the steering wheel. His hands gripped the pebbled surface of the wheel tightly.

"I can't pick up their damned trail. They could have gone anywhere," Remo said testily.

"They have not gone anywhere," Chiun snipped. "They have gone to steal my gold."

"I liked you a lot better when all you cared about was building statues of comedians."

"I am through with that," Chiun announced huffily. "Jesters come and go. Only gold lasts forever."

The jeep radio suddenly squawked to life. The anxious, accented voice of Colonel Heine came on. He spoke in English.

"This is Colonel Heine of the German Federal Border Police to the driver of my jeep. Come in, please." He had never bothered to learn Remo's name. His voice was anxious.

"Answer it," Chiun demanded, pointing to the radio.

"Um..." Remo said.

"You do not know how," Chiun said accusingly.

"Do, too," Remo replied.

"Prove it."

Remo answered the radio. For some reason he couldn't fathom, the windshield wipers came on.

"I told you," Chiun said.

"It is urgent," said Heine's voice. "Please respond."

"*You* do it." Remo aimed his chin defiantly at the radio.

"It is beneath me." Chiun crossed his arms.

"You don't know how, either," Remo challenged.

"Please respond," begged Heine.

"I'll admit I don't know how if you admit you don't know how," Remo offered cagily.

Chiun appraised the radio. "It is a model with which I am not entirely familiar," he admitted.

"Fine," said Remo. "Let's answer it together."

THEY DIDN'T HAVE to dig as long here.

The rim of stone Heidi had uncovered by hand turned out to be the topmost portion of four buried walls. The excavation went down only about six feet in this narrow enclosure before the first shovel clanked on solid rock.

As before, they used their hands to clear off a flat stone. It rested level in the buried square of rock. A horizontal door.

The edges of the stone were cleared away, revealing a stone casing. Again icy water was brought from the nearby river to wash off the ancient accumulation of dirt.

When they were finished, a narrow gap was visible between the large stone and the strips of interlocking rock that bordered it.

"We need to pry this up," Heidi called up to Kluge. She was squatting in the hole atop the stone. With her hand, she felt around the edge of the ancient slab of settled rock.

There were two skinheads still inside the pit. They were on their knees assisting Heidi.

"Get the crowbars," Kluge told a few of the border police who were standing with him at the edge of the hole. The men ran obediently off.

Inside the shallow pit, Heidi was trying desperately to contain her excitement. She had to keep reminding herself that under the circumstances it did not matter if this was the right spot. The discovery would do her no good if she was dead. Somehow she had to get out of this alive. And she could. If only the others showed up in time...

"It is a pity you didn't see me following you," Kluge called in mock sympathy from the edge of the pit. "From your perspective, of course," he quickly added. "After you turned onto the access road, it became a simple enough matter. There are no paths leading off it. Those twisted genetic bastards had the right idea for once, it seems. They had sense enough to steal my trucks and make a run for it. Not you. You led me directly here."

As Kluge thought of the missing blond-haired Numbers from the IV village, his face suddenly clouded over. He peered more closely at Heidi Stolpe. All at once, his eyes opened in delighted surprise. It was a spark of joyous realization.

"You are one of them, aren't you?" he asked happily. He beamed as the truth of his words sank in. "I *knew* you looked familiar when I first laid eyes on you. But I never knew our friend Dr. von Breslau created a female lab rat. Perhaps you were an accident? An improvement on the men, I must admit. You at least can talk. That is, until now." He smiled a wet, superior smile.

In the pit, covered with dirt, Heidi tried to hold his condescending gaze. She nearly succeeded. But as she stared into the fiery blue-gray eyes of Adolf Kluge, a sinking feeling of inferiority seemed to settle like a fog over her slender frame. Her shoulders sank. She averted her eyes, ashamed.

Kluge knew in that instant that he had guessed

correctly. Somehow Heidi Stolpe was the freakish sister to the hundreds of Aryan males mass-produced by IV more than thirty years before.

He would have been fascinated to learn more about her life. About how she alone of all the embryos concocted in that Nazi lab in South America had been born female. About how she had come to be where she was today. About her apparent knowledge of IV. But it turned out that Heidi was not the only one surprised at that moment.

Kluge felt a rough shove between his shoulder blades. The air was knocked from his lungs from the severity of the blow. He toppled forward into the open hole.

Kluge thudded hollowly atop the huge stone slab beside Heidi, banging his knees painfully against the rock.

He rolled over onto his back on the cold chunk of stone. Kluge was shocked to see, framed in the square of light above him, a familiar mud-splattered yellow kimono. Above it was an enraged parchment face.

"Claim jumpers!" the Master of Sinanju announced.

The two skinheads who remained in the hole with Heidi helped Kluge to his feet.

The IV leader had to think quickly.

"Ah, you made it," Kluge called up to Chiun. "Excellent." He smiled weakly.

Remo Williams slipped into view beside the old Korean.

"Don't bullshit a bullshitter," he advised Kluge.

"No, *really*," Kluge insisted. "It was bedlam back there. I am genuinely pleased that all of the interested parties have found their way here."

"It wasn't luck," Remo said. "The German air force spotted your stupid convoy headed this way. They radioed your position to the border police, who put us on your tail."

"It is fortunate that I knew how to operate the radio device," Chiun announced. "Or we might still be driving aimlessly through this bleak forest."

"Hey, I thought we were going to share the credit for the radio," Remo complained.

"Oh, please, Remo," Chiun remarked testily. "While you occasionally display signs of almost being a good son, I live in constant fear that you will someday die in a bathroom after misremembering the operation of the doorknob."

"Man, you're nasty when you're greedy," Remo said. He left the edge of the hole to go off and sulk near the river.

Chiun was too busy to be concerned with Remo's fragile state of mind.

From beyond Kluge's and Heidi's limited field of vision, the Master of Sinanju produced two handfuls of long metal crowbars. Each weighed approximately fifteen pounds. Chiun held them in his hands as if they were plastic drinking straws. He flung the bars to the bottom of the pit where they clanged in an angry pile.

"Remove the stone," he commanded imperiously.

IT TOOK LONGER than either Kluge or Heidi had expected. Perhaps they had imagined it would not be so difficult after seeing Chiun fling the previous stone with such ease.

It would have taken Chiun no time at all to pull the ancient stone from its age-old resting place, but the Master of Sinanju was not about to dirty his hands this time. He let the others strain and tug along with the neo-Nazis and former border police.

It took twenty minutes.

Remo tried to remain aloof for most of the time, but curiosity eventually got the better of even him. He stood above the hole alongside the Master of Sinanju.

Panting from her exertions, Heidi joined them up above, allowing the men to pry and tug at the stubborn edges of the fifteen-hundred-year-old block of buried stone. Her eyes strayed only once to the woods at the edge of the field.

After many long minutes of grunting and straining, the stone finally popped loose. A burst of fetid, swampy air poured up from around the edges of the dislodged slab of ancient rock. The men in the pit struggled to avoid the urge to vomit at the stench.

The worst of the smell passed as they labored to stand the rock door on its side. With difficulty, the men managed to lean the huge piece of stone up against the dirt-smeared rock wall of the shallow pit.

Below the spot where the ancient stone had rested for more than a millennium was an empty blackness. Stone stairs led away into darkness.

The Master of Sinanju couldn't contain his joy. He bounced happily on his sandaled feet.

"Come, Remo," he enthused. "Let us reclaim the treasure of poor maligned Master Bal-Mung." He headed for the edge of the hole.

"What about them?" Remo asked, indicating the skinheads and border police who were still standing in the small field.

Chiun paused, looking at the collection of men. There were only about twenty of them in all. "We will need them to transport my treasure," Chiun said merrily.

He hopped down into the hole.

Remo and Heidi followed, along with the curious group of neo-Nazis and Nazi sympathizers.

The moss-coated stairs led deep underground.

As the motley collection of treasure hunters made their way down the long, treacherous flight, more than one skinhead slipped and fell. Once, Remo had to grab Heidi when the heels of her boots slid out from beneath her. Only Remo and Chiun descended the ancient staircase with ease.

The waning late-afternoon sunlight from above grew dim when they were only halfway down the stairs. Their group had only two weak flashlights, which they played along the slime-coated walls and slick staircase. Adolf Kluge held one of the lights as

he stepped gingerly down the stairs immediately behind the Master of Sinanju.

The staircase led into a narrow, stone-hewed hallway. There was a shelf set into the wall on which
rested dozens of slender rock-carved torches.

Siegfried must have considered the possibility that
the treasure might languish down there for many
years. While it would have been traditional to fashion a torch from wood, wood rotted. Stone did not.

Chiun took one of the unlit torches down from the
wall. As Kluge shone a flashlight on him, the Master
of Sinanju made an unhappy face.

The torch had a wide cup that tapered down into
a long handle. It was like an oversize golf tee. Chiun
dipped his index finger into the hollow at the top of
the rock torch. He removed it, pressing the finger to
his tongue.

Angry, Chiun spit the drop of oily substance between Adolf Kluge's boots.

"Your ancestor's final theft," he said to Kluge.

Chiun continued forward down the corridor, toying with the top of the torch.

As the Master of Sinanju walked away, Remo
took down one of the torches. He smelled the end,
nodding.

"What is it?" Kluge asked, confused.

"Old family recipe," Remo explained. "Lasts for
years."

Far down the corridor, Chiun's torch flared to life.
The narrow walls were instantly illuminated in a

brilliant flash of white-hot light. The light from the torch then faded to a steady yellow incandescence.

Remo instructed the men with them to gather up several of the torches. As he and Heidi walked past Kluge, the IV leader could see Remo rubbing his thumb and index finger rapidly together above the bowl of the torch. Somehow the friction he produced caused his own torch to burst aflame.

Remo used his flame to ignite the other torches.

The mass of men moved down the hallway. Adolf Kluge lagged behind.

A feeling of intense claustrophobia had enveloped Kluge. He couldn't allow it to get the better of him. Not if he hoped to succeed in his plan to kill the others. Steeling himself, Kluge trailed the rest down the hallway.

"Why are there skeletons everywhere we go lately?" Remo griped as he picked his way through a litter of bones.

The hallway had ended in a large chamber. Above them could be heard the muted roar of the Danube. The chamber had been constructed in such a way that—even after all these years—the river had not burst through.

The broken bones of murder victims were spread all around this large room. In spite of the dampness, they cracked like scattered potato chips beneath the heels of the intruders.

"Siegfried would not want his secret made known," Chiun explained. "Doubtless these are the bodies of those who constructed this place."

"They are likely the men who moved the gold, as well," Heidi offered from her spot at Remo's elbow.

"What did he do if you *didn't* help him?" Remo asked.

There was a sconce at the wall just inside the door. Remo put his torch there. It was bright enough to illuminate the entire room, which was roughly the size of a high-school classroom from the time when such rooms held more than five students, one teacher and fifteen teacher's aides.

There were at least two more rooms leading off of the one they were in. Weird shadows danced along the moist, moss-covered walls.

Beyond the skeletal remains on either side of the chamber were two large piles of slime-coated rock. Lichens and moss sprouted from every conceivable crevice in the huge stone piles. A narrow space ran up between the mass of slippery rock into the next chamber.

Beyond the right pile, a relentless drip reminded them of the nearness of the Danube above their heads. An elaborate sluice system constructed at the sides of the slightly slanted floors carried the dripping water away.

"I guess ol' Siegfried did it to you again, Chiun," Remo commented sadly, looking around the fungus and ooze filled room. "I've got to hand it to him, though. I almost believed this one."

The Master of Sinanju wasn't listening. His eyes

held an eager glow as he handed his torch back to Remo. Remo took it, confused.

"What's with him?" he asked, turning to Heidi.

She wasn't listening, either. Both Heidi and Kluge broke away from the pack, their faces awed. They moved with nervous reverence after the Master of Sinanju.

When they came up behind him, Chiun was already crouched next to the nearest pile of moss-covered stone. Heidi and Kluge didn't look at one another. Didn't blink. Didn't dare take their wide eyes off the hands of the old Korean.

Chiun snaked a bony hand toward the rock pile.

Remo had no time to voice his disgust before the Master of Sinanju had clasped firmly on to one of the slippery stones atop the main pile. Spiriting it to his chest, Chiun used his free hand to brush away the years of slimy growth that had built up atop the stone.

Remo had just opened his mouth to complain when he spied an odd glimmer in the bright torch-light within the cavern. It came from Chiun's hand.

And its color was gold.

Stunned, Remo took a step forward.

Both Heidi and Kluge watched in wonder as Chiun's long fingernails expertly wiped away years of residue that had built up atop the object that all of them now knew was not merely a piece of rock.

It came clean with surprising ease. When he was finished, Chiun held in his hand a single brick of solid gold. He turned to Remo.

"Behold," Chiun said, with quiet awe. He held a grand arm out toward the mossy piles within the cavern, "the long shame of Master Bal-Mung is lifted. I give to you the Nibelungen Hoard."

oThe decision was made by the Master of Sinanju to haul the entire Nibelungen Hoard from its ancient resting place in one massive move.

Every available man, with the exclusion of Chiun himself, formed a line into the farthest rooms within the underground catacombs. Piece by piece, the lumps of gold were passed forward. There were also crates brimming over with fabulous jewels. Although the wooden boxes had originally been preserved in the same manner as the block carving map, given the soggy conditions of the tunnels in which they had been stored, they had not held up as well. However, most were strong enough to survive being passed down the line of waiting men.

When the back room was clear, the line leapfrogged out into the next room, passing the gold farther out into the corridor. From the corridor, they moved to the stairs, and from the stairs, outside.

In this manner, the rear room was cleared out in just under five hours.

When they were only halfway through the first room and he realized just how monumental an undertaking this was going to be, Remo had Heidi help him to contact Colonel Heine on the radio.

When Heine had informed him earlier of the location of Kluge's trucks, Remo had warned the colonel to hold his men back while he and Chiun dealt with the neo-Nazi situation. Having seen with his own eyes the way Remo had walked through the heaviest firefight of his career, Heine was loath to upset the American.

Remo now told the colonel that the situation was under control. Heine spluttered for a moment until Remo reminded him of the pain he caused the colonel's hand. The colonel promptly agreed to abandon the Black Forest.

They worked for twelve hours straight. Kluge and his Border Police defectors had only three trucks on hand. They weren't enough to put so much as a dent in the huge pile of gold and jewels stacked around the windswept clearing.

Dawn was breaking on their second day of back-breaking labor. The skinheads still hauled treasure up from below. They were weary from their many hours of ceaseless effort.

Remo was just coming back from getting a drink at the river. Chiun danced happily up beside him.

"It is a magnificent sight, is it not?" the Master of Sinanju proclaimed as he viewed the massive stack of moss-encrusted treasure.

"Metal and rocks," Remo said with a bland shrug. He wiped at the grime on his forehead.

Chiun waggled a playfully admonishing finger at him.

"Do not sulk, Remo. It does not suit you."

Chiun flapped over to inspect a crate of flawless diamonds that hadn't seen the warming rays of the morning sun in fifteen centuries.

"Funny. *I* think it suits me just fine," Remo grumbled. He trudged back over to the mouth of the cavern.

AS THE WINTER SUN broke over the damp riverside meadow, Adolf Kluge was as far away from its warming rays as he could have imagined. Filthy and sweating profusely, he was crawling on his belly in a narrow shaft that ran parallel to the long corridor at the bottom of the old stone stairs.

The dull yellow glow of his flashlight shone brightly off the slippery walls of the man-made tunnel. The air was thick with the smell of overgrown moss. For Kluge, it was like crawling through a massive, fungus-filled laboratory petri dish. The years of mossy growth felt like one giant sponge. As he squished ahead on all fours, his pants and jacket grew sopped at the front.

The feeling of claustrophobia Kluge had experienced in the corridor outside was magnified a hundredfold in this cramped interior.

As he made his way along the cave, he pulled in deep, measured breaths. He had heard that this was supposed to have a calming effect. Kluge found that it did not.

It should only be a few feet up ahead. Everything else had been the way the map had described. There was no reason to think that it wouldn't be here, as well.

It was the Siegfried map that held the key. The Nibelungen king might have planned for the Hoard to be uncovered in a far distant future, but the future he had envisioned would have been measured in a few short decades. His fifth-century mind could not have considered that the cave would lie undiscovered until the twentieth century.

Siegfried had imagined all along that this storehouse of treasure would be divided in his lifetime. But if it happened that the gold was uncovered at a time when he was aged and his mind was failing him, he wanted to be sure that he of all the interested parties would still hold a winning hand. That was why his section of the block carving was the only one to show a detailed route to the ancient booby trap.

The narrow tunnel opened into a long vertical shaft. Kluge found that he was able to stand upright.

He shone his flashlight up the slick walls of the cramped enclosure. The ceiling was invisible behind a gnarled ganglia of dangling roots. To Kluge it was rather like being trapped at the bottom of a capped well.

Kluge turned the flashlight to his feet. He found what he was looking for immediately. It was a chiseled chunk of stone about three feet long. It appeared to be holding up another much longer support beam.

This long stone brace rose up to the ceiling, disappearing amid an interlocking series of carved rocks.

Siegfried had anticipated that he might be infirm when at last he used this shaft, so it would have been designed to dislodge easily. But that was many years ago. There was no telling whether or not Kluge would be able to budge it.

The IV leader sat down at the mouth of the tunnel through which he had just crawled. The moisture from the cave seeped in uncomfortably at the seat of his trousers.

Twisting unhappily, he braced one foot up against the slimy side of the propped stone.

Kluge reached into the pocket of his filthy jacket, pulling out a walkie-talkie he had packed along with the rest of the provisions and turned it on.

The muted sounds of low voices and shuffling feet came through the tiny speaker.

He heard Remo and Heidi. But not Chiun.

When Remo had opted not to come along initially, Kluge thought he would have to abandon his plan. Not anymore. But it would still work only if *both* Masters of Sinanju were beyond the main corridor.

Feeling the chilly wetness of the cramped tunnel, Adolf Kluge sat patiently. And waited.

"THAT'S THE LAST OF IT," Remo said as he walked back into the first of the three chambers that had held the Nibelungen Hoard. The final batch of gold had been moved down the corridor and was waiting in a pile at the bottom of the stone staircase.

"I am just double-checking," Heidi said.

She had brought in one of the unlit stone torches from the hallway shelf. Heidi was using the handle end to push beneath the piles of smelly moss that had been left behind.

Now that there was no longer any treasure stored beneath them, the brownish green lumps of slime looked like deflated weed balloons. Although it didn't seem as if a scrap of the Hoard remained, Heidi was meticulous in her search.

Remo heard echoing laughter from inside the two adjacent rooms. Heidi had enlisted some of Kluge's men to help her in rummaging through the mildewy chambers.

"I wonder how much loot those felons have pocketed," Remo commented, nodding to the skinheads.

"I am certain Chiun will not allow them to take anything that is not theirs," Heidi commented absently.

"You got that right," Remo snorted. "I'm still wondering how he plans on hauling all of this junk out of the country."

"Half," Heidi said.

Remo smiled. "You still think you're getting a piece of the action?" he asked innocently.

Heidi stopped digging beneath the moss. She turned to Remo, her face unhappy. "We have a contract," she said.

"Are you sure he didn't write it in disappearing ink?"

She shook her head firmly. "Masters of Sinanju are not known for duplicity."

"That's 'cause no one lives to tell the tales," Remo said. He seemed genuinely surprised at her. "Do you mean to tell me that it honestly never occurred to you that Chiun might have considered your contract null and void the minute you and Kluge ditched him?"

"I barely escaped with my life," Heidi insisted.

"And Kluge?"

"We were never working together. At least, not after the gunfight. That man is a monster. His kind still thinks that they are some kind of master race. And he is the worst offender of all. He is an intellectual midget who fancies himself a giant. He is superior to nothing. Least of all to me." She thrust her chin forward angrily.

Remo was baffled by the passion in her voice. "Where the hell did that come from?" he asked.

Her embarrassment at her outburst was almost instantaneous. "I did not—" She paused, collecting herself. "I have a deal with the House of Sinanju," she said, firmly, coming back to her original point. "I expect the House to honor it."

Chiun came through the door at that moment. The radiant joy that beamed from every crevice in his wrinkled face was not diminished by the darkness in the dank underground.

"Have you finished?" he lilted.

"Not quite," Heidi replied. She redoubled her efforts searching through the slimy growth.

"Carry on," Chiun said. He waved a delighted hand as he skipped over to the other side of the room. Searching with his feet, he began kicking through the debris.

"Have you given any thought to how you're going to move all this garbage?" Remo complained to Chiun.

"I believe I have that taken care of," Heidi offered.

Surprised, Remo turned to her. "Oh?" he asked. Chiun interrupted her before she could respond.

"What is this?" the Master of Sinanju asked. He had just unearthed something from beneath a brackish green lump. Picking the object up, he displayed it to Heidi and Remo. Although strips of moss still clung to its surface, the device was visible enough. And it had clearly not been down there for fifteen hundred years.

"It looks like a walkie-talkie," Remo said, puzzled.

As he reached for the small instrument, Remo suddenly became aware of a low rumble above and around them. He had grown used to the sound of the rushing water directly over their heads. This was an entirely different noise.

Heidi got to her feet, curious. Remo glanced over at her, hoping that she might shed some light on what they were hearing. But she was clearly as puzzled as he was.

All at once, the room began to shake. As if from some unseen cue, a gigantic slab of rock fell with impossible slowness from above the door, tumbling to the floor with a room-shaking, thunderous crash.

Chiun dropped the walkie-talkie.

"Run, Remo!" the Master of Sinanju shouted.

His warning came too late.

As they raced for the exit, the wall before them began to buckle. It collapsed inward at the midpoint, scattering massive stones like toppled blocks. An avalanche of stone and muddy earth rained down from above, sealing the corridor.

They didn't have time to consider their options.

Without the support of the far wall, the ceiling began to bulge downward with horrifying slowness. It creaked as the resettling earth pushed in on it.

At a frantic run, the skinheads from the inner room joined them. They looked up in fear at the groaning roof.

"Is there another way out of here?" Remo asked warily.

Heidi's eyes were wide. "No," she said softly.

And with that, the ceiling collapsed in a shower of dirt and crashing boulders. Like a deluge from some bygone era of biblical vengeance, the full fury of the Danube River exploded in all around them.

26

Kluge felt the walls of the cramped tunnel rumble all around him as he made his frantic way back out to the staircase. He tore ragged holes in his coat and pants as he crawled recklessly through the pitch-dark wetness.

The support stone had kicked away with surprising ease. The series of key stones had interlocked like some ancient puzzle. As soon as the cornerstone was gone, the others began collapsing in around it.

He had dropped his flashlight in his haste.

The walls drummed like thunder all around him as the corridor and rooms collapsed. He only knew he was going in the right direction because it was impossible to get lost in the long burrow.

His claustrophobia had nearly robbed him of all sense. He wanted to scream, wanted to panic. Logically he knew that it would do no good, but logic had nothing to do with the almost paralyzing terror he felt. It was like being trapped in the black epicenter of a massive earthquake.

Scurrying like a rat in a hole, Kluge suddenly slammed against something solid with his head.

Panicked now, he grabbed forward, shoving hard against the object. The stone toppled away. It was the same one he had pulled in place behind him upon entering the tunnel.

He scampered out beneath the stairs—lungs aching, heart pounding.

He was alive!

There was enough weak light filtering down the stairs to illuminate the small pile of gold that still remained. The corridor was gone. Buried behind a wall of rock and earth.

Get the panic under control.

Deep breaths. No! Save it for outside.

Outside.

He headed for the stairs, casting one final glance at his end of the collapsed corridor.

The others were dead. The gold was all his. He could collect whatever was left at the bottom of the stairs later.

Exhilarated by his success, Adolf Kluge raced up the staircase to the distant square of light.

THE ICY WATER CRASHED down in an enormous burst of frothy, churning white. The floor flooded in seconds.

"Back!" Chiun commanded.

The skinheads were already running in panic through the waist-deep water toward the rear rooms.

"I don't think that'll do any good!" Remo shouted over the roar of the waterfall.

"It will give us time!" Chiun insisted.

Bony arms pumping in furious motion, the Master of Sinanju fought against the lethal, swirling current. Remo followed. Heidi struggled after them.

Heidi had not taken more than a few fumbling steps when she tripped against a shattered chunk of toppled stone. She fell beneath the rapidly rising water. Thrown forward on the waves, she lost all sense of direction. She swam for what she thought was up, bumping against the floor of the flooding cavern. Or was it the wall?

No time to decide. She kicked off, pushing up to the surface. A wave caught her midway, tumbling her sideways. She no longer had any sense of up or down.

Heidi began to panic.

Strong arms suddenly grabbed her by the armpits. She was hauled, spluttering above the water by Remo. It was now as high as their chests.

Remo carried her along with him, taking a few swift strides across the room. The water was at their chins by the time they made it into the second room.

The skinheads were in hysterics. They were clawing at the walls and at one another, trying to climb above the water. Screaming and crying, they pushed up on the shoulders of their confederates. One body floated face down in the water. Another skinhead attempted to ride it like a raft.

Chiun was treading water.

"There's no way out of here!" Remo shouted to him.

"There is one!" Chiun yelled back.

Beyond the door, they could see the river pouring relentlessly through the broken ceiling. It was so steady it was like a single, huge column of water.

"It's too dangerous!" Remo shouted.

"I am open to suggestions!"

There was a massive rumble. They watched as a new section of the outer ceiling began to give way. It fell in huge irregular blocks to the rising, churning water.

The water was only a few feet from the ceiling now and rising ever more rapidly.

"Go!" Remo yelled to Chiun over the roar of the river.

The Master of Sinanju nodded sharply. Twisting up, he ducked below the waves. His spindly legs appeared for an instant as he jackknifed underwater. Then he was gone.

They were at the ceiling now. Heidi held her face up to the approaching rock, breathing desperately.

"Take a deep breath!" Remo yelled.

She was so disoriented she didn't know where Remo was any longer. The skinheads were screaming as the water swirled up around them. Heidi craned her neck to see Remo.

"What?"

"Do it!"

Heidi did as she was told. The instant she had filled her lungs, Remo grabbed her around the waist. Pulling her close to him, he threw himself into the swirling torrent.

The push of water was like a fist shoving against

him. Dragging Heidi beside him, Remo kicked hard against the racing current.

The freezing water was murky and filled with swirling plants and mud.

As they passed out into the remnants of the outer room, Remo felt a series of muted booms behind them. The roof of the room they had been in was collapsing. The stones of the ceiling were crashing in slow motion to the new riverbed.

A few scissorlike kicks brought them to the largest waterfall. It was like fighting against the mighty spray of a jet-powered firehose.

Remo pushed them into the center of the driving water.

He had to fight against the force of the incoming river. It was hard enough to do alone; carrying someone else made it all the more difficult.

The roar of the flooding water pounded against his ears as he propelled the two of them forward. His limbs were like leaden weights.

Chiun's fault. He had forced Remo to haul his precious booty for almost twenty hours. The heavy labor had taken its toll on his arms and legs.

Remo's muscles ached as he pushed up through the remnants of ceiling and earth. For an instant, it seemed as if he might be thrown back down through the opening.

He kicked a final time, hard.

They were propelled upward against the tide. A new current caught him, pushing him away from the ragged opening. The legitimate bed of the Danube began to slide rapidly beneath him.

Remo caught the bottom of the river with the tips of his toes and pushed. The force was gauged to bring them at an angle through the racing current of water. Remo and Heidi were propelled up to the surface. In an instant, sunlight exploded all around them.

Heidi pulled in a ragged gulp of air.

Remo gave her little time to fill her lungs. Cutting across the roaring river, he swam swiftly to the shore, dragging her behind him.

In a few seconds, they were pulling themselves up onto the grassy riverbank, drenched and weary. But alive.

The Master of Sinanju was there to greet them.

"He has stolen my gold!" Chiun cried. His sopped kimono clung in mud-encrusted sheets to his bony frame.

"Who?" Remo asked, pulling himself to his feet. His clothes dripped icy water.

"The thieving scion of the scoundrel Siegfried and his army of pinheads, of course," Chiun huffed. "Hurry!" He bounced, dripping wet up the weed-strewn bank.

Remo climbed up the embankment and looked out over the meadow. Most of the Nibelungen Hoard was still there, but Kluge's trucks were gone from the nearby access road. There was no sign of the skinheads or defecting border police.

"He only took some of it," Remo offered.

"It was not his right to take one precious ingot!" Chiun said, stomping his feet.

"Fine," Remo said, exhaling tired frustration. "We'll go after him. But you've got to promise me, Chiun. When we find him, we kill him. I've had it up to here with this stupid gold fever of yours."

"We will kill him," Chiun replied icily.

"Good," Remo said.

"For stealing my treasure."

Rolling his eyes, Remo turned to Heidi.

She was panting and drenched behind them. Her blond bangs clung in dripping sheets to her forehead.

"Keep an eye on this stuff till we get back?" he asked.

"Only if our fifty/fifty deal still stands," she said.

"Fine with me."

Chiun jumped forward. "I do not trust her."

Heidi began to speak, but Remo interjected. "All that's left is my crummy rental car," he complained. "She's not hauling all of this out in that." He indicated the field and its piles upon piles of gold and jewels with a sweeping motion of his hand.

Chiun was faced with a vexing problem. To part with the bulk of the treasure in pursuit of a small portion, or to sacrifice a small portion to guard the larger mass.

His eyes passed indecisively from the access road to his mounds of precious booty. He finally reached a decision, though it obviously gave him little happiness.

"I warn you," he said threateningly, raising a long fingernail to Heidi.

The old Korean said not another word. He spun on his heel and raced for Remo's borrowed jeep.

"Do us both a favor," Remo warned with a knowing nod.

Leaving Heidi alone, dripping, shivering and surrounded by the Nibelungen Hoard, Remo took off through the field after Chiun.

27

Adolf Kluge waited alone in the small Berlin warehouse.

He didn't dare leave. Not with the amount of gold piled on the floor.

The few skinheads who remained after he had collapsed the underground storehouse had returned with him to the city. Kluge sent them out to rent more trucks and gather more men.

It was unbelievable. The actual Nibelungen Hoard.

The treasure piled in this warehouse didn't seem like much compared to the huge amount he knew was waiting for him in that desolate clearing next to the Danube, but he knew as he looked down upon it that he was gazing at a fortune.

He had enough here alone to reestablish IV. The secret neo-Nazi organization would be stronger than it ever had been in the past. With the wealth at his disposal, it might even be time to begin considering the true mission of IV.

A global fascist government.

With himself as its leader.

He had never dreamed he would have the operating capital to carry out such a plan. But now...

Now it could be a reality. Kluge had come to believe only recently that anything was possible.

Stooping, he picked up one of the gold bars. It was still flecked with dark fungus. He scraped the growth away with his thumbnail. Pulling out his handkerchief, he buffed the surface to a high luster.

Anything was possible. Anything at all.

Kluge smiled as he held the bar up to examine it in the weak light of the warehouse.

He caught something reflected in its gleaming surface. A pair of dark shapes silhouetted in the door. Men. But the door was closed and bolted from the inside.

Kluge turned around slowly, still holding the gold bar.

"Here's a tip. If you want to keep your hideout a secret, don't trust skinheads," Remo Williams said, stepping into the room.

Chiun took this as a cue. He marched over to Kluge and snatched the heavy gold bar from his hand. He examined it as if it were a baby the IV leader had physically assaulted.

"Thief," the Master of Sinanju announced. Cradling the gold bar delicately, he walked back over to the door.

"He told me he was careful," Kluge gasped. He looked as if he were seeing a pair of ghosts. "I even told him to use a false name when he rented this place. How are you alive?"

Remo ignored the question. "He used a false name, all right," he said. "The same one he used to rent one of those trucks. These baldies aren't the brightest bulbs on the circuit, Dolph."

"The truck?" Kluge asked. He was totally bewildered. He obviously didn't see a connection.

"I don't know how my boss does it," Remo said with a shrug. "Chiun remembered the number on the truck. Smith managed to use his computer to track you. Now we're here."

"Smith," Kluge said. He was coming back to his senses.

"Yeah," Remo said "The guy you knocked on the head. He sends his thanks for that, by the way. I just found out he's going into the hospital today. They're going to have to drain fluid from around his brain because of the crack you gave him. I don't like him, but I respect him. For that, you suffer." Smiling grimly, he advanced on Kluge.

"This is not how the House of Sinanju is supposed to do business," Kluge called quickly over to Chiun.

"Did you not read your contract?" Chiun asked blandly.

"Of course," Kluge said. "We had an ironclad deal."

"You obviously did not read the section written in Korean," Chiun noted.

"I do not understand Korean."

"Do not blame me for your inadequacies," Chiun said simply. He heated the gold bar in his hand with a warm puff of breath, polishing off the condensation with the sleeve of his clean, sea green kimono.

"The one thing I don't get," Remo interjected, "is why you sent all those letters."

"Letters?" Kluge asked. "What letters?"

"The E-mail you sent to the bank people, the chancellor, even the freaking border police."

Kluge was shaking his head in bewilderment. "I sent no letters."

"Well, one of your lackeys did. They mentioned Four, the Hoard. Even the fact that you were searching in the Black Forest. You're like a guy who wants to be caught."

Kluge was baffled. He kept trying to think of who would report on them or even know that they had set out to find the Hoard. And why E-mail? They might just as easily have used a phone.

Then it struck him.

"They would not be able to use a phone," he said numbly to himself. He remembered the trucks that had escaped during the firefight with the Border Police. The men in them were not skinheads. They were Numbers. It was *her*. *She* wanted a diversion so that she would be able to search on her own.

Remo was nearly upon him.

"Wait!" Kluge cried desperately. He was grasping at straws, desperate to avoid what he knew was coming. "That woman. The one you were with."

"Heidi?" Remo asked, stopping.

"Yes. She is not normal," Kluge insisted.

"Given your friends, Cuddles, I don't think

you're the best judge of that," said Remo. He strode toward Kluge.

"You do not understand," Kluge begged. "She is a Number. They are the ones who E-mailed. They cannot use a telephone. They must be working with her."

Remo stopped once more. "What are you talking about?"

"The blond-haired men," Kluge explained hastily. "The identical mutes? They are called Numbers. They were part of a wrong-headed genetic experiment."

"And Heidi is one of them?" Remo asked. He sounded doubtful.

"Somehow," Kluge admitted. "The rest of them were freaks by design. They were created to be fiercely loyal to Four. I don't know if she has that as part of her genetic programming or not. But if she does, and it has somehow mutated, she could pose a far greater threat than my organization ever did."

"What do you mean?" Remo asked.

"It was a program designed to create the perfect Aryan man. There were not supposed to be any women. I don't know how she even came to be." He shook his head, as if he were speaking to a complete moron. "Do you not understand? She should not exist. And she should never have opposed me in my search for the Hoard."

"Does this affect my treasure?" Chiun asked from across the room. He was clearly anxious to leave.

"What?" Kluge said. "No. No, of course not."

Chiun promptly walked out the door.

Remo advanced on Kluge.

"I can help you," the IV head offered desperately. "With her. With the Hoard. I have men coming."

Remo shook his head. "I'd rather go this one alone," he replied. "Thanks just the same."

And because Remo had seen so much killing in the past few weeks and was so bone-tired, he simply reached out and crushed Adolf Kluge's skull.

Afterward, as he looked down on the crumpled body of the dead IV leader, Remo had no feeling of satisfaction.

Hauling Kluge up off the floor, he carried the corpse over to the concrete wall of the warehouse where a series of pegs jutted from the wall. He hung Kluge from these, arms spread across the pegs, legs dangling.

Finding a half-empty bucket of red paint in a store room, Remo painted a large swastika on the bare wall next to Kluge. He enclosed it in a circle, cutting a single red line across the symbol of hate it contained. It was the international sign for "No."

Beside it, he painted a simple legend in English. A few brief words: IV Ends Here.

Remo left the warehouse to find Chiun.

THE MASTER OF SINANJU insisted that they first had to store the gold Kluge had stolen somewhere. Only when this was done were they allowed to return to the Danube. They weren't able to go back until early the next morning.

When they came to the end of the access road, Remo felt a sinking feeling in the pit of his stomach.

Beside him in the jeep, Chiun let out a pained wail. He was out of the jeep before Remo had even slowed down.

"No, no, no!" Chiun cried, running across the empty field.

Heidi was nowhere to be seen.

The only signs that anything heavy had been stored in the meadow were the large indentations in the earth and the huge patches of crushed grass. The treasure itself was gone.

Remo checked down the dank staircase. The area down below had begun to fill with slowly seeping water, but the level was low enough for Remo to see that what little gold had remained down there was gone, as well.

He came up and shrugged.

"Sorry, Chiun," Remo said helplessly.

The Master of Sinanju didn't appear to even hear him.

He just kept repeating the same word over and over as he wandered aimlessly around the field.

"No, no, no, no, no..."

After a half hour of this, Chiun got hold of himself. Afterward Remo—feeling intensely guilty— helped Chiun search the clearing for hours for even a single ruby or diamond. They found nothing.

Not a scrap of the Nibelungen Hoard remained.

28

One week later, Remo was on the phone in the kitchen of his home back in the United States.

"The fluid buildup was causing severe pressure on my brain," the lemony voice of Harold W. Smith said over the phone. "The doctors assure me that with it drained, my recovery will be complete."

"That's great, Smitty," Remo said. "What about those headaches you were having?"

"They were a symptom of the pressure that was building up. I have not had one since the operation."

Remo heard a relentless tapping in the background.

"What is that noise?" he asked, annoyed.

"My laptop computer," Smith explained. "My ill health may require a certain amount of bed rest, but it does not mean I have to be completely indolent while I am here."

Remo tried to picture Harold W. Smith—head swathed in bandages—banging away at a laptop computer in the bed of his hospital room. Oddly it was a mental image that didn't stretch Remo's imagination.

"As long as you're working anyway," Remo said, "is there any sign of Chiun's money?"

"No," Smith admitted. "And I find it more than a little alarming that one person could control that much raw wealth. You said her name was Heidi Stolpe?"

"That's what she told me."

"There is no one of that name anywhere in the world that fits the description you gave me," Smith said. "The castle in the Harz Mountains is virtually abandoned. The family who owned it died out in the 1960s. Nearby villagers will occasionally ferry tourists up there for sight-seeing expeditions, but it is otherwise empty. You are certain you found nothing on your subsequent search?"

"Chiun and I went through the place with a fine tooth comb for days. Heidi wasn't there, and neither was the loot."

"I don't know what to say," Smith told him. "I will do my best, but you must tell Chiun that I think it unlikely he will see the Nibelungen Hoard again."

At that moment, Remo heard the front door open hastily and slam shut. The Master of Sinanju's ninety-pound body sounded like a herd of stampeding elephants coming down the hallway to the kitchen.

"I've got to go, Smitty," Remo said hastily. He hung up the phone just as Chiun burst excitedly into the kitchen.

"Oh, joy of joys! Oh, happy day!" Chiun announced. His face beamed pure bliss. It was a marked change from his sulking behavior of the past week.

"What is it?" Remo asked, happy at anything that could change the Master of Sinanju's mood.

"Only this," Chiun said, his voice elated. He raised high a piece of mail.

Chiun had kept a mysterious mail drop for years. Today was the day of the month he had its contents transferred to their current residence. He received a bizarre assortment of mail there, which he generally shielded from Remo. This letter, however, he waved like a trophy above his bald head.

Remo had to snatch the letter from Chiun's hand. As he scanned it, he saw that it was written in a language he didn't understand.

"Care to fill me in?" he asked.

Chiun snatched the note back.

"It is from the enchanting Valkyrie," he said, "The delightful daughter of Gunther of the *Nibelungenlied*."

"Heidi?" Remo asked. He tried to grab the letter again, but Chiun spirited it out of his reach.

"She tells how she has secreted half of the Hoard in something called a storage facility in Bonn." Chiun reached into the folds of his kimono. He held aloft a single shiny silver key. "Behold, the passkey to the wondrous unit number 18. Therein we will find both gold and keys to chambers 19 through 22. We need only find a way to transport the Hoard out of Germany."

"If that doesn't cause Smith to throw an embolism, I don't know what will," Remo said dryly.

Chiun didn't even hear Remo. He was practically singing. "Apparently my gold has taken up many spaces at this repository. The dear girl has even paid expenses on this place of storage from out of her own sweet pocket." Chiun sighed wistfully. "Do you think, Remo, that at my age it is possible to find true love?"

Remo was leaning against the kitchen counter, arms crossed in disgust. "Don't ask me," he said sourly. "Check your bank book."

EPILOGUE

Heidi waited three months before returning to the castle of her ancestors. She made certain first that Remo and Chiun had moved their half of the gold from Bonn.

The last thing she wanted was a confrontation with either Master of Sinanju. Kluge had made that mistake. It was his mismanagement of IV that had brought the organization crashing down around his ears.

Heidi had chosen a secret location beneath the ancient chapel to hide her half of the Hoard. Beneath the shifted stone altar, two huge oaken doors that otherwise meshed with the hardwood floor had been flung open.

She watched as the few remaining Numbers carried her portion of the Hoard down into the treasure chamber hidden deep beneath the Harz Mountain castle. There were only thirty of the blond-haired men left. Thirty of her brothers.

Numbers. The term was so dehumanizing. Not fitting for the men who were supposed to be the future

masters of the world. She would have to come up
with something else to call them.

When they were finished hiding the treasure, one
of the Numbers came over to her. It was the same
man who had followed Remo from Berlin months
ago. The one who had been on his way to report to
Kluge when he was spotted by Heidi. He had instantly recognized her as the genetic superior to
them all. He had been the one to tell her where the
IV village was located. It wasn't a betrayal of Kluge.
She was superior to the dead IV leader. The Number
recognized that.

Everything after their chance meeting had been
easy. Including the massive undertaking of moving
the entire Nibelungen Hoard.

As the man stood, stone-faced, before her, Heidi
smiled. She nodded her pleasure at his work.

"Seal it off," she said, indicating the chamber.

The men across the room flung down the massive
wooden doors. They landed with a crash, upsetting
a huge plume of dust. It rose up into the dim light
that filtered in through the stained glass of the castle
room.

"From now on, Four will move cautiously,"
Heidi said with a smile. "And swiftly."

Take
2 explosive books
plus a
mystery bonus
FREE

Mail to: Gold Eagle Reader Service
          3010 Walden Ave.
          P.O. Box 1394
          Buffalo, NY 14240-1394

YEAH! Rush me 2 FREE Gold Eagle novels and my FREE mystery bonus.
Then send me 4 brand-new novels every other month as they come off
the presses. Bill me at the low price of just $16.80* for each shipment.
There is NO extra charge for postage and handling! There is no minimum
number of books I must buy. I can always cancel at any time simply by returning a shipment at your cost or by returning any shipping statement marked
"cancel." Even if I never buy another book from Gold Eagle, the 2 free books
and mystery bonus are mine to keep forever.

164 AEN CH7R

Name	(PLEASE PRINT)	
Address		Apt. No.
City	State	Zip

Signature (if under 18, parent or guardian must sign)

* Terms and prices subject to change without notice. Sales tax applicable in
  N.Y. This offer is limited to one order per household and not valid to
  present subscribers. Offer not available in Canada.

GE2-98

Follow Remo and Chiun on more of their extraordinary adventures....

#63220	SCORCHED EARTH	$5.50 U.S.	☐
		$6.50 CAN.	☐
#63221	WHITE WATER	$5.50 U.S.	☐
		$6.50 CAN.	☐
#63222	FEAST OR FAMINE	$5.50 U.S.	☐
		$6.50 CAN.	☐
#63223	BAMBOO DRAGON	$5.50 U.S.	☐
		$6.50 CAN.	☐
#63224	AMERICAN OBSESSION	$5.50 U.S.	☐
		$6.50 CAN.	☐

(limited quantities available on certain titles)

TOTAL AMOUNT	$
POSTAGE & HANDLING	$
($1.00 for one book, 50¢ for each additional)	
APPLICABLE TAXES*	$ _____
TOTAL PAYABLE	$ _____

(check or money order—please do not send cash)

To order, complete this form and send it, along with a check or money order for the total above, payable to Gold Eagle Books, to: **In the U.S.:** 3010 Walden Avenue, P.O. Box 9077, Buffalo, NY 14269-9077; **In Canada:** P.O. Box 636, Fort Erie, Ontario, L2A 5X3.

Name: _____

Address: _____ City: _____

State/Prov.: _____ Zip/Postal Code: _____

*New York residents remit applicable sales taxes.
 Canadian residents remit applicable GST and provincial taxes.

GOLD EAGLE®

GDEBACK1